IMAGINE THIS

Also by Vickie Stringer

Let That Be the Reason

IMAGINE THIS

A Novel

VICKIE M. STRINGER

ATRIA BOOKS

NEW YORK   LONDON   TORONTO   SYDNEY

ATRIA BOOKS

1230 Avenue of the Americas
New York, NY 10020

ISBN: 0-7394-4503-0

First Atria Books trade paperback edition August 2004

ATRIA BOOKS is a trademark of Simon & Schuster, Inc.

Manufactured in the United States of America

This book is dedicated to those doing federal time under the Mandatory Sentencing Guidelines.

To my son, Valen Mychal, I am because of you.

To my girl, Leah Whitney, you gangstress when it comes to having my back, ain't you? Bulletproof Thanks!

To my darling Clifford Benton, I hope your VS makes you proud.

Mommie, I love you!

ACKNOWLEDGMENTS

God, your grace is sufficient for me, and I know to whom much is given, much is required. Favor is a privilege, and privileges are to be treated as such. You are faithful and have never failed me. For this I am so grateful.

When it comes to acknowledgments, I find myself struggling not to forget anyone. Why? The answer to that question is that everyone has played a role in shaping who I am today. How do you forget the person that smiled at you on the morning of a bad day and changed your entire outlook for the rest of the week? I could fill pages with acknowledgments, thanking everyone who God has used to miraculously touch and transform my life. That said, I would like to thank all of those I've encountered on my journey and been allowed to grow and learn from, including my exceptional family, unconditional friends, committed fans and supporters. A heartfelt thank you goes out to you all.

To my legal and professional support, who manage my career, thank you!

To my authors: What an honor it is to be your publisher! What you have given me, I pray that you receive in return. Triple Crown Publications, because of your sincere and genuine input, continues to be about dreams coming true, choices, and opportunity.

Shannon Holmes, I am here, I am your friend, waiting to understand you.

IMAGINE
THIS

PROLOGUE

FRANKLIN COUNTY JAIL

4:35 P.M.

"Carmen . . . Carmen!" Delano repeated, snapping me out of my trance. "Did you hear me? You left something somewhere. Where do you want me to look?" Delano asked as I sat there smiling, thinking to myself that trouble don't last always. It gets greater later, and *let that be the reason* I come home to my son.

All I could do was smile.

MONTH THREE

I had a beautiful two-year-old son named Antonio. And I was in the Franklin County Jail being held without bond for federal drug trafficking offenses.

I had been left for dead, abandoned by my so-called peeps. Sad and embarrassed to admit it, even my baby's daddy, Chino, was still getting his hustle on—slangin' them *"thangs."* Chino continued to get his grind on for that cheddar even after the feds laid me down like fresh tar on pavement. I was looking at football numbers—you know, four score and seven years, trying to be true to the code. The street code of *don't tell,* Chino instilled that in me: Ball 'til you fall, and button-your-lip-type shit. Well, I did ball. I did fall. And my mouth was shut. But something was going on inside my head. A fight was raging between me, Pammy, and my alter ego, Carmen.

Pammy wanted to be with her son and out of this game. Pammy wanted to be free.

Carmen wanted to be in prison. Carmen wanted to be locked. She didn't mind an all-expenses-paid vacation to rest a spell and recoup. She really had no issue that the feds *laid a bitch down for a minute.*

Carmen was a baller—a hustler—a dealer—a playa. A *goin'-for-mine-by-any-means-necessary*-type bitch.

To talk, or not to talk, Shakespeare ain't had shit on me. This was my dilemma, for real. I could talk and walk, or shut up and fry 'til I die. On the other hand, talking could mean, well, death. Shit. I was fucked either way and there was no turning back.

There was a city in the Midwest that from outside appearances was a slow, conservative family town. But lurking underneath was an underworld where drugs flowed throughout the city like blood coursing through veins.

This blood kept alive the disposable income that supported the hustlers' lifestyle in the city. Like a shark drawn to the smell of blood in the water, so did it draw the out-of-town ballers from the east coast. Like a pilgrimage to Mecca, they were coming for the expected promise—wealth by any means necessary. And it was uncommon to encounter anyone who was actually born and raised in Columbus. The majority of the residents were transplanted from other places, seeking opportunity.

In the center of downtown Columbus was a tall, granite building. Gothic looking with mesh-covered windows, it was a city block wide. This was the Franklin County Jail.

From above, inmates pressed their faces close to the paint-tinted windows for a glimpse of freedom. On a sunny day, cars driving by and the hustle and bustle of the downtown working class could be seen.

The business suits and skirts scurried past the building, knowing all too well that the dregs of society lived within the granite walls. Paralegals used the side entrance to clerks' quarters. Attorneys entered through the center tunnel, passing security guards of the underground parking for the legal elite. Commoners circled the block, time after time, in search of a parking meter that allowed limited minutes to go to court in support of a loved one.

The rat race was obvious and apparent and continued day after day, week after week, and eventually month after month for the detained criminal who was assumed guilty until proven innocent.

Sometimes I didn't think that I was going to make it. Shit, death had become a welcome remedy. I saw those like me take deals from the advisement of their lawyers, generally referred to as "lips" by inmates. Some did it because their innocence gave way to ignorance. Others did it because they abandoned the street code: *Death before dishonor*.

It had been a wonderful surprise to see Delano. He was to me what sunlight is to a withering flower. He had proven himself to be a good man.

Delano had cut his hair close to his head, removing the small ringlets of curls. He was tall, thick and tempting. His skin was sun kissed, and he had full, deep-set eyes hiding behind lashes a girl would truly die for. His dark brows matched a perfectly trimmed mustache and five o'clock shadow beard. Although he had gotten rid of the curls, a defined pattern where they once mingled was left behind on his head. He was also packin' a thick, long and satisfying dick of any girl's dream. Just to smell his dick at this point would be a fulfilling fantasy. When I first laid eyes on him, he was in my living room playing with my son. At the sight of him, there was a flutter in my heart. That was when I knew my heart wasn't frozen and that I could believe again . . . that I could love again. He came along and put my heart on simmers, bringing back to life a part of me that I seriously thought was dead. The baritone rhythm of his voice sent chills up my spine as his eyes roamed my body from head to toe. I needed more time with Delano. I sure as hell wasn't in no hurry to get back to those bitches who had been my cellmates for the past three months. More importantly, I needed to know if this nigga was really down for me or just on some penitentiary shit—you know, saying what I want to hear. That "I miss you, Boo" and "You the one for me." That is, until a nigga gets free.

"Come on, CO I just got here," I protested. "CO" is short for correctional officer. It's actually an insult that is often overlooked, considering the long list of other names inmates called them. I was ready to spew all the ones I knew—security guard, paid robo cop, unarmed Shaft—and was poised to add a few to the list if she denied me my request for more time.

She flipped through her logbook and began writing as if she never heard a word I'd said. Delano's eyes were telling me to calm down as mine narrowed to match my sharp tongue. Before I could say another word, she said, "Five minutes," without looking up from her logbook. The temperature was chillier than a December morning, so I stretched my long-johns sleeves over my hands for warmth. The temperature was kept low, similar to a hospital, to minimize the germs, I was told.

I turned my attention back to Delano, my composure completely restored, donning a million-dollar smile. "Delano, it was really nice seeing you. Thanks for the visit," I said. As if on cue, he said what I was hoping he would say.

"Carmen, do you need anything?"

Chino began talking about the killings he had committed and how I was his weak link because I had that gun information on him. I knew how he ran with the nine millimeter, unable to wipe his prints off 'cause he was butt naked. Getting into the Good Samaritan white man's car with the gun, he used the change of clothes given to him to remove his fingerprints. When Chino confessed his crime to me, he and I buried the gun together, sealing our secret. Then Chino began to talk about the location of the gun. "Yeah, I went back and got that gun just in case you flipped on me. I can't even trust you no more. I have no more use for you. Pooh, your ass has got to go. Have you said your prayers, love?"

I looked over my shoulder at the overpaid security guard, knowing that the attention she was giving her logbook was a ploy to listen in on our conversation. Thinking fast, I prayed that Delano would understand the Pig Latin that I was about to drop on him. In the seventies, this dialect gave the street hustler the ability to converse in the presence of the police and others of opposition. But as informants infiltrated the crime world, they learned the lingo and exposed it. I was gambling on the youthfulness of my captor, who looked to be only about twenty-one—tops. The fact that the language had been considered dead, old-school dialogue was an added plus. I brought my index finger to my lips to hush him. I looked into his deep-set eyes, then I rolled the dice.

"No, I don't need anything. *Ogay ota rena ina etay burbay ofay nublay. Unday otey boatay ockday eriday isa hedsay tathay usay orfay.*" This meant: Go to the park out near the suburb of Dublin. Under the boat dock, there is a shed that they use for storing rope for the boats. Walk about twenty grown-man steps going north. There will be a green steel bench next to a water fountain. Beside the fountain, there is a drain that allows for the overflow of water from the fountain. With a crowbar, the grate can be removed. Lift the grate and place your hand inside. You need to wear a glove because it's slimy. Tell me what you find wrapped in a gray bag.

He winked his eye and nodded his head, letting me know that he understood the Pig Latin. All the time growing up in the hood playing around with this as kids had finally paid off.

Delano rubbed his sexy chin and winked his eye. "I'll be here next Saturday. I'll give you an answer then. If I find *it*, what do you want me to do with it?" Since he presented himself like he was my knight in shining armor, I felt like I was giving him the location to uncover the mysteries of Excalibur. With it, he could protect me from those who sought to harm me. That was the fantasy that played through my mind, but the only thing I asked of him was to keep it in a safe place.

"Cool. There are some things I need to take care of. I'm

going Up Top, to New York, this weekend. I'll get back at you when I return."

I studied him, wondering what that entailed. Was it business or pleasure? Going "Up Top" usually meant to re-up on some of them *"thangs."*

"Xavier! Visit's up!" I heard the stinkin', tobacco-chewing, Inspector Gadget-looking, Ms. Dudley Do-Right action ass announce.

Delano wanted me to put my hand on the glass as if he was Patrick Swayze in *Ghost.* I did yearn to touch his strong hand and feel his sensational warmth one more time.

I remembered the first time he stroked the side of my face and nape of my neck ever so gently while the sweat from our naked bodies dried in the air-conditioned bedroom. Remembering the last time he made love to me in the Hyatt hotel after dinner and a carriage ride caused goose bumps to surface. Not understanding how the fate of his occupation, that of a drug dealer, brought us together to find love, and hopefully happiness, I felt apprehensive about him going to New York.

New York was the land of opportunity for a baller looking to get paid. The city represented itself as the certified port for drugs into the country. Delano and others like him stood at its shores, waiting to welcome it home: coca. I wanted him to stay clear from that. I wanted him to be safe. Perhaps I was the example. I went to jail so he wouldn't have to. He continued to reassure me that all was well as he spoke calmly into the receiver.

"You'll be all right," Delano said and gazed squarely at me. I sensed that he could feel or see the internal turmoil I was going through. Over the next several weeks I had some hard decisions to make. I could take a plea on the conspiracy to distribute narcotics, money laundering and aiding and abetting charges without cooperation, or I could take a plea with cooperation—in other words, snitch. I could also

simply tell the court to pick twelve and make the government prove their case. My eyes obviously disclosed my
dilemma, because Delano leaned closer and spoke directly
into the phone. "Baby, you have to do what's best for you
and yours. You know what I mean?" he said.

I shook my head slowly. If I was reading Delano right,
and I was sure that I was, my baby, my love and my heart,
was asking me or telling me that I should flip. If I had learned
one thing from Chino, it was to respect the game and to
honor its code. Now a nigga that I loved and might one day
marry was asking me, no, telling me, to bitch up, snitch and
become a fuck for the feds. I was hurt. But more than being
hurt, I was disappointed. I had seen Delano as a man's man,
a nigga that walked it like he talked it. I was sadly mistaken.
Niggas knew, and I am sure Delano did, that you played the
game at your own risk. Delano repeated himself. "Do what's
best for you, you know what I mean?"

His instructions for me to go for self made me question
his integrity. A true baller played the cards he was dealt.
Even if the shit was fucked up, he put on his game face like
he was holdin' four aces. Also, a true baller knew the most
fundamental rule of the game: He knew when to hold 'em
and when to fold 'em. I knew it was easy to play a good
hand well. It was the woman or the man who could play a
bad hand well that distinguished the real from the fake, a
gangster from a prankster. Delano's advice made me feel
sad, for I realized that I was truly out of my league. I loved
Delano, but not only didn't he really know me, he had me
fucked up. Yeah, I was scared to death and I didn't want to
do life, but I wasn't going to be no snitch either.

Delano made a feeble attempt to assure me that things
weren't as bad as they seemed. Although I appreciated his
comforting words embracing my broken spirit, I could not
stop the tears from streaking my face nor feeling faint. He
whispered into the receiver. "Carmen, they are not thinking
about you." I began to cry tears of pain. "Don't cry, you'll be

fine," Delano continued, and I felt the warmth of his words and tasted the salty residue from my tears as it rested upon my top lip. Breaking before his eyes, I had to end the visit. I rushed the words out of my mouth.

"Delano, I gotta go, bye!" I motioned for the turnkey to let her know that I was ready to go back to my housing unit. Delano blew me a kiss, and made the *call me* sign with his thumb and pinky finger before he got onto the elevator.

I stood in my cage, holding onto the bars for support. I felt like I had consumed a gallon of Absolute vodka, and the box I was in was being twirled like a piñata. I felt nauseous and my legs started to give way. The rent-a-cop's words barely registered when she told me, "Nah, you sit your happy ass down and wait for me, now. I've gotta do this paper work. It's shift change. Second shift will . . ."

This trick cop had gotten on my last nerve. I wanted to straight wile out on this bitch, but I was too weak. I held onto the bars for dear life. I wasn't about to sit in the filth that covered the once white tiles. But facing double digits only made me sicker and the more I thought about it, the more appealing the floor became. I eventually sat down.

I couldn't believe that I was doing time and facing football numbers. However, God was sustaining me, and I hadn't given up yet. I still had hope. Besides, I had to come home to my son. He was waiting on me. I was living a nightmare. I imagined that all inmates felt this way—wanting to wake up and resume their previous lives. On the other side of the coin was relief, though, because getting knocked meant having a sense of peace; the demanding lifestyle of a hustler could be very hectic, containing a mixture of all sorts of things that eventually came out smelling like shit. It all ended in bullshit, if you asked me.

Now I was really trippin' 'cause Delano came to see me. I thought he had forgotten all about me, just like the others had. All my so-called friends, where were they now? Three months and counting, and I still hadn't heard from Chino, my baby daddy. I knew I shouldn't have expected more from him. Bastard! My thoughts were tainted with the presumptions that would never prove true.

I don't know how long I sat there on the floor, knees up and head hanging between them as if I was literally trying to kiss my ass good-bye, waiting to be returned to my unit. That's just how jail was. It was always "hurry up" and "wait." In jail you simply went nowhere. Your life came to a halt and became defined as meaningless. None of your concerns mattered. You didn't matter. This withered the spirit and broke the pride.

In my daydreams I was with my son. We were in a flower field with bubbles and laughing as his little finger popped each one. He said, "Momma, look," as beautiful birds took flight and performed an aerial display of loops and turns, then gracefully soared high up into the cotton-candy-shaped clouds. This reminded me of my former life. I went from overcoming the hurdles of dropping out of college *("You can't succeed in this world without a degree")* to owning a hair salon *("Pammy, here's fifty thousand, go do your shop, baby")* to selling my ass to feed my son *("Hello May I Help You?")* to becoming a major figure in the drug game *("Motherfuckas better have my money!")* only to end up in this bullshit *("You have the right to remain silent. . . .")*.

As I sat on the cold floor, somewhat tired, I must have nodded off. The jingling of keys and the turning of the cell lock brought me back to my senses. When I looked up, Deputy Allison Brinkley, the coolest deputy in the county, was smiling down at me. I was pleased to see that she had started her shift. She was cool as hell and constantly hooked a sistah up. Favors such as extended visits, extra food trays, phone calls and extra sheets, towels and blankets in jail made the time easier.

"Xavier, let's go. How long were you sitting in there?" Deputy Brinkley asked. Most deputies have a holier-than-thou, standoffish *fuck you* attitude. That wasn't the case with Brinkley. If she could do you a favor, and it didn't hurt her, then you could consider it done. At least that was the way it was between her and me. I stretched my legs and answered her question.

"Too long. That pimple-face CO left me in there. I'm glad you're on, though. I had a visit with a man, girl. She was trying to rush me, but I kept straight talking like she didn't exist, so she left me in there until you came on. It's cool, though. She's just jealous because nobody wants to see her ugly ass."

"That's right, keep a positive attitude. There was another article in the newspaper about you and your case," she said as she fidgeted, trying to find the right key to unlock the visiting door. I got more press than the daily weather.

I sucked my teeth and asked, "Really? What did it say? Did you bring it?" Finally she unlocked the visiting door, slid it to the left and escorted me down the hallway.

"Yeah, I got it. The headline said you counted over a million dollars every weekend. Is that true?" Brinkley queried.

"Nah, they trippin'," I replied trying to avoid the hype.

"Also they did a tour through your house in Murifield last night during the news. That newscaster, you know the one, Wendy Williams, was going through your house with her camera crew describing your lavish lifestyle to the viewers. I mean, really. Why did you have all those pairs of unworn shoes and clothes with the price tags still on them? Like, rows and rows of outfits," Brinkley inquired.

"Girl, you know the media be trippin'," I said.

"Xavier, it was *your* house, *your* address. Are you saying that they made all that stuff up?" I hated lying to her. I trusted her, but shit, it felt like she wanted a true confession or some shit. I couldn't really tell. The snitch on my case, G-Money, was cool, too, but look where my black ass was now.

"Don't you know the feds will stage shit just to see who

comes forward? Nah, they buggin'. It wasn't even like dat. Fa real," I said.

"Wendy was putting on your fur and leather coats and spraying perfumes from what seemed like hundreds of bottles on your dresser. They showed hidden wall safes in your basement laundry room. It was wild. They devoted like a thirty-minute show to the war on drugs and how drug dealers live. They even interviewed the arresting officers in your case that said you had over forty thousand dollars worth of jewelry on at the time of your arrest."

"Girl, where my diamonds at?" I asked her, laughin' it off. Motherfuckers had all my shit.

"Oh, and they found a photo album in one of the extra bedrooms in the house—held them to the camera. It looked like the pics were taken at that nightclub downtown called the Pulse. You know how they got that rainfall backdrop in the photo booth. It was you in some white hottie shorts along with some other dudes."

"What you know about that spot, miss I-don't-go-nowhere?" Brinkley smiled and continued her endless questions.

"Your hair was really long. Next you'll be asking me for a relaxer, right?"

Damn, I hope I'm not questioned about those photos from that night with Infa and T-Love, I thought to myself. I allowed the silence to hold the air like a secret. My business was still just that, *my* business.

"I'll show you the article later. I'll bring you into the hall or something so you can read it," Brinkley stated.

"I really appreciate all you do for me." I turned to give her a friendly smile.

"I know you do, that's why I try to help you. I just can't lose my job helping you—especially since you don't have that money to take care of us," she joked.

"Yeah, right? They should allow us to have newspaper

articles in here," I said, slapping my oversized flip-flops on the cold floor.

"They won't because drugs can be smuggled in on the paper, and it would cause lots of confusion. LSD is often laced on paper articles for smuggling." *They already have that in here*, I thought to myself. But I gave her the *act-like-you-know* look. "Besides, you know everyone is in everyone's business," Brinkley added. "Well, I've got a surprise for you. You'll see later. Get in your dorm before I get into trouble," she said firmly, inserting her key and pulling my dorm door open.

I mouthed "Thanks" as she walked away.

Deputy Brinkley's personality was definitely nothing short of uplifting. There was a respect in her eyes for me that the other female guards dared not reveal. Her cordiality comforted me. Perhaps, under different circumstances, we would have been friends.

On the walk back to the housing unit, I felt a little better. Unfortunately, when Brinkley let me into the sixteen-woman tank in the belly of the beast where the brilliance of the sun could never be seen, I was assaulted by the hopelessness that I saw in the shadows on the faces of the other women.

I laid on my steel bunk, barely cushioned with a thin, two-inch mattress, its stuffing shifted to the bottom. Its plastic covering was ripped in so many places that it could've been a prop in a Freddy Kruger movie. Many times I woke up with scratches all over me. Today, the busted mattress could have been a Serta with goose down pillows, as tired as I was.

The occupancy number in jail varied because people came and went, went and came. They got bonded out, released, sentenced and shipped. There were seventeen steel bunk beds with extra thin mattresses in the unit. Many inmates slept on the floor because they were old, or pregnant and extra fat and couldn't climb on to the top bunk. Sometimes someone would trade her bunk. This was rare. Oftentimes that someone was me, but not anymore because I had to think of me, my back and my behind. Strange things happened to a person in close quarters. I saw too many fights break out over *"Who let out a fart?"* *"Who's looking at what?"* and *"Who knew who on the street and got the story straight or not?"* In jail people were tried and found guilty from the clink of the handcuff. If you had any idiosyncrasies about feet touching you or stinking-ass breath in the morning, you could hang that shit up at the fingerprint station 'cause jail was just like that—the slumber party from hell, and nobody was getting picked up in the morning. Only the strong survived in the county jail.

Then there was one toilet behind a little wall, three feet high and five feet wide, for so-called privacy. My first month in, I got constipated so bad that my stomach almost exploded trying to hold in my shit, too ashamed to take a dump in front of people—hearing inmates yell and scream at other inmates to *"Flush the fucking toilet! Your ass is rotten, what crawled up in you and died?"* After landing on medical, getting an enema and having to drink a bottle of magnesium stearate, I finally took a shit. I trained myself to take dumps at night in order to avoid the drama ever since.

There was a night side and a day side of the dorm. On the day side of the dorm there was a broken-down TV rigged with aluminum foil antennas. It had two channels, and there were two picnic tables made of steel, which could never be eaten on because they were always covered with clothes. There was one phone and a pencil sharpener. The dorm had about eight narrow windows, but they were all painted shut so that no one could see the light of day. The only time I saw daylight or received fresh air was when I went to court. It had been a while. The feds were so fuckin' slow with their shit! I had not gone to court in three months, and my attorney, Myer Levin, didn't know when I would go again. At least that was what he told me, so I just sat doing county time.

We ate our last meal of the day at about 4:30 P.M.—way too early, but that's jail. Once the rules of jail were learned, it wasn't hard to figure out which ones could be bent and which ones could be broken. There was only one shower, and although there were a lot of women, there was no line to stand in to freshen up. Now the phone line was something else; for that, the line was never ending. A phone in jail was an entirely different situation. It was our link to the outside. We all used it to compensate for the things we had no control over—our lives, our men who could care less and our shaky business matters. But the fact was that nothing was run behind the wall but our mouths. And some knew not to even do that. In many ways we were helpless dependents, left only to our consequential fate.

"Who's next on the phone?" I asked.

"I am," answered a fellow inmate named Shorty Rock. She was little, about 4'11" and a hundred pounds soaking wet. Shorty Rock's sidekick was named Cricket. Cricket was a he-she, or should I say, she-he. Cricket had a light complexion, and she was fine in the dyke sense. She-he looked like a dude, and she-he got massive attention and all the commissary she-he could pimp off the ladies. She-he wore her khakis saggin', a low-top fade, and had a pimp walk that would put an ol' *G* to shame. Shorty Rock and Cricket were an obvious couple and kept the dorm up most nights bumpin' pussies under the covers, lickin' and lappin' each other.

Shorty Rock slapped her dominoes on the table and said, "Xavier, you can go before me since ya just came in from yo' visit."

"Thanks, Shorty Rock," I said cuffing my pants for the fifth time that day. I heard her mumble some sucka shit under her breath but I simply didn't give a fuck. She wore a fake smile and started asking questions.

"Any good news, girl?" she asked, with her nosy ass, as she tapped the sides of her bones on the table.

"It was a personal visit, not a pro visit. But it was interesting. Rock, Vanessa, y'all wanna play some bid whist later on?" I said, nipping any further conversation about my business in the bud.

"Yeah, no doubt," Vanessa replied—another dude lookalike.

"Cool, let's play after my shower." Before that, though, I decided that I would call my sister. I went over to the phone and wiped off the germs with my shirtsleeve. "Please be home, Sissy," I said as the phone rang.

"Hello?"

"You have a collect call from the Franklin county jail. To accept this call, please say yes after the tone." Beeeeeep!

"YES!" My sister Lori screamed into the receiver.

"Hi, Sissy," I said.

"Hi, Pammy, how are you?" Lori asked.

"I'm hanging in there and still alive. What's up with you?" I said twisting the phone cord. I kept the same habit of twisting the phone cord from back in the day.

"Not too much, just the usual, working and worrying about you. Are there any dykes in there? Do they try to get at you?"

"Stop that," I said, not wanting to get into that discussion with my sister as a dyke was staring me down so hard that I had to turn my back to her.

"Have you heard anything about your case or from your brother?" Lori asked, and I turned my back to the card table to whisper into the phone.

"No, I'm still waiting. I wrote Ty and he hasn't written me back. Ty is so slow writing me back. My lawyer is supposed to come see me soon. He said that he filed a discovery motion," I said.

"What is 'motion of discovery' or 'discovery motion'?" Like most people who had only been in court for traffic tickets, my sister knew very little, if anything, about criminal law. Truthfully, that wasn't so surprising, for it seemed as if most supposed lawyers didn't know jack shit either. I certainly wasn't any Johnnie Cochran, but I was learning, albeit the hard way.

"Sis, let me see if I can make it as simple as possible. The courts are supposed to serve as a forum for the judgment process to play itself out. What that means in layman terms is this: Your lawyer and the prosecutor are on opposite sides of the fence. Your lawyer is hired to prove your innocence or make the prosecutor prove your guilt to a jury beyond a reasonable doubt. It's a fight. The judge is supposed to be an impartial referee. The prosecutor has two obligations before the battle begins. One is to serve you with an indictment, a fancy word accusing you of whatever it is you are supposed have done. Two, to turn over any information they might have, or have access to, that could potentially prove your innocence. These documents are called Brady, Giglio and Jencks material."

"Say what?"

"Yeah, for instance, if you committed a murder or was charged with committing one, but some witness said that they saw a white woman running away from the murder scene, and the investigators took her statement, that's considered Brady material."

"Why do they call it that?"

"Hell if I know. But anything that the prosecutor has in his files along these lines must be turned over to you before trial. Even statements that people have made implicating you must also be turned over to your defense team. The process that you or your lawyer uses to get this information is called a discovery motion. The shit sounds complicated, Sis, but it really ain't all that mysterious. This will allow us to see where we're at, or shall I say, how much trouble I'm in." I rolled my eyes at a nosy spectator.

"Yes, 'cause you are definitely in trouble," Lori said.

"My lawyer also filed a motion for severance. Basically, it's a motion to the court asking the judge to give me a trial separate from my so-called codefendants. For instance, if I had implicated Chino and Chino implicated me or said that I was the real King Pin or culprit, then we would have what the court calls mutually exclusive and antagonistic defenses. Realistically, we could conceivably get separate trials. But all this motion stuff will help us see and get an idea of how long I might have to do."

"When do you get this motion stuff back?"

"I'm not sure, but my lawyer has sent me copies of all the ones he's filed on my behalf. He even filed one for separate counsel tables, so I can be tried alone and not as a coconspirator—a lot of mumbo jumbo legal stuff."

"Well, it sounds like you're learning the law."

"I'm trying to stay with this litigation thing. Things are moving slow in one sense and fast in another. It's moving fast because they're trying to send me away for a long time," I said.

"Remember, we're not claiming all that time. Do you want me to call your lawyer?" Lori asked.

"No, let's give him two more weeks."

"All right. Do you need anything? I'll be down there to visit around eight," Lori said.

"Oh, I almost forgot, you can't come because I've had my visit for today. I hate this one-visit-per-day rule."

"Who came to see you?"

"Guess. No, you'll never, ever guess in a million years," I said with a smile on my face.

"Chino?" She couldn't hold back her laughter and I interjected loudly.

"Hell no!" I said with disgust. Just the mention of his name made my blood boil like hot lava. "That sorry-ass motherfucker!" I took the phone from my ear and began to beat it on the wall.

"See, that's why the phone stay broke!" A girl from the card table began to yell at me and say some smart shit out of her mouth.

"Fuck you!" I looked back at her and screamed. I placed the phone back to my ear, trying to respect my sister's phone bill and her time.

"Are you sane in there?" Lori asked.

"Yeah, I am."

"Maybe he will finally one day over the rainbow come through," Lori said into the receiver.

"Anyway, guess who came to visit me?" I said anxious to tell her how Delano came through like a trouper should.

"Hmmm . . . okay, I give up, who?" Lori asked.

"Delano!"

"Delano," she repeated.

"Yes, Delano, and it was a nice visit."

"Where has he been hiding? I hardly hear from him, and his pager number is changed or disconnected or something. Plus, your niece, Kristen, asks about him all the time."

"I didn't ask him where he's been. I imagine surviving all this drama."

"Yeah, much drama. You were in the newspaper again," Lori informed. There was silence. "I know they upset you so much," Lori continued.

"Have you talked to Mom?" I asked.

"Yes, this morning. She is having some sort of custody hearing for the baby."

"Why?" I quizzed.

"Somethin' to do with your arrest. It's no big deal. Call her and she'll explain, but she'll be in Columbus, and we both will come see you."

I explained to my sister how and why I didn't want her to bring my son to see me living like an animal in a cage—how I couldn't bear him feeling rejected due to the fact that I could not touch him and feel the warmth of his body against my face. How would I explain why we couldn't touch? She continued to plead, but my heart was dead set against a noncontact visit with my son. The time ran faster than a marathon athlete as the beeps cut into our conversation.

"Thirty seconds remaining!" and we said our last good-byes with promises of visits and next-time opportunities to see each other.

"I love you, too, Lori." *Click!* I hung up the phone and went to go lie down in the dorm. The screeching sounds of a rigid-wheeled cart echoed down the hall.

"Trraaaays! Trraaays! Cups up, ladies."

"Does anyone know what they havin' for dinner?" I asked like we were at a restaurant.

A voice from underneath the covers screamed, "Whatever any of y'all don't want, I want it."

"Okay, anything that I don't want, you've got it."

The same routine every day—trustees ordering trays and cups up for juice or colored water, the county jail's Kool-Aid. The food was cold and the juice was always hot. It was like they had it in reverse or something. The strangest looking officer on staff called us for meal. "Get in line for trays, ladies," the CO yelled.

"Hey, Officer Neal," I yelled from the back of the line trying to get some play. A butch dyke from Chi-Town was beckoning me to the front of the line. I shook my head and said, "Nah, I'm straight," and walked away. I went and stood next to a crackhead that had come in the night before. She was wiping sleep out of her eyes. They called her Diamond. She'd been asleep in a crack coma for two days.

"Whew. C'mon wit' the food!" Diamond said. "We were up in Big Mama's house gettin' higher than a cloud—blazin! Before the raid, it was like *dat!*" Diamond said to another addict trying to edge closer to the front of the line.

"Xavier, those people involved in that drug raid got it goin' on." Diamond had been in and out the jail so much that she made my head spin. On each and every return she had something to say about that, tried to pry into my shit or bring back some off-the-streets drama.

"Hold that shit down," said a girl from the front of the line. We tryin' to eat."

"Shit, I know you gon' let me talk, right?" Diamond said. She couldn't have weighed a hundred pounds. "Like I said, that drug bust got everyone wondering, Xavier, if you gon' tell." She played it off as if she was trying to make a statement, but she really wanted it to be a question for the dorm to ponder. Motherfuckers spent their days ear hustlin' about the next man's business. No doubt that she was buying rocks from someone from my past. But I didn't know if she was friend or foe, informant or hoe the way she ran up in the spot and seemingly had a get-out-of-jail-free card. The police used crackheads as snitches. They would have them do a buy and then raid the house afterwards.

"Hi, Xavier, you want an extra tray?" Officer Neal asked, shifting the focus to the food. I told myself the best thing to do was ignore the crackhead, but then again, I wanted to put her in check about my business. I ended up simply letting let it slide. I walked past the Chi-Town butch and she winked her eye at me. *Damn, now I gotta sleep with one eye open.*

"Sure, thanks," I said and sashayed back to the metal picnic table holding two trays like I had pull. Yep, pull in the joint was still a status symbol, just like on the streets. The meat and the soup on the trays were a mystery. I was hungry, but not that damn hungry. "Anyone want this extra tray?" Now I was about to get mobbed.

"Yes, I do," White Girl Susan said eagerly.

"Here, take this shit. You can have this one, and Yvette, you can have this one," I said to another inmate. I gave the trays away and began to sift through my commissary bag searching for a Nutty Buddy.

"Thanks, Xavier."

"Mmmaaaail call!" The officer yelled and the girls swarmed the door. I stood in the rear of the room waiting to see if my name got blown up.

"Smith, Flowers, Jones, Stringer, Xavier . . ." I walked to the front and grabbed the letter from the officer's hand. It was from my brother, finally. I plopped down on my bunk, ripped open the letter and pulled out a candy stick. I began sucking on it and read:

What's up Sissy,

Hope you doing all right over there on your end of the jail. I got your letter and want you to know that I am praying for you. I am praying for us. Shit, hopefully this will be over soon. I spoke to Mom and Lori and they seem to be doing fine. I tried to call Carla. I mean, she is the sorriest baby mama I could have ever chose to have. She got a block on her phone, so I don't know how my kids are doing. Mom said she would try to get in touch with her through her fake-ass mother.

Guess who came up in here last night? Okay, you give? That motherfucker they called Tony. You know, the one that sold clothes to G-Money's ass. I'm trying to pick his brain to find out what is up with that snitch. Tony said he still in Columbus, trying to lay low. He also said that the feds got an undercover out in Columbus taking niggas down. Sneaky bastards.

I walked past Diaz's dorm on my way to my pro visit and he was up in the dorm looking like a girl. Them fags done put it down wit' his ass.

So what's up with your attorney? They want you to flip da script? They want me to do the same thing. And I can't speak for you, but I'm going to stay the course and do my time. They ain't got shit on me. Quite frankly, I need a vacation. Tired of all the shit I left out on the streets. I got caught up in your shit, but only God knows what I am really doing time for. I'm looking at aiding and abetting. That runs about twenty-one months, if don't nobody else put no shit in the game.

I heard Chino got a new car and still fucking with them thangs on the streets. Sis, don't even worry, he gon' get his. He lucky that I'm in here. I just sit back on my bunk sometimes and think about how in the hell I got into this shit. It seems like yesterday that you had your salon before you and Chino broke up. It seems like yesterday I was going to my prom and you were outside taking photos of me.

I know you miss your son and I know you wonder how Chino could leave you for dead. Sis, I wonder the same thing myself. But try not to worry about it. Keep your head up and your mouth shut. Let little bro' give you the advice this time. Everyone over here wonders if you gon' tell. I get tired of hearing that shit. I know you a stand-up woman. I tell them to go to hell with that bullshit.

I know this is silly, but this morning I remembered when they arrested me, I had a hamburger in the microwave. I wonder if it's still there?

Take care and when you speak to the fam, give them my love and I will do the same.

Young Ty

Following the evening mail call, they had Visit Package Delivery. Visit Package Delivery was when your visitor left a package for you prior to the visit. The staff inspected the package, and it was later delivered that night. My favorite deputy, Brinkley, came in with a brown paper bag that had my name written across it. She motioned for me to come closer and whispered into my ear, "This was my surprise. You're up to your limit on items, but I let these lovely things get through." I grabbed the bag and walked over to my area. I read the package slip and saw that it was from Delano. I thought, *Sweetie lookin' out. Yeah, that's what I'm talkin' 'bout.* Doing time wasn't so bad when there was someone loving you from the streets, showing loyalty just because. My ass was up a creek without a paddle, and Delano was still there for me.

My nose was filled with the scent of Delano's cologne as I removed a white chenille bathrobe from the bag along with white footie socks with the little balls on the back, wife beater Polo T-shirts with matching undies and cotton pajamas. Delano's Dolce & Gabana fragrance covered me like a blanket on a winter night.

At the bottom of the bag were *Don Diva, Essence* and *Urban Trendsetters* magazines. Lining the last layer of treats were books by my favorite authors: *Street Dreams,* by K'wan, David Walker's *Appeal* and *Sheisty* by T. N. Baker.

It felt like Christmas in the county jail. I held the robe to my face and inhaled, wishing Delano was here, near me, and thankful that he had not left me for dead.

I was so relieved to have the one and only street bible, *Don Diva Magazine.* I flipped through the pages looking for advice. *Don Diva* advised me, "Don't tell. . . ." *Don Diva* knew about *the choice.* It understood the street code.

I headed for the shower.

There is nothing like a hot shower. In this place, standing under the water was more than invigorating. It provided more than relief to my sore, aching body. It was also a place where I could escape. In here, I didn't have to worry about answering questions that none of us could really answer, nor listening to the stories of grandeur that the women invented to build up their self-esteem. I didn't have to listen to complaints made by women with charges that didn't amount to shit compared to what I faced. My shower was where I could find uninterrupted solitude. And this is where I prayed.

God, I want to thank you for my life, health and strength. Thank you. Oh, God, I miss my baby. Antonio, Mommy is so sorry. I'm sorry, son. Father, thank you for the strength to endure another day. Father protect my family, comfort my son and give me the wisdom and vision needed to go through this. Thank you for your grace and many blessings.

Amen.

As the water pounded against my skin, washing away the stench and grime that permeated my body, I couldn't help but think about the visit I had with Delano . . . so sudden . . . so strange . . . so needed. Then I cried.

Sudsing between my legs, making sure that I scrubbed any foul smells away, I heard a voice calling me from just outside the shower curtain.

"Hey, Pam, I got a towel waiting for you when you get out." Rinsing off the last remains of soapsuds, I recognized the voice to be that of the Chi-Town butch.

MONTH FOUR

By the fourth month, I was on the verge of becoming completely stressed out. I was ready to go! Today started off fucked up and it didn't look like it was going to get any better.

Common practice in jail was to wash your clothes by hand in the only sink in the tank. The same sink was also used for washing dishes and taking birdbaths. That was a problem, because many of the women were infected with venereal diseases. They tried to wash away the parasites feeding and nesting within their pubic hairs, and they made vigorous efforts to wash the stinking, yellowish discharge that was oozing from their coochies with Dial soap as if it was a miracle cure. The stainless steel sink was also the only source of drinking water. Therefore, I was constantly washing it out and praying that whatever microscopic organisms gestating there wouldn't kill me.

Last night I placed my clothes on the picnic table to dry, and someone stole my underwear—again—used underwear! I couldn't believe that shit, and I was mad as hell. Where was the honor among these thieves? Some of these women came in here with charges for grand theft, stealing nothing but top-shelf merchandise, so for the life of me, I couldn't understand how secondhand underwear was such a hot commodity. Then I realized how fortunate I really was.

Inmates, upon being processed into the jail, were not allowed to keep any undergarments that weren't white. This even included women who were on their period. Imagine that! Women were running around trying to hold sanitary pads in place with just their pants, and those new inmates who came into the jail were virtually *ass out* if their people didn't bring them any *whites*. They had to steal some if push came to shove, and I had seen a whole lot of pushin' and shovin'. I really did have to count my blessings. My sister, Lori, kept me fully stocked. My being fully stocked brought out the hater-aid in others.

As luck would have it, the day of my arrest, I had on my white satin panty set from Victoria's Secret. The thought of that made me laugh. Those were the same ones that I purchased from G-Money for my escort service girls. Needless to say, I was never without.

I looked over at the telephone. My desire to talk with my son became compelling. A Latino girl sport'n' a fresh black eye was whining to someone who apparently didn't give a fuck about how long she had to stay in this hell hole. I saw a couple of girls staking their claim to the phone. To jump the phone line in county was no good. It meant war. My desire to hear my son's voice made me care nothing about the pecking order. I made up my mind that as soon as the Latino girl hung up the phone, I was on it. I watched for signs that her phone call was nearing its end. When she rubbed her nose, I made my move. I bumped someone as I ran to the phone, lifted the receiver and commenced dialing.

"Hey, I'm next!" I heard someone shout over my shoulder. I looked back to see the roughest looking bitch I had ever seen. Big Baby was every bit of 6'2", and she weighed about two hundred pounds. Her skin was so badly blotched that it looked as if she had been pepper sprayed her whole life, and her nose flared like a silverback gorilla protecting her young.

"No! I'm using the phone. I need to call my son," I retorted.

"Oh, well, so do I," she countered. The threat was evident in her voice.

"No phone checkin' here—not here, not now!"

I put my back to the wall and faced her while she continued to protest. "You don't own that phone," she said clenching her teeth. I continued to hold onto the phone for dear life. My fingers rapidly punched the numbers.

After dialing the phone, I tried my best to count the number of rings I heard while keeping a watchful eye on Magilla Gorrilla. I was anxious to hear the excitement in my son's greeting that would undoubtedly comfort me. Each ring seemed to last an eternity. Mixed feelings of disappointment and frustration raced through my veins. I slammed the receiver down on the lever. I'd had enough of this funny-built bitch.

The noise drew the attention of some girls who were engaged in a game of dirty hearts.

"Come on, Xavier, you got the phone. Leave that shit alone. It's not worth it," warned a girl who seemed scared for me. But the way I was feeling, ol' girl could have been the daughter of King Kong. The shit was on.

I lunged at Magilla, throwing a wild hook that caught her square on the jaw. It forced her back, but she regained her composure fast. She rushed me as my fist connected with her nose. The girls began banging on the steel bars and shouting, "FIGHT! FIGHT!" Magilla was grunting when she grabbed a handful of my hair. She tried to yank me down to the floor, but I was stronger than she thought, so she just held onto it. As I hit her in the stomach, I heard the wind come out of her. Somebody should have told that bitch that my brother was a Golden Gloves boxer and he'd taught me a few tricks.

Seconds later, the goon squad, which wasn't nothin'

but wannabe SWAT, busted in, rushed me to the floor and broke us up. They wore navy blue riot gear with helmets and hood-beater sticks strapped to their left hip. They'd beat the shit out of shit if they had to. They dragged me down to the booking area and put me in a tiny urine-smellin' holding cell. Following behind me shouting threats was Big Baby. They placed her in the holding cell next to mine. As they stopped to open her door, she peered into my area and sang through the vent. *"Ain't nothin' but a blanket p-a-r-r-t-y . . ."* For three hours, I sat in there waiting to find out what would happen next.

What seemed like two days passed and the corporal finally came to see me. He was a Barney Fife-looking motherfucker carrying my write-up for fighting. They called them "tickets." My destination was segregation. The images I held of solitary confinement came from the movies I had seen, like *Shawshank Redemption,* where the character, Andy, was tossed into a cell that was completely dark and roach infested, and the only thing he had to eat was bread and water. I thought about the guards that would break my door in the middle of the night and torture me, if for no other reason, their own enjoyment.

I was led to another room. It was as if I was being toyed with—being put on display, like a public execution was about to take place.

A buffed male officer wearing his tight polyester dick-imprinted pants came from behind the desk to take off the handcuffs, which were cutting into my wrists. Then he told me that he needed to photograph me. "For what?" I asked him.

"Because we need it along with a listing of your injuries," he replied. Beside my head being tender from that primate trying to use my hair to swing from, I was cool.

"Do you want to press charges?"

"What?" I asked, confused.

"These are standard questions. Just answer them so we can get this over with. Now, what happened? Do you want to give a statement?" he said, irritated by having to do his job.

"No!"

"All right. Because this is your first fight, you lose your visit this week and a week's commissary privileges. You'll also have a dorm change and spend three days in segregation. I will not have fighting in my jail."

I wanted to laugh in his face. I had been fighting every day since my arrest. I fought against the two-million-dollar cash bond that was placed on my head and the incompetent lawyers who took my case because they saw me as a gold mine. I fought against the endless number of charges that were being thrown at me. I fought against the vulture who was trying to strip me from everything I worked so hard to get. I fought to keep my son from being taken from me by agencies that were still practicing something being prescribed for slavery. I fought for the right to throw the food they served me into midair because it didn't look, or taste, like it was fit for human consumption. I fought to get a good night's rest. But most of all, I fought to keep my sanity through all this crazy shit.

The door to my new cell in solitary slid shut. I felt I had walked into a catacomb. I was indifferent to my living arrangements because I had assessed it as being nothing more than another aspect of jail. The girls had coined it "The Hotel." After I cleaned the toilet, sink and floor, it wasn't all that bad. It was dark, though, but not entirely; there was enough light coming from the corridor that allowed me to read. The dim lighting added to the diminished spirit. It multiplied the reality of being punished. The silence heightened my senses, and I was able to hear things that I had not heard and smell the odors oozing from the concrete walls.

Jail always had a way of fully exposing one's nature; people who were assholes on the streets and came to jail became even bigger assholes. I lived by the axiom, "Life is what you make it." No matter where I was, I intended to do just that. Eventually I found peace.

Two cells down and across from mine was an elderly woman pacing the length of the four-by-six-foot cell, shouting, "Hallelujah! Thank you, Jesus!" When I peered through the cell, across the small hall, I saw her peering out of the bars. She looked me in the eyes with such confidence that it gave me chills. Before I could ask her *Do you know me?* she said, "God cares."

This woman reminded me of a grandmother. The only thing she was missing was one of those duster dresses that grandmas wore early in the morning. She was well into her seventies, and she had a strained look on her face that conveyed that she was simply fed up with it all. "Every shut eye ain't sleep, every good-bye ain't gone."

I took a step backward, not knowing how to respond to her. But she didn't wait for any response and turned away from the bars. "Ma'am . . . Ma'am . . . what did you say?" She remained silent the rest of the night. I fluffed out my mattress, rolled my sweatshirt underneath my head and fell asleep.

In the middle of the night, I awoke to someone saying, "1 . . . 2 . . . 3 . . . 4 . . . breathe." There were several officers standing at my door. Two of them were male. One of them was looking at me with a dumb-ass look, as though I had caught him staring. I got off my bed, and he motioned for me to stop, even though the door was locked.

"What's going on, CO?" I asked.

"Nothing! Get away from the doors," he screamed at me. I could see a gurney positioned on the floor and the medical staff. It looked like they were a couple of cells down.

"Xavier, you up?" a girl that I had befriended during a game of spades asked.

"Yeah. What's goin' on?"

"That ol' bitch hung herself."

I couldn't believe it. Her last words resonated in my mind. "God cares. Every shut eye ain't sleep, every good-bye ain't gone." I felt sympathy and betrayal—sympathy for the obvious and betrayal for receiving a message that seemed like a contradiction.

Three hours later, the cell doors were opened and everyone was allowed out. A few of us girls met in front of the empty cell. I thought about my friend, Young Mike, who took his life at the age of twenty-three, and I wondered *why?* Right then, I vowed that I would not go out like that. I would fight to the bitter end.

I sat on my bunk and pulled out the last letter that I had received from my brother. A smile graced my face as I thought that he had held the same letter I was now holding. I pulled out my notepad and began to write him a response letter.

Young Ty,

I got your letter, finally. Nigga what you doing over there? You ain't got nothing to do but play cards and write me back. It takes you weeks to get back at your big sis. What part of the game is that? Well, I made it to the hole for chin-checkin' a bitch about mine. I am so sick of this shit. You talking about do the time. Let me tell you, a part of me wish like a motherfucker I still had my salon and lived legal. Then if I had to get some fast money, I could have gotten it through the escort service. I mean, what does pandering carry? Not nearly the time dope does. I still wonder if my baby daddy ever loved me. I mean, this nigga really left me for dead, yo. Moms all upset, Lori is stressin' and I miss the hell out of my son, Ty. I wish could run into G's ass. Fuckin' snitch set me up. I am so sorry that I stopped by your apartment that day. If I would have kept goin', the feds would have never got you caught up in this conspiracy case. I really don't see many people that I know come through here. I didn't know a lot of women on the streets, but they sure as hell know me. And what about them niggas slangin' all that crack on High Street with the Short North Posse. My attorney said they got so many secret indictments on them it's pitiful. You could build a football stadium with the numbers they about to give them. This doing-time shit ain't the glitter the hustlers made it out to be. Young Ty, I wanna go home. But please, keep ya head up. And don't let them niggas punk you. Do they give you guys rec on the men's side? We don't rec or gym; they keep us locked up completely.

I saw a girl that reminded me of China that came in here last night. Hurt me to my heart to think about all that she could have become. Then I thought of her daughter.

I miss you, baby brother. Hold ya head up. It still gets greater later, and don't drop the fuckin' soap! Smile.

Love you,
Sissy

After my three days in the hole were up, I was ordered to pack my things for transfer. *Transfer?* I thought. I had only heard this term used for inmates who had been sentenced to the Ohio Reformatory for Women in Marysville. There had to be some kind of mistake. Federal prisoners didn't serve time there. Then I was overcome by the thought that my bond might have been paid. Maybe I hadn't been for-gotten after all. It just took a little time to come up with that kind of money. I started thinking of all those who could have assisted in my release. I knew that my moms and sister combined couldn't have accumulated such a large sum of money, so I scratched them off my mental list. I thought about my Chino. I wanted to believe that he would not leave the mother of his son in a place like this. Despite the fact that we weren't together as we said we would always be, and that he forgave me for shooting him, he knew that I loved him still. But the more that I thought about it, the more I tried to dismiss that fantasy. Chino was only for himself, the essence of a true baller. Was it possible for Delano to pull off a stunt like this and pay my bond? Had I, again, underestimated the stature of this man like I did when I first met him and he was driving his *hooptie?*

As I contemplated the possibilities, a sudden chill crept down my spine, for who else might have been negotiating my release—Dragos? The Columbians were coming for me. They wanted what money I didn't have, and they wanted to make sure I kept the secrets that I had within, that I remained silent. Dragos once bragged to me about how he killed this informant once. He got a surgeon to anesthetize this guy. Then he got a big-ass rat and had the rat anesthetized. Next, the surgeon opened the guy's stomach and put the sleeping rat inside of him. The guy finally awoke, and the rat woke up not long after inside of his stomach. *Damn! What have I gotten myself into?* I thought about all the things that could happen to my son. *Would I see his face on the back of a milk carton?*

I looked for an exit. My only chance was to make a run for it. I felt the pressure of an officer's hand around my arm as I was being led out to get dressed. It was as if he sensed the urgency flowing through my veins. Escape was impossible now, so I prayed for an opportunity to present itself in the near future.

To my dismay and relief, I wasn't being released on bond. I was on my way to the Federal Detention Center in Circleville, Ohio. With my leg irons and handcuffs in place, I rested in the back of the unmarked federal van. I knew that being behind the wall didn't mean that I was untouchable. Even with the right connections, no one was untouchable. And for all intents and purposes, I couldn't shake the eerie feeling that someone was somewhere watching, plotting, waiting.

CHINO

"Man, how in da fuck did you get out? Nigga, you slip-perier than a duck in an oil spill. I thought they had yo' ass for good after I saw your shit plastered on the news. I just knew your shit was fucked up," Sean, the barber, stated.

Chino squirmed a little to get comfortable in the bar-ber's chair and thought of a response to the comment as he got his hair cut. It had been a long time since he came into the barbershop, and he knew that there would be questions from the locals of his escape from the publicized drug bust. But he didn't really give a fuck. His rep stood on its own, and it was enough for others to know he didn't tell to get out. Besides, nobody would believe that he left his baby mama for dead. Anyway, he and his partner were free, and it was business as usual. He brushed off his silk pants leg, being careful not to ruffle the material, and responded to the barber's comments.

"Yeah, you gots to be slick these days to stay out of other people's mix. I got caught up on some bullshit, but you know I got that Jew lawyer and he handled his busi-ness. I'm going to fight this case. They ain't got shit on me. And if worse comes to worse, with the feds, I can fight this case for at least three years." Chino touched his head as if to check on the progression of his cut and suggest to Sean to hurry up and stop asking him questions.

"Nigga, just fade me. I ain't on the witness stand. Stop pressin' me. You press hoes and clothes, not me," Chino said, glancing at the glittering diamond on his left index finger.

Chino was one of Sean's best customers, so he did as he was told. Sean allowed him to cut in front of other clients and get in his chair without waiting his turn. The barbershop was called Legends due to its clientele. It boasted, or rather, Sean boasted, of doing every money-gettin' nigga in Columbus. No other barber could touch his skill in the city and his reputation held a captive audience. Sean even stopped someone's shave to do Chino. Chino dropped fifty spots on him just for a simple cut. Chino was a customer Sean couldn't afford to lose, so he went the suck-up route.

"Noticed you got a new ride. Honey sitting out there is fly. You know you dat nigga! I respect yo hustle!" Sean said as he finished up. He flung the cape off Chino like he was a magician doing a magic trick. Chino put Sean's money in the palm of his hand with what seemed like a handshake without another word. He left the shop and slid into his new whip with his latest hoochie in the passenger seat.

Chino rubbed his chin and screamed into the air, speaking to no one in particular. "Pooh flunked! I give her a straight *F.* No longer playing the game, she is being played. Now it's her turn to learn lessons. Pammy's first lesson: Never trust nobody, not even yo'self. She trusted a mark with her freedom, now she got me caught up in her bullshit. I wouldn't be mad if we were caught up on a humble—the kind of case you catch when shit goes bad, or because of a traffic stop or a wrong place, wrong time type of situation. I can handle that. But to be set up by somebody she should have known would cross her. I warned her against trusting niggas. Fuck that, she on her own. Listen, I taught her to know a person. She should have known G-Money's kind would flip the script in a heartbeat. But no, now her ass on lockdown and the feds breathing hard down her back, and soon they'll be breathing down mine."

He looked at his passenger, LaShone, with a coldness that chilled her more than the air blasting from the vents. "Death before dishonor. I hope she remembers this rule. It's the rule you play by once you knocked. I told her to watch the snitches and slick-ass bitches." Chino returned his eyes to the road. He tried with vain effort to silence the voices in his head: *I gotta get paid. Pooh left customers out here that need to be taken care of, and I will oblige them. I'm already serving two of her customers. P and his crew still takin' kilos a week. Let's face it, when you get knocked, there's always someone else in line for your customers.* "Shit don't stop 'cause a bitch get locked. Pooh, if you can still hear me, your ass flunked. Oh, well . . ."

Chino turned up the sounds in his off-the-showroom-floor, triple white Benz, patted the leg of his hoochie of the week and took the exit ramp south heading into Kentucky. The Kentucky Derby was the spot for horse lovers and ballers of the Midwest.

They came to gamble, snort coca, pop ecstasy and pick up pussy for the evening. Chino was free and coveted his freedom like a newfound jewel. He began to think more and more about the laws of retribution. What was in store for a person who had done all the dirt that he had done? Where was the bullet or beatdown with his name written on it? Sometimes a motherfucker got what his hand called for. Chino had done so much dirt that he knew if he was his own judge and jury he would have been ass out months before. He made a vow to do all he could as the sand in his hourglass ran short.

MONTH FIVE

STILL ON LOCKDOWN.

"This facility is much better," the officer assured me. But I couldn't tell. This jail was cold as well, and the flimsy, thermal underwear I wore didn't help at all. So far, everything was similar to what I had experienced in Downtown Columbus—different address, same problems. In less than thirty minutes of my arrival at the new facility, I was humiliated when ordered to strip ass-hole naked, to bend over, squat, spread my ass cheeks and cough. My property was again taken from me and inspected for weapons, drugs and other contraband. In addition, I was asked a whole bunch of questions that my interrogators already knew the answers to.

My attorney visited me within the first couple of hours of my arrival at the new facility. He told me that the feds wanted me to cooperate with their investigation, and this change of scenery was a good-faith gesture that I would receive the best possible treatment.

The only differences, so far, that I saw up to this point were that I was sprayed for lice like I was a flea-ridden dog, and instead of the ugly green shirt and pants the county provided, I was issued a set of tan khakis to wear.

I was placed in a dorm on the east side of the jail. Stank-ass toilets, stank-ass bitches, stank COs, fucked-up phones with split and twisted cords, stank food and jacked-up commissary options. My eyes searched the room for a vacant bunk, to no avail. The room was filled over the capacity limit. Salty as hell, I held a screw face as I stepped over several people, who had made a home on the little space on the floor, and threw my mat down. The amount of personal belongings that I had brought with me let those who were looking for a mark know that I wasn't new to this. Bidding four months in the county was doing hard time.

I counted forty-one women in a room that was originally designed for seventeen. The evidence of the breakdown in our social structure was strong. No one showed the courtesy to offer their bunk to the two elderly ladies among us. Even when top bunks became vacant and available, no one bothered to move up and offer either of them a lower bunk. Each night the older women struggled for what seemed like an hour, simply to get up on the top bunk. Thankfully, they seemed to find solace in each other. There was no generational bridge between them to try and cross. They had no idea what a *whip* was, or what *killin' niggas for chips* meant, and they didn't seem to care. The appreciation for their sacrifices and the lessons that they handed down had been forgotten. The prevalent attitude of pure unadulterated selfishness dominated the atmosphere. Amongst the girls in the dorm, there was no appreciation for the sacrifice these two women made in their lives, the burdens carried or the dreams of their youth, long gone. They were toothless lionesses in a world of jackals and hyenas—once respected and maybe even feared, but now easy prey.

I continued to examine the conditions of my new environment, looking for what was "better" about this place. Among the federally detained, there were still state detainees as well. This mixture simply caused more confusion, as jailhouse lawyers attempted to elaborate on laws governing the state actions, as well as federal actions. This seldom left anyone with any more insight than the day of arrest.

I camped out on the day side of the room in front of a broken-down television that allowed viewing of two of the nine channels Columbus offered. I sat my things on one of the two steel picnic tables and started taking down my hair that was now nappy as hell.

Separating the entwined pieces of hair one loop at a time, I felt some eyes on the side of my face. I turned to see who those eyes belonged to, and *lo and behold,* it was the bitch that called my house on numerous occasions, chasing down my man, Chino. The way I was feeling, I could have immediately put something on that ass on G.P. (general principle). Before I could play the position, she slid under her blanket and feigned sleep. Didn't nobody want none of this can of kick-ass I was waiting to open. With almost three braids left to go, I dropped my arms to give them a rest. Another young lady walked over and hopped up on the table across from me.

"Hi, my name is Mychala. I see you got a fed case and you wearin' a Rolex." She was making reference to my armband. It was mandatory that each inmate wore one. The color corresponded with the severity of the charge against the felon: white for misdemeanors and orange for felonies. Mine was yellow.

I looked Mychala up and down, making note of the burns on her thumbs and the blotches on her face. *Crackhead.*

Although she was neat in her appearance, my first impression of her was that she was another nosy crackhead who thought she knew me or saw me on TV and hoped I could hook her up like I had kilos rolled up in my blanket. I was in need of a shower and conversation was the last thing on my mind. But I was polite and gave her my name, which was boldly written with a black magic marker on my armband. She took that as an invitation to continue.

"My husband is Dominican. He caught a federal case,

too," Mychala said staring at me. Now she had my undivided attention. I thought that the chances of me meeting someone who could help me make sense of all this was slim to none. The extent of knowledge that most of these women had about federal cases was that if you had one you were in deep shit, and they were glad they weren't in my shoes.

"So, how long did he get?" I asked her.

She tossed a handful of peanuts in her mouth as if she needed something to help her keep her mouth closed. I could tell she was trying to discern whether I could be trusted enough to discuss such a sensitive subject. Since trust was earned and rarely given, I didn't ask again. Instead, I asked her if she liked to read.

"Shit, up in here, what else is there to do?" she said while looking over the book I handed her, but ignoring my bookmark.

"I don't want a dog-eared book. Please use this bookmarker."

She sucked her teeth as if my request was too much to ask. Then she read the title of the book aloud: "*Woman Thou Art Loosed*, by T. D. Jakes. A church book, huh?"

"Yeah, it's good."

"Well, I can dig it. I just didn't figure you for the church-going type. Before crack got me, I was headed for the ministry."

Here we go, I thought to myself. *Every nigga in jail finds religion*. They were all making some kind of promise not to sin again if God would just get them out of this mess. The expression on my face betrayed the dubious thoughts that were going through my mind.

A sense of seriousness came over her as if she was trying to summon the power to part the Red Sea. "No, really, when I don't have my legs up in the air to support my habit, I even have the gift of prophecy."

She spoke with an intelligence that was uncommon to

the average inmate. Her voice was controlled, and she
enunciated each word as if she had studied Shakespeare.
There was an air of realness about her. The more I looked
at her, the prettier she became. Instinctively I knew she
was somebody I wanted to know.

Mychala was about 5'4", and she had a deep chocolate
complexion. Her keen, Indian-like features were promi-
nent, and she wore her hair in a weave ponytail. Her eyes
were a light hazel brown, and she had a large gap between
her front teeth and full lips that illuminated her smile.

While we were talking, the deputy passed out commissary slips for us to order hygiene products and snacks that
cost an arm and a leg. Here, again, I saw the disparity
amongst the women. Every time I received my groceries,
even at the other place, I would catch the evil eye—haters,
no doubt. But their hate wasn't directed towards me, per
se. It was reserved for those who they thought would be
there for them unconditionally, but had given up. We were
also given a "kite," a form used as a method of correspon-
ding with the other departments within the jail freely, without the need for postage.

Consumed by Mychala's stories, I forgot my worries for
a while. She should have chosen comedy as her career. She
kept the unit up all night with impersonations, giving
Jamie Foxx a run for his money. "Pammy, what do you call
a dog with no legs?" she asked.

"I dunno. What do you call him?"

"It don't matter what you call him. He can't come anyway, he ain't got no legs." She cracked herself up more than
those listening to her jokes. Mychala began to wave her
hands, motioning the dorm towards her. "Gather 'round
ladies: Once there was a man that drove a cab. He picked
up a fare in the downtown area near the theater. The passenger had a mysterious bag with him, so the cabbie said,
'Hey, what's in the bag?' The passenger said, 'None of your
damn business.' Of course it made the cab driver curious.

After about five miles or so, they had reached the passenger's destination. He paid the fare and got out of the cab. The cabbie turned and watched the man leave, realizing that he had left the bag in the rear of the cab. In his excitement, he grabbed the bag and looked inside to finally see what was in the bag." Mychala held us captive with her joke; we all wanted to know what was in the bag.

"What was in the bag?" a girl asked with tiny spots of toothpaste covering her acne.

"None of your damn business . . . get it? Hee . . . hee . . ." Then Mychala was at it again. "Okay what about the joke where the two men were walking down the street, right. And then . . . wait . . . I can't remember."

"Ah, you wrong for that one, Mychala." I threw my hand at her. We were now both tired. Mychala returned to her bed, and I laid my head down with my hair only half braided. I wondered what the fate of my son and me would be. He was still considered a ward of the state, although he was temporarily in the custody of my mom. She and her husband were well into their sixties, and I feared that Children's Services would consider them too old.

As my thoughts remained on my son, I observed Mychala, stretching and getting into the center of the room, yelling, "You can do the electric slide!" As the laughter filled the room and everyone watched her hustle, doing two steps to the right, zigzaggin' to the rear and finger poppin', my thoughts drifted.

For some reason, I couldn't get that old woman's statement that "God cares" out of my mind. Before I realized it, I had addressed the kite to the chaplain. I didn't know if any of my prayers were being heard, but I figured the chaplain would have more pull with *The Man Upstairs* than me. Despite that, I said another prayer and pulled the sheet over my face to hide my tears. Another day leading toward the unknown had passed.

• • •

"Mail call! Xavier!"

I jumped off the table and took the letter from the extended hand of the CO It was a letter from my brother, Young Ty:

Big sissy,

So you went to the hotel. Got your cherry broke, huh? I know you did the left-right on her like I taught you. Did you give that bitch one to her body, the other to her head and send her to bed? See, all that play fighting was preparing you for this shit. These niggas so 'BIG' over here, like they been eatin' some blow-up. I need a motherfuckin' baseball bat, fa real. Shit, I'm light and quick on my feet, but ain't nowhere to run in county jail. Strength is the winner when you fighting in close quarters. When I have beef, and it's mostly over that damn phone, all I'm thinking about is breakin' a nigga's nose or some shit like that. You do the same. If you ain't learned by now, I know you know, hit first and wonder what happened last. The other day a nigga got smashed over the head with his tray by an old head. These old heads ain't no joke. Did you hear about Mom? Lori said the doctors found a lump. Hope it ain't cancer. I worry about her health all the time. The doctors won't tell anyone if it's terminal, and you know Mom won't talk about it.

What's up with your boy Delano? I hear he out on the streets doin' it. Do you hear from him?

Yo, I heard you got transferred to another facility. I hear Circleville is sweet. Is it? My attorney said my time depends on what you gon' do. Sissy, tell me and let me hear it from your own lips, or should I say handwriting. Are you gon' tell? Are you gon' take a deal? Sis, I personally got to honor the code, and I would want you, no, expect you, to do the same. But as my sis, and thinking about how dirty these niggas did you, I wanna tell you to do what you gotta do. Go home to my nephew if you gotta tell on me. If I could do

your time, I would. I'll love and support you, whatever you
decide. Now, I may get into some fights about it, but hey,
little brother can handle his, sis. For once, do you.

Young Ty

I folded the letter, placed it back in the envelope and
slipped it inside my commissary bag. I laid back on my
bunk and watched the others open and read their letters.
Mail call did something for an inmate. It was the highlight
of the day, even if it was for just a quick five minutes or so.
It was a temporary, euphoric high. We behind the wall
looked forward to our mail—capturing the feeling of love
from the outside. I thought about my son and my choices,
then, once again, about my son. Would anyone mess with
him?

MONTH SIX

"Xavier, you got a visit!" I heard a male officer announce.

I was dog tired. My eyes looked like I had just smoked a pound of weed, and my hair was still a wreck. The officer looked me up and down, and I could almost see him making comparisons with the newspaper articles that he had read about me.

As I was being escorted to where I thought would be the visiting room, I learned that I was on my way to see the chaplain. That was a relief. I expected to meet a George Burns-looking bastard who was demented enough to think he was God. Instead, I was greeted by a clear-skinned, bald, immaculately groomed, handsome African-American brotha of above average height. He was smiling at me as if this was a family reunion and I was his long lost sister. I thought, *If this brother's practicing celibacy, I'm gonna put him to the test. Can a sistah get a quickie?*

"Hello, sistah. My name is Chaplain John Matthews. How are you doing?"

"Fine," I said, feeling everything but that.

"I recognized your name from all the publicity you've been getting. You're quite a celebrity around here. You're not at all what I expected," the chaplain said.

"What did you expect, may I ask?" I said sitting in his

small office. He looked at me quizzically, sizing me up as I blew away his typical stereotype of a felon.

"Well, a hard-core criminal," he responded. I instantly let out a chuckle.

I liked him for his realness. "Making assumptions can be dangerous," I said teasingly.

"So, sistah, what can I do for you? Your kite said that you wanted to talk."

"More like cry. I want prayer for my son. I miss him so much. Then there's this custody issue."

"Have you accepted Jesus as your Lord and Savior?"

"Is that a prerequisite for prayer?" I snapped, feeling the pressure to convert. "No, I have not."

"Then let's start there, because anything you ask in His name, He will do."

"I feel more comfortable if you just pray for my son. If I want to accept Jesus, I will kite you and say that. I don't want to barter for prayer. Either you will pray with me or not."

"Humph, I see. I got to remember that." He extended his forefinger after dabbing it with olive oil and rubbed my forehead and said, "Let us pray. As I anoint you with this oil, I ask, in Jesus' name, to protect you and your son. Lord, give her the strength to endure her trials and tribulations. Watch over her, O Lord, and keep her near your bosom. Amen."

With the words penetrating my core, I was eight years old again, sitting on the front pew of my grandfather's church. I appreciated his prayer. "Thank you, Chaplain Matthews. I didn't mean to be so impatient. I just needed someone to talk to me."

"Anything you say stays in here, between you, God and me. Would you like a Seven-Up?" That was an impressive way to lighten the mood. I had not had a cold soda in five months. It tasted like it was sent from a heavenly fountain.

The chaplain never mentioned Jesus to me again, nor

did we discuss the details of my case. I simply enjoyed his company, as he told me about the bizarre path that led him to the ministry.

He had taken a strange, and some might say, bizarre route to the ministry. Raised on the east side of Baltimore, and the middle child in a family of five brothers, the chaplain's early life seemed to suggest anything but involvement with God. In a family of all boys brought up by a mother whose husband left after the last child was born, Chaplain John grew up fighting. Taking what he wanted from his younger brothers and having to protect what he had taken from the older ones, the chaplain learned the art of fisticuffs at an early age. By the time the brothers, whose ages, like stair steps, were all very close in range, had reached their teens, they were the dregs of their neighborhood. Each brother, without exception, had at least one encounter with the local police department.

John's older brother, whom he idolized, was the leader of a crew. He bought a gun from a neighborhood crackhead, and took to sticking up local dope boys. One day, as the brothers sat on the porch of their row house, a black SUV with tinted windows pulled up and came to a sudden stop. Suddenly, a fusillade of gunfire erupted from the passenger side of the four-wheel drive. As the brothers dove for cover, their mother, hearing the gunshots coming from the front of the house, ran from the kitchen in her nightgown to make sure that all of her kids were safe.

A nine-millimeter bullet tore through her nightgown, ripped through her stomach and encased itself in her bladder. Ambulances seemed to take their time arriving to the scene of a shooting in the inner city, so by the time one had appeared, Mrs. Matthews was no longer conscious.

The Matthewses were not a religious family, but the boys huddled together as their mother lay unconscious in the emergency room of the hospital, praying for her survival. When the doctor came out, he informed the boys that their mother had lost a great deal of blood. He told them that he and his staff would do all that they could, and he asked them to pray for a miracle.

It was then that both John and one of his older brothers each made a silent vow to God. One promised vengeance, and the other promised that he would spend the rest of his life serving God if his mother's life were saved. Mrs. Matthews's recovery from the operation was slow but certain, and both of her sons lived up to their separate vows. The older brother, true to his word, sought out the driver of the SUV and handled his business, pumping hollow-point bullets into his head. John would also be true to his oath; after finishing Dunbar High School, he enrolled into the seminary. Putting his past behind him, he left Baltimore and relocated to Columbus, Ohio. His first position was that of chaplain. He still visited Baltimore, where three times a year he traveled to the state prison, where his oldest brother was still on death row for the vengeance murder that he committed on that night years ago when he was just a teen. Yes, the chaplain knew the world that Pamela Xavier came from. He knew it all too well.

"Pamela, listen to me, and listen well. As long as there is life, there is hope. My life hasn't always been some bed of roses. I've seen difficult times, but I've prayed to God and kept the faith. I believe, sweetheart, that God doesn't close a door unless he opens a window. But you'll never know, Pam, where or when your window has been opened if you foolishly choose to take your own life. I often worry that inmates facing long sentences contemplate taking their own lives. Maybe you'll go to jail, Pam, and maybe you won't. Only God knows that for sure. But let me tell you this: Jail doesn't have to be a living hell. Like life, jail tends to be what you make of it. For the time that you're locked up, be it one year or twenty years, make your stay a

period of evolution and growth. You are much too beautiful a person, both outwardly and inwardly, to give up on
yourself, to give up and abandon the child you profess to
love."

The chaplain's story made me forget about my own
problems—for a moment. Suddenly, I noticed something
different about him. It was as if he was no longer interested in my reaction to what he was saying. His whole
being seemed to be fixed on something that wasn't tangi-
ble, and I soon understood that he was listening to a voice
within him. Then, as quickly as he had gone into a trance, I
regained his full attention.

"Do you need to make any phone calls while you're
here? I can let you make one as long as it's local," the chaplain said.

"Really? Can I call my friend's cell phone?" I asked.

"Only if it's a call that you think you really need to
make. I'll do it for you."

"Yeah, it is. He's looking for something for me, and I
need to know if he found it." I could not believe my luck. I
had been trying desperately to get in contact with Delano
since our last visit. We tried to play the contact careful, not
knowing if any day he would somehow become my codefendant or be visited with a warrant for his arrest. I knew
that he was back from New York. Rumors said that he had
been seen around, but I didn't know where he was. One
mutual friend said he was acting "funny," and that worried
me. It had been over a month since Delano's last visit, and I
was anxious to know if he found the gun that Chino hid.
This would answer several questions for me.

Chaplain Matthews handed me a cordless phone, then
turned on a Sony bookshelf stereo system. As the phone
rang on the other end, Teddy Riley and the Winans were
singing about change.

After three rings, I heard Delano's New York accent.
"Yeah?"

"D, it's Carmen." One of the chaplain's eyebrows raised; he knew me as Pamela Xavier, and most of the time, that was who I was. But years ago, I developed an alter ego to help me cope with what I was doing in the sex industry. Running an escort service required traits that Pamela didn't have. I was a *Thelma and Louise* all rolled up into one young black woman. Pamela was the innocent, fun loving, caring person who always got good grades, followed the rules and watched her manners. Pamela was sugar and spice and everything nice, because that's what girls were made of. Carmen, on the other hand, was different; she was sly, careful, cunning and untrusting. If shit had to get handled, Carmen stepped up to the plate. Carmen, on any occasion, could be that bitch for real.

"Hey, baby, how are you calling me? What's up?" I looked over at the chaplain and wondered if Delano believed in miracles.

"I'll tell you later. So, did you find that thing?" My heart began to beat faster than an African drum. The phone went silent, and I paused, awaiting his response. I thought about my promise to Chino, about our secret that was now being uncovered.

"Is this phone cool, Carmen?" Delano cautiously asked. I thought about what Chino had asked me: *"Pammy, promise me, on everything you love, that you won't ever tell anyone what we did with that gun."*

"Chino, I promise."

"It's the coolest we gon' get. What's up, love?" I said and asked again, "Was it there?" My palms sweated.

"It was right where you said it would be. What's up?"

"Wait. Let me hear you." I pushed my free ear closed with my index finger and pressed my other ear into the phone to hear clearly what I thought I had just heard.

"Yes, Carmen, heavy heater, baby? I got it. Well, I got it put up. Now what?" I was speechless. Truth was, I didn't expect the gun to be there. During my last argument with

Chino, he said that he moved it because he could no longer trust me. That hurt. Delano now had the gun that was used in the murders, the gun that the police were looking for, to tie someone to the murders. I had the weapon, and after all these years, Chino had not moved the gun, as we vowed we wouldn't, unless we both decided to do so. Many times we wanted to, but thought it too risky to move a murder weapon. We regretted our decision to not toss it into the river instead of hiding it.

People on the streets from the set that kidnapped Chino knew he did the murders and told the police as much. But with no more than rivalry beef as a motive and no weapon, they had no case. Later, the only witness, that Good Samaritan, came forward. He admitted to giving a naked man a ride to my car, which he recorded no license plate number for and said he thought the car was black instead of midnight blue; so he was no help to the officials. However, with a murder weapon and a photo of Chino, perhaps this witness's mind could be refreshed. With my corroborating story, that would surely put Chino on death row for a double homicide. I believed Chino when he said that he lost trust in me. Now that Delano said that he had the gun, I needed to be sure of what I was going to do. I couldn't believe my ears. Chino had never lost trust in me, and at this point, what was that trust worth? What was the murder weapon worth? "Hello, hello," Delano continued into his cell phone.

"Delano, I'm still here. Was it in a gray bag?" I asked, wanting to be crystal clear that I had exactly what I needed to be free.

"Carmen, yes, and it was where you told me to look. I put it in a safe place—now what?" I paused, having no answer to Delano's question, and I began to think about Chino and how we had been through so much together. I had endured so much because of him. I thought if I could just rewind the tape to each point of our relationship that got me to where I was today, and press erase, then maybe things would be different. But so many things went wrong. I gave him my friendship, and he became my archenemy. I believed in him, but he failed to believe in me. I shared with him my dreams, and he turned them into nightmares. He was never there for me.

Arriving at the hospital, Chino warned me, "Pooh, if you come in, do not say you shot me. Darren, take her home."

I pleaded. "No, I want to stay with you." We ran to the entrance, gaining the medical staff's attention. They rushed to the car with a gurney and assisted Chino onto it. I began to kiss the sides of his face and pleaded, announcing to everyone within earshot distance that I shot him and how sorry I was and how they had to help him. Inside the hospital, everyone was racing about as Chino began to lose consciousness.

"Pooh, go home. Darren, take her home." Those were his last words. Darren pulled me by the arm and pushed me out of the hospital door towards his car. He stuffed me into the front passenger seat, got behind the wheel and drove off in silence. The sirens of an approaching police car sounded loudly. Sobering, I watched the bright, neon vehicle speed by us onto the hospital grounds.

Darren reached over, patted my leg and said, "You know, Chino let you go free. That's love, baby girl. That's love."

"Fuck him and his trust."

"Carmen, now what?" Delano said again, sounding agitated this time.

"Delano, I don't know," I said sadly into the phone.

"A'ight. Let me know . . . I got a surprise for you," Delano said.

"What?" I said. He was full of surprises. That was one of the things that I liked about him. I remembered when he surprised me with two dozen yellow roses at the airport upon my return from New York. No one had ever bought me flowers before. That was really special to me.

"I got your name tattooed on my neck last night. It's wicked." He placed his hand over the phone, but I still heard what sounded like a female in the background.

"What, D? What did you say?"

"It's done in cursive letters." A female voice in the background asked him whom he was talking to. Delano's hand covered the phone again, and I heard him tell someone, or *her*, that he was on the phone and to be quiet. "Sorry, baby, motherfucka can't even talk on the damn phone without interruption. The tattoo says *Carmen*. Hangin' from the *N* is a teardrop." My mind began to get heated and jealous, wanting to know who da bitch was in the background. But I decided against using our precious time to argue. Delano continued to talk. "You are so beautiful to me, baby. I never knew that love could be so special—this deep. And I love you, Carmen. I miss you, girl."

I came to know several kinds of love. Sometimes people had love for one another because they walked the same path; they graduated from the same school of thought, had the same business interest. I knew love based on association, wealth and power, when everyone, based on common goals, was moving in the same direction. Then there was the kind of love that satisfied a passing desire.

I realized that Chino's love was in a whole different category than Delano's. Chino's love was fear. Chino's love was: Is that my baby? Delano's love was peace, rest and security. But I never told him, and I regretted the wasted chances that I had to be with him, perhaps the chance to ever be happy with a man. I couldn't believe that he thought me worthy of inking my name on his neck. That was eternal.

"Did the tattoo hurt?" I asked

"Love is pain, baby," stated Delano.

"Oh, you got jokes," I said smiling from ear to ear.

"I see you don't understand. My body is precious, Carmen. I just don't go and put shit on my skin just to be doin' it. It ain't no fashion statement," Delano said, and we were silent for a moment, as I had not thought of what this tattoo really meant. He continued to whisper into the phone. "This tattoo means that you're now a part of me—a part of my flesh."

"I know, and I understand, D," I replied.

"Baby, I will be there in two weeks. We'll talk then. Carmen, I want you to use what's in this package to come home to me. I'm setting things up for you as we speak. You'll be taken care of and never, ever have to worry about money again. I need to go back to New York. I'm workin' out with my cousin." I couldn't help but love his accent and the way he said New York, like it had an *"aw"* instead of an *"or"* in the middle.

I never liked his cousin, and for him to be *workin' out* with him was insane. Workin' out was far from exercising. It was a light term for *ballin'* in the streets—gettin' down for yo' crown! His cousin was one of those shady mutherfuckas who was always pissing off the wrong people, the kind of people who didn't have a problem with getting what you owed them out of your ass. But I knew Delano was still hustling, despite what had happened to me, so all I could do was hope for the best. Maybe he would be the one to make it out of the game. Perhaps he was smarter than me. My mistakes would not be his. The rhythm of his voice continued to vibrate through the receiver.

"Carmen, what I'm out here doing is for us. You gonna be all right. I'm still lookin' for Chino. Me and my cousin are gonna see him one of these days. You my heart, girl."

"Delano, same here—one."

The phone went dead and I handed it to the chaplain, who looked deeply into my eyes. He asked, "So, was that closure of something or the beginning?"

"I hope it was the end of one thing and the beginning of something else."

"Well, let's take you back to your dorm, and if you need me, send me a kite. Hopefully, next time, you'll seek Jesus."

I winked my eye and said, "Who knows, maybe I will." The chaplain escorted me down the hall, cement block after cement block. As I passed the other dorms, I peered in and saw the same cramped quarters as my own. The guard let me back into my cell, and I waved good-bye and mouthed a thank you. I lay on my little mattress and savored the taste of ice-cold soda in my mouth.

I rested my head on my pillow, thinking of receiving Jesus, but I knew it would only be for the predicament I was in and not from my heart. I was skeptical about jail-house religion and didn't want to be a hypocrite. I watched my cousin come home from his ten-year bid the first week with a knitted cap on his head and a prayer rug. Before long, he was eating a Polish sausage sandwich and smoking a blunt. All of this after sending me letter after letter stating that he was now to be called Kwame Muhammad. *Kwame Muhammad! We still call that nigga June Bug!* I just couldn't go out like that.

I thought about the prayer sent out for my son. I felt relieved that he was in the hands of the angels. Then the voice of Delano, my love, filled my head. Damn! Why didn't I believe in his love when I was a free woman? My mind drifted to Chino and the day we placed the gun in the park.

"Pooh, those motherfuckas tried to play me," Chino said.

"It's okay, you're home now," I assured him. "What happened?"

"Pooh, this is murder one, baby, no turning back. From this point on, you my accomplice, or you can turn and leave, now."

"Chino, you know you got me, boo. Now, what's up? No doubt they got what their hand called for."

"Pooh, baby, this is murder, and without this weapon, they got nothing."

"Chino, let's do what we gotta do." I looked into his eyes and he embraced me, placing my face to his chin. I was able to smell the stale scent of dried blood on his breath. I inhaled it deeply into my nostrils. This was my baby and he almost left here, and if need be, I would do whatever it took to be there for him. He kissed my forehead and then bit the side of my cheek, whispering into my ear, "You all I got, Pooh."

Then we drove to the park, a spot where we used to take walks and talk. Chino selected the site to bury the weapon. We kneeled and prayed that nothing but death would come between us. "Pooh, this is the spot, and you hold the secret to my freedom. You not my wife, legally, but in my heart I trust you with my life."

Mychala was finishing up her phone conversation as I came into the room. She hung up and stared at the phone as if she was deciding whether or not to call the person back. Judging by her mood, whoever it was she was talking to said something she didn't like.

"What's up, girl, you a'ight?" I quizzed.

"Yeah, I'm cool. I just had to take care of somethin'. Where were you?" Mychala asked. "I woke up and you were gone."

"I got called to the chaplain's office." I hopped up on the picnic table.

"Is everything okay? I mean, they usually don't call you to see the chaplain unless someone died or something." Mychala took the seat next to mine.

"Nah, it ain't nothin' like dat. I kited him so he could pray for my son."

"Oh, that's good. Gotta keep him protected, don't we?" she said while patting my leg.

"I'm just worried about what's gonna happen tomorrow. Children's Services wants to take him from me, but I'll be damned if I let that happen. Those motherfuckas are always trying to justify breakin' up families. They say that it's best for the child. But how can that be? They scream 'Dysfunctional' in the courtrooms, then take our children and place them in foster homes with strangers who could care less about our kids as long as they receive a paycheck. To make matters worse, while the foster parents are sitting on the couch licking chicken grease off their fingers and watching *As the World Turns*, the children under their care are abusing the hell out of each other. And this is their idea of a good home? Yeah, right. Fuck that," I said.

"I feel you. I wish I could see my girls," Mychala stated.

"What are you talking about? You said that you don't have any kids." I gave her a look of confusion and straight bullshit.

"Right. Well, it feels like it sometimes. I lost them to the state a long time ago. They said that I was an unfit mother, but dat was a lie. I worked two jobs to provide for them. I needed a babysitter, and this girl that I trusted to watch my twins let her boyfriend molest them. The state charged them both with abuse, and me, child endangerment and neglect. For the longest time I asked God why He wouldn't allow me to see that coming with my gift. But the Lord told me to be still, for my thoughts are not His thoughts, neither my ways His ways . . . Isaiah chapter fifty-five verse eight. I wasn't married then to my second husband, Emanuel, and that's the only part of my past that I never told him."

Her anguish was contagious. I fought back the tears that were stinging my eyes, and I gave her the only thing that another mother in her position could give—a hug.

That evening I called my mom. I didn't want her to bring my son to the upcoming court proceedings. I didn't want to let him see me as an inmate. As much as I wanted to hold my son in my arms and relish the scent of him, I didn't know if I'd be allowed to touch him. That would have been too much for me to bear.

The authorities didn't know my son's actual whereabouts. For all they knew, he was in the care of my sister, and I planned to keep it that way. My intuition told me that it was better this way.

The following morning, two U.S. marshals, David Jeffries and Walter Kilburn, arrived to escort me to my son's custody hearing. There was nothing outstanding or special about them—nothing that distinguished them from any other man on the street—no insignia, no visible weapons set in quick-release holsters like cowboys preparing for a gunfight at high noon.

Agent Kilburn didn't smile as Agent Jeffries did. He didn't bother himself with congeniality. I figured by the paleness of his skin that he was a pencil pusher, and quite possibly, this was his first time in the field.

I could tell right away that Kilburn was one of those hard-nosed cops whose dick got hard every time one of the good guys took down one of society's lowlifes. After all, the world was a better place without them. He appeared to be uncompromising in this belief. When he looked at me, it wasn't with eyes of professionalism; it was with eyes that were deadly . . . cold . . . contemptuous.

Agent Jeffries had one of those laid-back personalities. When he spoke to me, he addressed me by my first name. His receding hairline suggested that he was much older than his partner. However, he had at least twenty years to go before he was able to retire. Nevertheless, he looked strong.

Both men wore black, soft, comfortable shoes that were buffed to a shine, dark-colored slacks, a crispy white dress shirt and a sports coat.

Agent Jeffries was always kind enough to keep me abreast of what was happening. Even when he shackled me he would say, "Pamela, we need to get you ready now. I hate to do this to you, but I have to. Kilburn over there wouldn't have it any other way."

"Thank you. Could you loosen them up just a bit? They *are* a little tight," I said.

"Sure, no problem," he replied. "I have to put you in a holding cell for a minute. We'll be back to transport you back downtown, okay?" I never gave a response, and the cell door slammed shut.

Twenty minutes later, wearing a pumpkin orange jumpsuit, I was being stuffed into the back seat of a gray Mercury Cougar. There wasn't any bulletproof glass separating us, which was common in police cruisers.

As we pulled out of the parking garage, we merged into traffic and got on I-71 North. I couldn't help but notice how polished the feds were compared to the state authorities.

The closer we got to downtown, the more nervous I became. During the whole trip, I didn't hear one word of the marshals' conversation; I was too busy taking in everything else—the sun gleaming off the bumpers of the cars that passed us—the way the car glided over the bumps on the highway. I paid attention to grass as if it was my first time seeing it. I tried to hold the vision of the outside world in my mind, because if the feds had their way, I wouldn't see the light of day for the next twenty-six years.

"Let's stop to get something to eat. I'm starving," Jeffries said to Kilburn.

"W-w-what? You know we never deviate from our route!" Kilburn said, scolding his partner.

"Sheesh, relax. I was just kidding. Learn to lighten up, why don't you?" Kilburn looked at Jeffries like he wanted to stop the car and put his ass out. Jeffries ignored him and turned the radio on to a rock station, WNCI. "Have you heard about those Colombians from the East Coast?" he asked, pacifying Kilburn.

"Nah, what's the latest on them?" Kilburn replied.

"Those crazy-ass people are stopping at nothing to get what they want."

"Maybe we need to change our territory. If they want you dead, it's just a matter of time."

When we got to the courthouse, I was placed in another holding cell behind the state courtroom until my case was heard. In the cell there was an exposed toilet of stainless steel, and there was a piece of sheetrock above a three-foot-tall sink. On the left side of the cell was a wooden bench. The door to the cell was not barred. It was a mere mesh-covered gate that went from the floor to the ceiling and it had a center lock. In the middle of the gate was an opening where items could be passed back and forth. There was an eerie echo in the corridor, as voices could be heard mumbling from the court sessions in progress. I felt as though I was trapped inside of a metal sarcophagus.

Finally, my case was called, and before I knew it, my son's custody was being discussed. Standing in front of the courtroom, the baliff cleared his throat and said, "In the case of the State of Ohio versus Pamela Xavier for the custody decision of the child, Antonio Xavier, the attorney for the child representing Children's Services can approach the courts," said the bailiff.

A dark-skinned sistah stood up. She looked as though she could have been raised in Africa, but right away I could tell that even if that were true, she had fully adapted to the ideas of Western civilization. For all intents and purposes, she was nothing more than a white woman with a helluva tan. Her hair was straightened and styled like a Barbie doll and she wore blue contacts as if they would make her uncompromisingly Negroid features more acceptable. If my eyes were closed, I would not have been able to detect her ethnicity when she spoke:

"In this matter, your honor, the parents of the said child are both facing sentences with a federal mandatory minimum of ten years. Notice was served at the address on record for the listed father, with no reply or answer of service. And as for as the mother, she's facing a lengthy sentence and needs to have a home for the child.

"An inspection, interview and evaluation of her sister were conducted. It has been determined that her home would be suitable placement for the child. The grandparents request visitation, which includes, but is not limited to, summers, vacations and holidays. However, the state requests that primary residence be with the child's aunt, Lori McCaskill."

My sister and I stood side by side. I wanted to hold her hand, partly to convey my gratitude, and partly to support me from falling out. The decision would allow me no physical contact with my son whatsoever.

The judge spoke. "Very well, then. The new legal guardian of Antonio Xavier is Lori McCaskill. Is there anything that you'd like to say, Ms. Xavier?" the judge asked me. I couldn't speak. I was devastated. I watched my tears drip onto the plastic sandals I was given to wear. All I could do was shake my head no. What *could* I have said? I lost the one reason I was living for. The judge banged his gavel, and I wanted to grab it and bash my own brains out with it. That would have improved my emotional state.

My sister looked over at the guard for permission to console me while clenching her soiled Kleenex tissue in her hand. He gave her the okay and she embraced me, but I was numb from shock. Nothing really mattered at that point. My life was shit and going downhill fast. My shit was fucked up.

My mom did a wonderful job of raising me, and I knew she'd do the same with my son. But the problem was that he was my only child, and I wanted a chance to parent him.

After divorcing my father, my mother had gotten remarried to a difficult and complicated man. He was a good provider, which I was certain attracted my mother to him. My mother had always been accustomed to the very best, and, like her, I inherited her taste for the finer things in life.

No one could replace my dad, although he wasn't worth much more than the paper his name was written on. He was my father, and from all reports, I was cut from the same cloth as him. My father was smart, had business savvy and was an entrepreneur. He was an older version of Chino; he was horrible and he hustled back in the day as well. His hustle was heroin on the streets of Detroit. My father, "T-Mack," as he was called, lived here and there. "Papa Was a Rollin' Stone" was his anthem. He lived the good life in the beginning. Then the feds stopped that when they gave him four years on a twenty-year sentence. In the seventies, the feds believed in parole. They also believed in rehabilitation and furlough and allowed my father to earn a degree in engineering from the University of Massachusetts while doing his bid.

My father emerged a different man. He had decided that prison was not for him. Having lost everything, including my mother while he was away, he came home to change his life legally and move forward. I saw my father irregularly and tried to gain his attention through excelling in school. Like my father I was smart, and school was easy for me. But it was also boring.

As fate would have it, my stepfather proved to be an almost impossible person to get along with. Raised as an army brat on various bases that his family had lived on, Herbert Hampton decided when he married my mother that some discipline and order would be instilled in both my brother and me. Promising to whip us into shape, dinner was served promptly at "eighteen hundred hours." If either of us failed to get to the dinner table on time, he would threaten to put us on half rations. We were subject to room inspections before breakfast, and he expected our beds to be made with hospital corners before we left for school.

I don't know, I guess the rebel started in me then and never let up. I rebelled against the inspections. I rebelled against the half rations, and I damn sure wasn't going for any corporal punishment. The turning point came for me when one night Herbert, dear old step daddy, decided he was going to check my brother's behind. He raised the belt to hit Ty, and I grabbed it. When he raised his hand as if to smack me, I ran to the kitchen and grabbed the butcher knife off the cutting block. He stood across from me, glaring, and I stood only a few feet away from him, trembling, hoping he would make my day. My mother, to my relief, entered the kitchen but sided with her husband. This caused a rift between her and Ty and me. I ran to my room and barricaded myself behind the door and dreamed of the day I would eventually leave home. The rift between my mother and me would heal, but a rebel had been born.

As a result, my brother and I formed a bond that was stronger than the normal sibling bond. He was my baby brother, and I was his big sister who he idolized to a degree. Having become his legal guardian when my mother could no longer handle him was as normal as breathing, as I would have it no other way; Ty became a son to Chino and me. Taking me from my thoughts, my sister asked, "Are you going to be all right?" When I looked up to reply, I saw one of Dragos's men standing in the rear of the courtroom. A chill went up my spine. He was standing in the gallery as if he was a friend of the family. The cartel was keeping close tabs on me.

Back at the dorm, I retreated to my secluded place of refuge—the shower. This time it didn't relax me, nor did it provide the medicinal effect on my body like it usually did. It wasn't the hot and steamy water that I had grown accustomed to. On this particular day it was cold—ice cold. Nevertheless, I stood in there and let it beat against my body. It was my penance for all the wrongs that I had done as a woman and as a mother. And even though I probably deserved worse than this cold water, I knew that I didn't deserve what they were doing to me.

I knew that my son was in good care with my mom and my sis. He was safe and secure, and that was the only thing that comforted me. I knew that they would love and take care of him like he was their very own. I had no doubt that my mom would do the same with him as she had with me, but he was my son; I wanted the chance to parent him. I prayed that I didn't have to be away from him for too long.

After my shower, Mychala and I watched the evening news. The news was the highlight of the day. Everyone wanted to see who got arrested and what was going on in the world outside. There was always a morbid expectation to see someone familiar. We knew all too well the lives our friends and associates lived. Perhaps we were waiting to confirm the only possible and satisfying outcome for that—to say, "I told you so."

I made a habit of watching the news before I came to jail. It only made sense for me to tune in to see if one of my customers got knocked. If they resurfaced as if nothing ever happened after trying to cop something from me, I knew that nigga was *hot*.

The noise level in the TV room was consistent with what I had endured in the last facility. The volume on the TV couldn't be raised any higher. Despite the fact that it was blaring, I still had trouble hearing over the women talking. Consequently, I learned a valuable thing: to read lips and speak at a close distance when my conversations were being eavesdropped.

Mychala asked me how court went. After thinking about all of the strain I had undergone, I made note of the fact that jail had been good to Mychala. I often heard peo-

ple say that jail rescued them. I was starting to understand
that paradox as I watched Mychala's skin on her face clear
up and the oil deposits from the crack addiction that black-
ened her knuckles lighten up. But I didn't feel like talking
about my son, so I gave her a fake smile and told her that it
went fine.

"Pam, I have three children. Being out there on my mis-
sions has kept me away from them, so I understand how you
feel. But God will protect the bond you have with your son,"
Mychala stated, popping peanuts into her mouth.

I know I heard her say three children. How come she
didn't mention that when she first told me about her kids?
The first time it was twins, and this time it was three kids.
This bitch was straight up lying. Something wasn't right
with this chick, but I just couldn't figure out what.

"Thank you," I said and focused my attention on the
evening news. I folded my sweatshirt in half and placed it
on the metal table for cushion. Tracey Taylor was
announcing that a man was found dead in an abandoned
garage on the Eastside this morning. I heard someone try
to "Shush" the talkers so we could hear the details of the
city's latest homicide victim. It was the seventy-ninth murder this year.

"An Eastside woman discovered a man who has yet to
be identified by authorities. He was naked, gagged and
bound to a chair in the garage of an abandoned home.
Apparently, while she was walking her dog, the animal
picked up the scent of the lifeless body. Police are saying
that this was an execution-style murder. They have no
motive and no suspects.

"Officials are comfirming that . . ."

I turned to look at Mychala in disbelief. Three years
earlier I found Chino in our living room covered in blood
from being pistol whipped. He told me that he, too, had
been stripped naked before his abductors. But he fought
for his life, killing all three men. I wondered if this man

had tried to fight for his life. More so, I wondered how men could be so cruel to one another.

As Tracey Taylor was wrapping up her report, she gave the number to the Crime Stopper's Hotline in the event that information could be provided leading to an arrest or the identity of the unknown man.

"Oh my God, don't let it be someone that I know . . . a tattoo . . . Delano just got a tattoo on the right side of his neck. Could it be D? A name, no not my sweetheart, in scripted lettering, please, God, please . . . that spells . . . that spells what, come on, say it, what, spells what? Goddamnit, say it, spells . . . Carmen!"

WHY?

My lungs were still functioning, but it felt like the air had suddenly been sucked out of me. I jumped from the table and ran to the TV to be sure that she said what I thought she had said. "Please, God. N-o-o-o-o!"

"And now our local weather. Today's highs were . . ."

"What did she say? Did she say *Carmen?* Did she say that he had a tattoo on the side of his neck that said *Carmen?*" I frantically asked.

Some of the girls were shaking their head in agreement. Others were yelling at me for being in front of the TV. Mychala rushed over to me and held me. I was crying uncontrollably, knowing in my heart that Delano was dead.

"Yes, Pamela. She said *Carmen,*" Mychala confirmed. "Do you know him or Carmen?" she added and kept asking me if I knew him or not.

I pushed Mychala back, desperately hoping that she would say something different . . . hoping that she would make it all better.

My eyes darted over to the phone and I thought about calling my sister. Unfortunately some goofy bitch was hugged up on it, and it was going to be turned off at 11:30 P.M. It was obvious that she was oblivious to everything that was going on. I needed to see if I could find out where Delano was—see if Lori had heard from him recently.

I stood behind the girl on the phone and asked her to end her call. She looked at me as if I was crazy, then resumed telling someone how much she loved them. I wanted to snatch the phone right out of her hand and beat her with it. I heard the newscaster signing off and knew that there was no way I would get a call out in time.

I started to pace the floor. My emotions were caught in a vortex of frustration, sadness, confusion, anger and total loss. When I looked around the room, everything seemed to be drawing closer to me as if the walls were slowly being pushed together. I was no longer able to control myself. I heaved once, but nothing came out.

"Pam! Calm down! You're not even sure. It might not be him," Mychala screamed trying to calm me.

"I KNOW. I feel it in my heart. It hurts, Mychala. N-O-O-O . . . ! Dear God! N-o-o-o! WHY? WHY? WHY, DEE? I TOLD YOU THE STREETS ARE BAD! WHO DID THIS?"

The inmates began to bang on the door for help. Mychala began screaming, "Call the guards. She needs help!"

When the officers arrived, one of them spoke through an opening that was cut out of the door to pass food trays through.

They were hesitant to enter the room and deal with a hysterical woman. "Stop all that screaming in there!"

"Fuck you!" I screamed back at them. "Fuck you!" I yelled again.

Then they called for backup. Mychala ran to the door and told them I just heard that my friend was killed on the news. Luckily, the guard that she was talking to was one who I got along with. "Please, help her," Mychala begged for me. "Don't let them send her to the hole. She needs help. She went to court today about custody of her son, too."

I fell on my knees and curled up into the fetal position, and the officers rushed in and placed my hysterical ass in a strait jacket. Then I was strapped to an apparatus that looked like a stretcher, but they called it a "boat" and I was rushed to the medical side of the prison where I was placed in a holding cell. I lay there unmoving, for the contraption was designed to tighten up more and more every time I moved. After a while, I was even afraid to blink. I looked like a comatose victim, as I was thinking of everything I was losing and had lost.

The only man who had ever loved me, and I couldn't trust his love to be true. Why didn't I just believe him? God, why did I do such fucked up things in my life? "Delano, I love you, I love you, I love you," I whispered, hoping that his spirit could hear me. "I never told you how much I wanted to be with you." I turned my head to the side and felt my tears rest on the plastic boat. My hysterics began to set in again and I asked, "Oh, God, why did you take him from me? Who did this? Who in the fuck did this? Who beat and killed Delano? Why? He did not deserve this." I released the pain in my mind and opened my mouth and yelled. "AAAAAAAGGGHH!!!" "AAAAAAAGGGHH!!!" "AAAAAAAGGGHH!!!" I screamed with my eyes fixed to the tissue paper that was stuck to the ceiling.

After that episode subsided, I wondered how in the hell I got myself into this bullshit. I'd fucked up my life. A nurse came into the cell with a needle. I felt a pinch in my arm and then I felt whatever was in that syringe take effect. A calm came over me. My eyes rolled back into my head, and I thought of Delano—how I would never see him again, never be able to say good-bye, or hear his voice or say the things I wanted to say to him. I did this. I'm responsible for all this shit. If only I didn't have to be so fuckin' greedy. Why didn't he just leave me for dead and go on with his life—legal?

It was over. I couldn't even pay my respects at the funeral. Why should I have kept on living? I wished I was dead; they weren't gonna let me out. There was nothing to live for.

Blackness covered the room. I had lost the three things that I held dear: My son, my love, my freedom.

PAUL

"Shorty, you need to get down with the home team!" Chino said, giving Paul some dap.

"Yeah, I was thinking about it. I see you. Can I get your numbers?" Paul asked cautiously. That was how it all got started.

Paul paced back and forth inside the hotel room earlier, nervous, contemplating his decision to do business with the notorious Chino. It had been over a year since his hand held any cocaine, and the possibility of drug dealing with a supplier again made him move constantly about, his nose dripping from the mixture of nervousness and excitement, just as a junkie would with the anticipation of the next hit.

Paul had gone cold turkey. He was more or less scared straight after the arrest and media coverage that the Pamela Xavier drug ring had gotten. He had never, ever been arrested and had only sold drugs to help support his legal ventures. Paul, also known as "P," wanted nothing to do with prison life. Although he had survived a year on his stash acquired from business ventures—rental properties and investing in a fried chicken carryout—it was still not enough. His girl, along with their three children, was as addicted to the fast money as the addicts that purchased the product.

Paul thought of working a legal gig, but his pride wouldn't allow him to stoop so low. What job could he possibly get that would pay him like coca did? He had to get enough money to make it out of the game—to come out of the game ahead—to win. After all, Carmen was a girl that had made a stupid mistake, and he would be smarter than her.

One particularly sunny day, Chino approached him at the car wash with a simple nod of the head to say what's up. Paul made note of the fact that he still looked paid—how he still seemed to have it going on so effortlessly. Paul also noticed the new car and the ice that graced his neck and wrist—how the diamond-studded index finger's stone blinded his eye from the shine. His curiosity and low savings got the best of him, and he did exactly what Chino knew he eventually would do after dangling opportunity in his face every chance he got for the last three months.

Chino always had a rep for being unapproachable. Paul thought this friendly air about him was very unusual. A year earlier at Club Flo, upon his exit, Paul had seen Chino and tried to speak with him as he was entering the nightspot. Chino gave him a cold, "Do I know you?" and kept walking. Paul never tried to speak to him again.

But despite all of this and the uneasiness he felt inside, Paul took the bait. After being sold a dream, he felt chosen to be a part of Chino's crew.

Chino sized Paul up and decided to add him to his crew, knowing that he would eventually place him in a sucker's position. Addicting him to the money they would pull in, Chino gassed up his head and pulled him deeper into the game through an initiation. Paul didn't want to do all the things that were asked of him. He had never been pledged in order to get money before, but Chino said that they needed to have something on each other—to know how the other's heart was, and if he was a "ride or die" nigga; otherwise, he couldn't do business with him. Paul could remember Chino's words, specifically, on the day he convinced him of the task:

"P, sometimes it's more than money. All money ain't good money. Anyone can spend, but I don't spend with everyone. Sometimes you want to do business with a nigga that got a little more invested in this life than just money. I need to do business with niggas that got heart, 'cause when the money is gone and you fucked up or stankin', a person's heart is gonna bring him to the penitentiary for a visit or to the grave to show his respect—not money," Chino explained, crossing his arms and leaning back in his chair.

Paul hung onto Chino's utterances of wisdom like a child sitting at a teacher's feet in a classroom. Chino was a wonderful orator and used words and slang that he had never heard. Chino also represented, to him, the mentor that he never had in this game. Paul had learned to hustle from the contacts supplying him. Erik and T-Love, two New York hustlers, had taught him how to measure, and how to build clientele by using his relationship with the locals. But in the end, it was all for the benefit of the New York boys. Whenever they had gotten enough money, Paul was left with no opportunity until they wanted to hustle again, so he ultimately always worked for them, again and again. It was never a *Let's-just-get-money-no-matter-what* attitude like the one that Chino displayed. To Paul, choosing Chino over Erik was a no-brainer, but little did he know that his choice would result in serious consequences.

Paul rationalized that Chino was a homie. Although not from Columbus, Chino's hometown was Cleveland, and they were both tired of New York niggas raping the city like they had big dicks. The more Chino pounded this into his ear, the more Paul believed in him, saying what he had wanted him to say all the years that he was doing business with Erik and T-Love. And Chino said it better than Paul could: "Fuck them bitch-ass niggas from *Up Top!*"

As he rolled the dice, he awaited Chino's phone call. Chino would give him the meeting spot to discuss the particulars. So far, things had gone just as Chino had said.

And after Paul proved himself by passing the initiation, he would get thirty thousand dollars for joining the team. Finally, after the many nights of tossing, turning and repenting ahead of time for what he would have to do to prove himself, he found peace with the fact that *fair exchange ain't robbery*. And Delano, God help him, was only going to get exactly what Chino said he had coming to him.

It took Paul and Yellow (a long-standing gang member from Cali) and Chino to abduct him. Normally, Chino had others do his dirty work, but he wanted to be in on this one personally that fateful Thursday at the basketball court. Yellow called Delano over to the suburban truck he was driving, and he was surprised that a money-gettin' nigga would approach a car that he didn't recognize. Who said New York niggas were smart? Yellow didn't have a *Do-you have-the-time?* look. He had three teardrops hanging from his left eye, a name tattooed on his hand between the thumb and index finger, and he was dressed in all black. Yellow stood 6'4" and weighed 330 pounds. His look per-sonified pure danger. His arms, like a boa constrictor, at any given moment could put the squeeze on anything or anybody. It was only when Delano noticed Chino in the rear seat that he turned to run. Yellow lifted his gun and aimed at his legs, hitting him once in the back of the right knee bringing him to the ground. In broad daylight, they hoisted him into the truck and sped away.

"P, do that nigga!" Paul's stomach turned, and he felt sorry for the man sitting before him tied to the chair, beaten, bound and gagged. But there was nothing that he could do to help him. Chino pistol-whipped the shit out of him. Delano gave up a fight that Tyson would be proud of.

Initially, Delano thought, like a lot of the kidnappings that had taken place in New York, this would involve a ran-som request for money or cocaine. It was only after he had been shaken, smacked with a gun and losing consciousness, did his abductors show their hand. Delano sensed, at that point, that he was probably in deep trouble and might not escape this situation alive.

Delano gagged and began to throw up, but neither Chino nor the giant Yellow would show any mercy. If there was any doubt as to whether or not Chino intended to kill him, that doubt was now gone. Delano knew, and they had to know, that if he somehow escaped this nightmare alive, he would kill them, their mothers and firstborn children.

After Chino and Yellow repeatedly beat Delano and caused him to lose control of his bodily functions, Chino ripped off his soiled underwear and stuffed them into his mouth. They held his mouth shut and then duct taped it.

"So, you fuckin' Pamela, huh?" Blop! Chino yelled as he backhanded Delano across the face. "You fuckin' Pam, huh, New York?" Delano balanced and turned his head to face him and gained the strength to shake his head no. Chino took a closer look at the nigga that had fucked his Pooh, and saw the scripted "Carmen" tattooed on the side of his neck.

Seconds later, Delano felt what seemed like a bomb exploding off across the bridge of his nose. The pain shot up to the top of his head and seemed to settle somewhere between his stomach and his intestines. He began to gag. "What you say, muthafucka?" Chino screamed. "Yellow, take that duct tape off this bitch, and take them panties out his mouth." Yellow removed the soiled underwear as Chino continued his tirade. "Now what? Huh? We can't hear you!" Chino sang mockingly towards his victim. "Playa, playa." Chino tapped his forehead with the tip of his gun.

"I don't know what you talkin' 'bout, man. My woman's name is Carmen! What do you want?" Delano answered through swollen lips with blood and shit caked on the outside of his mouth.

Chino continued to allow Delano to speak what he knew would be his last words; it would quench his curiosity. It

made him furious that Pammy had given up the ass. He
didn't want her, but he didn't want anyone else to have her
either. "Take off these ropes and let's handle this like men . . ."
Delano struggled to speak, but his efforts were useless.

Chino jumped back and spun around doing a round-
house kick to his chest, almost toppling Delano over in his
chair.

Chino, Yellow and Paul all wore black, and the latex sur-
gical gloves they also wore were stained with blood. Chino
watched Paul's face closely to see his reaction. The way that
Paul hesitated confirmed that it was his first time. Chino
explained to him that first times were okay.

"P, baby, you okay? After the first time, you'll want to feel
that rush again. Like a vampire thirsting for blood, you'll
want that adrenaline high and then that rush of power, only
to be left empty, thirsting for that next victim." P trembled as
he held the gun to the back of Delano's dome, and as he
walked behind him to pull the trigger, Delano looked up into
his face, his eyes pleading for mercy from who seemed like
the only compassionate person in the place. Paul could not
bear to maintain eye contact with Delano, and he looked
away out of embarrassment. Chino pressed his face in closer
to Delano in order to look him dead in the eyes and told him,
"You a dead, New York bitch. Nigga, you a pussy!" Standing
erect, Chino gave the order. "Blast him, P, do that shit!"

Shaking, P grabbed the base of the gun to steady himself,
and Chino walked beside him and patted his shoulder.
Delano felt the coldness of the steel on the back of his head.
Sppt! Even with a silencer attached, Paul still thought the
sound echoed through the city and that someone, somewhere
had to hear what was going on. "Yeah!" yelled Yellow. Sppt,
sppt, sppt! Three more times in the head, and Delano's body
went limp, and he slumped far down in the chair with blood
running out of the corner of his mouth onto his bare chest. It
was over. Chino swaggered over to Paul and took the gun out
of his hand.

"P, I'll take that for you and put it where it can't be found." They left the garage looking over their shoulders, making a final check of being sure not to leave anything incriminating behind.

Eventually, Chino would have to take care of Paul, but not before he met and stole all of his contacts and perhaps even fucked his fine-ass girl that he was so in love with. Chino knew that eventually Paul would forget this whole scene, and the next time he had to pull the trigger he would become fearful and fold.

Over the next few days, Paul tried to shake the memory of his initiation. He began thinking of his future and how much safer it might be doing business with a homie in another state. But he failed to realize that even in that case, the feds would be a threatening presence and very hard to shake.

MONTH SEVEN

I spent twenty-four hours in the straitjacket before they felt that I was safe. I was then placed in medical on suicide watch in a one-woman cell. I was given an appointment to see the psychiatrist and talk about what was wrong with me. Contrary to what I expected, Dr. Pelt was a young man, casual and relaxed. He had one of those keen noses that looked like it was pinched with a clothespin. His fingers were long and slender, and he wore his nails a bit longer than the average man. As soon as I sat down I felt at ease with him, and a feeling of trust was immediately established.

Dr. Pelt's degree was on the wall, hanging above his head as he rested in a tall, black, cuddly leather chair. Sitting there, he looked like he had never experienced a bad day in his life, his manicured nails twirling a pencil. "So, Ms. Xavier, they say you want to kill yourself. Do you want to live?" he asked, now sitting erect and no longer twirling his pencil.

"I don't know," I said, shrugging my shoulders anxiously.

"Yes, you do," he said.

"No, I don't. I lost my boyfriend and custody of my son," I said, still thinking about how all of this happened.

"Well, you still have to live," he said sipping on a steaming cup of coffee.

"Why, so the feds can send me away for the rest of my life?" I asked.

"Let me tell you what I know. If you do the crime, you got to do the time. But also, this will build spiritual muscle. God has a way of putting us in a place to heal and change our lives. You are too beautiful and intelligent of a young lady to be sitting in here saying that your life is over, taking psych meds and giving up. You are a fighter, and you can make it through this. Your file says you lost custody of your son, so you just gonna leave him like your boyfriend left you—with unanswered questions? Life ain't fair. Only the strong survive, and I believe that you're one of the strong." I sat mute, staring at the clock on the wall. I couldn't remember the last time I had seen a clock. In the units there were no clocks. The old adage that an inmate doesn't need to know the time, while doing time, hit home at that moment.

Dr. Pelt changed the subject and said, "So, tell me about that yellow band you wear. You caught a federal case? Do you wanna at least talk about that?"

"No, I don't want to talk about that, I want to sleep. Can I have something to help me sleep?" I demanded.

"You want to sleep your time away? All inmates do. I'll give you a two-week prescription to help you sleep, and then I'll send you back to population. You're strong. I can see that. I want you, no matter how long you have to do, to go home to your son. Don't leave another black child out there abandoned. Do you hear me? You love your son, don't you?"

"Yes!" I snapped.

"Then do the right thing and return to him. Remember, this is building spiritual muscle. One day you will see. As for your boyfriend, unfortunately, it was his time to go. It was his fate."

"Why do people die in gruesome ways? I wonder if he was in pain before his death," I said like a naïve child.

"How did he die?" Dr. Pelt asked.

"Delano was beaten and shot four times in the back of the head," I informed the good doctor as tears began to well up in my eyes again. I had cried so much, I seriously wondered if my tear ducts would dry up.

"Well, that sounds painful, but I'm a Christian and I believe that God knows when it's your time to go, and He takes you before the pain. The only thing that's left is a shell of a person, and they never felt the pain that we think they felt. I think that like abused and molested children, when they die, God takes them before the pain, and they don't feel it. The assailant doesn't know it, but the individual has already gone, so if your friend was a nice person, as I am certain he was, then I don't think he felt it. I think that whoever did this to him was handling a shell of a person, and that God took him before his physical death."

I began to cry, as I wanted this to be true. I never wanted Delano to suffer, and the tragedy of his life was the way that he died. It made me think of Young Mike, Eddie, China and now Delano—all gone, dying senselessly in the streets.

"Do you believe in God?" Dr. Pelt asked.

I gave him a look of disgust and frowned up my face, letting a tear fall from my eye. "Yes, I *believed* in God, *before* my arrest, before all the sadness in my life. But if there was a God, would I be in jail? No! Well, I *used* to believe in God."

"Oh, so you believe in God as long as He is doing something for you—so long as things go your way. See, most inmates come to jail believing in God, but leave jail and forget God. Everything can't always go your way." Dr. Pelt took a sip of his coffee while staring at me and continued. "Yes, I know about bad days and disappointments. I didn't want to be a psychiatrist. I wanted to be a surgeon. . . ."

"So," I interrupted him, exercising bad attitude to the fullest.

"*So,*" he mimicked. "I was in medical school, and when you're in the operating room" *(What in the fuck does that have to do with me?),* "your mouth is covered by these sanitary masks. It was then, in medical school, that I noticed my hearing failing. Keep in mind that I had already been in school for seven years at this point, pursuing my dream. I was busting my ass to achieve the best grades. During a session in the operating room, I was assisting a surgeon and asked him one too many times to repeat himself. That is not acceptable in medical school. It was clear to everyone that my hearing was not what it was supposed to be, so I got on my knees and prayed and asked God to heal my hearing. I mean, He's God, right? He can do anything but fail, right?"

His story held my interest because I, too, felt like there was someone else let down by God. I relaxed my attitude and listened. "So, He didn't heal my hearing, which meant that I couldn't become a surgeon, which meant I had to choose a different field of medicine, which meant that God had failed me. Or rather, that is what I believed at first. My dream had exploded and I had to find another path." He turned his head, and I noticed a hearing aid in his right ear. "So I became a psychiatrist, someone dedicated to patiently listening to other people's problems. I also learned that God could do anything. But he also shuts the doors that we think we want opened. A strong man may push a boulder, but in the process, he not only builds physical muscle, he builds spiritual muscle. Maybe the stone will be moved, maybe not, but either way the obstacle will make the man stronger. He benefits from the process whether he succeeds or fails. I learned that God has a plan and a purpose. You may one day know the answers to the whys in your life. Pamela, it's by design that I'm sitting here with you. I am here to help. If you can just find something to believe in, if it's not God, then perhaps you can believe in being with your son, again, one day."

Dr. Pelt brought tears to my eyes, and I began to snivel, hoping that there was truth in what he was saying. I wanted him to make sense. I needed it all to make sense. He rolled his chair over next to mine and said, "Dry those tears, you don't want to die. You have something to live for, if not for yourself, then for your son. Don't leave him and have him feel lost and alone like you do without your friend. What was his name?"

"His name *is* Delano!"

"Be strong for your son. I've seen men do double digits and come out all right at the end. Women, too, it's not impossible."

"Thank you, Dr. Pelt."

"Do you feel better?"

"Yes, I do."

"Pamela Xavier, you are welcome. I'm going to allow you to remain on medical for observation and return you to your dorm next week. I'm going to give you the prescription drug Elavil. It'll help you sleep. It also helps with depression and anxiety." He extended his hand, and I held onto it, looking him in the eye. He whispered, "It's gonna be all right."

Dr. Pelt gave me the Elavil, and I returned to the medical ward. I slept like a baby that night, and I dreamed that I was free, lying in my bed at my mom's house in Detroit. We were lying in the bed, Delano and I, staring into each other's eyes, with my son between us. Nestling in Delano's arms, I was suddenly jolted awake by the nose of a rifle to the side of my ribcage and by the sound of angry voices. The voices were as clear as a sunny day.

"*El es un pequeño niño. No podemos perder una rata.*" (He is just a small boy. We can't use a rat.)

"*¡Podemos usar un ratón!*" (We can use a mouse instead!) I reached for my son and he was gone.

NEW YORK BOYZ

Erik and T-Love returned to their hometown of New York, the place they loved, after lying low for three months in various parts of unknown, small cities in the country. When the news spread of Carmen's arrest, they figured there was nothing to hide from. They knew that once the feds had you, it was a far stretch before your feet would hit them bricks again.

Erik and T-Love sat in the 220th Street Caribbean restaurant in the Bronx, waiting for Infa and Abudullah to join them. They were late, as usual, and T-Love was in his usual eating mode, licking his fingers and rubbing his potbelly. Erik needed all the patience he could muster if he was to put his plan in motion and make shit happen the way he had it planned in his head. It frustrated him that he had no one of his caliber to work with, but then again, he thought, "That's why you have leaders and followers. You'll always have something to distinguish rank." An old Jamaican wives' tale said it best: *Somebody got to go to hell.* The more he thought about it, the more sense it made to him. Hell, everybody couldn't be one of the chosen.

Erik had called the meeting to discuss business. He called his connect and they spoke very briefly, and although Erik would have liked to have thought that they had been playing phone tag, he couldn't really call it that;

he would blow Dragos's cell phone up, and every blue moon or if the feeling hit him, Dragos would call him back. Erik had a difficult time keeping him on the phone. "Dragos, just let me holler at you for five minutes," he pleaded.

"I'm busy. What do you want?" This infuriated Erik, as Dragos knew damn well what he wanted. He wanted some of them thangs at low prices. But Dragos would never talk business over the phone, and Erik could tell by his tone that he was not interested in anything he had to say.

It was clear that Dragos was still servin' up shorties and wouldn't fuck with him and T-Love. He hadn't cut them off entirely, and he kept them as close as an enemy, but not close enough to harm them. Dragos continued to feed Erik and T-Love hope that one day he would come around and speak with them. Dragos wished that they would take the hint and have some pride and leave it as a mutual split with no hard feelings. And still, if a blue moon appeared and they happened to be in the same space, they could at least speak to each other as former friends would in passing. But no, Erik would not stop, and the more Dragos resisted, the more Erik pushed. After a while, Dragos wanted to see just how hard he would push. The pushing would ultimately determine how and if he would deal with him. Dragos knew to never go back on his word and definitely not his intuition.

Dragos had enough money and more than enough people trying to meet him. A Colombian, cocaine, heroine connect, needed no new friends, so it was never hard to answer demand. Dragos began to be more selective with his clients. Since money no longer was a motivation, he became more amused with the creative and somewhat desperate approaches that people used to get at him. It was almost like a talent contest; the best approach won the prize. It had been about a year and a half since his last dealing with his still favorite client—Carmen. Of all the people he had ever dealt with, he liked her the most. He liked Carmen so much that he risked money and product in dealing with her. All those things could be and were replaced, but he eventually put himself at risk.

Dragos began to reminisce, and he explained the situation to his new protégé, Carlito. Carlito was his nephew and had recently reached twenty-one. He was now ready to get his cherry broken in the business. Dragos would have chosen a different route for his sister's son but the streets had gotten to him, and he felt obligated, since there was no hope in deterring him, to school him as he learned the ropes. Dragos also knew that although he could tell him *some* things, there would be certain things that Carlito would have to learn from experience. Since he knew that Erik and T-Love were basically harmless, he decided to hook his nephew up with them as his first customers.

As they walked alongside the Hudson River, Drago continued to tell his nephew of the lovely, young Carmen. He always taught in parables and wanted to share this last one before he sent him to meet Erik and the crew. "So, Carlito, like I said, even the financial loss that occurred as a result of her incarceration was minor. We can take a loss. Monetary losses you can recover from, so never let a setback force you to make a hasty decision. Make your decisions based on your gut and the practicality of your choices. Mistakes are also a part of life, and don't be so hard on yourself. I risked my freedom once dealing with Carmen on an intimate level."

His nephew looked at him with curious eyes, thinking of his aunt, Dragos's wife, and thought that perhaps he had been unfaithful. Carlito stopped and turned to his uncle as they walked side by side with bodyguard in the rear and asked, "What happened? Did you fuck her?"

Dragos laughed. "No, I didn't. Not to say I wouldn't have, but it wasn't like that; she wasn't that type of associate. Listen carefully so you can see how I risked my life. Carmen was a single mother with a small son. Her son's father showed her how to hustle coca, but then he left her to fend for herself. She was unable to maintain her lifestyle legally, for whatever reason, and decided to hustle."

Carlito interrupted, eager to show his uncle that he remembered what he'd told him before. "Carmen put a plan and a program together, and she was honest and spoke from the heart. She was true." They began to walk again.

"Exactly. She not only exposed her heart, but her hand. Although this isn't the wisest move, it's the best move, when you want something from someone and can't give him anything that he doesn't already have. Carmen gave me honesty, understanding that a man in my position rarely gets that. All I get is lies and people sucking up to me. Like you, nephew, you pretended to enjoy washing my cars and helping me in the store while you were visiting me just to get where you are right now. All you had to do was level with me when you were sixteen, and you would be retiring by now. But you faked it for five years and caught petty cases pretending not to want this life. That's another story that you'll figure out about yourself, and then come tell me when you've learned the lesson." Embarrassed, Carlito wanted to defend himself, but he knew his uncle was too wise, and besides, he knew he was close to getting put on. Who cared if he thought of him as an opportunist, he wanted to be plugged. It saddened Dragos that his nephew didn't want to clear up his perception of his intentions. A man with character wanted things understood when they weren't apparent through his actions. But the obvious was known, and he knew that eventually Carlito would catch a bid and come out with lessons learned—the hard way. Because he was family, they would go on working together, God willing.

Dragos continued his schooling. "But Carmen is a mother, first, and doing business with a mom is dangerous.

A mother is loyal to her children. When you find a woman who's not loyal to her kids, you can't trust her love, as she has none in her heart. Carmen was a curiosity for me; I wanted to see if she could handle this life and she proved that she could. But I knew that if she ever caught a case she would have to choose her son, and then I'd have to eliminate her." Carlito nodded in agreement and understanding. He always felt Carmen should have been stankin'.

"She was already risking her life out here with a child, so she got what she deserved." Dragos shook his head to affirm Carlito's statement and fixed a steady gaze on the river. "At first my feelings toward her were cold, but I grew to love her, son. Then I just wanted her to make it out of the game with some money. There were losses on my end, and I needed for her to keep working, so I even lowered her ticket. But greed and foolishness eventually took over, and she got caught out there. Now, she must be handled."

"Yeah, let me do it!" Carlito begged. Dragos shook his head and asked his nephew, "How do you plan to do that? Carmen's in the Federal Detention Center."

"I know a few people who can get to her. What you gon' do, Unc?" Carlito asked.

"I want to give her a chance to do a little time, but I'm afraid that she might fold, and I can't risk myself and my family." Dragos looked Carlito in the eye and said, *"Mi familia es número uno."* (My family is number one.) *"Sí,* Carmen will be handled. It's just a matter of time," Dragos informed.

"Unc, you got attached to her?" Carlito asked.

"Yes, and it happens, so keep your dick out of people, and if you get attached, cut them loose. It took me 'til forty-something to control my dick and fifty-something to control my emotions. But now, Carmen's situation is out of my hands anyway due to her choices. Carlito, I don't have a personal problem with her; it's business. In the streets, deal with those who have as much, if not more, to lose than you do. Power is when you can choose your own destiny—when you can control the outcome. Be in this to win."

"Thanks, Unc. I'll make you proud." They turned to each other and embraced. Dragos took a few steps back and grasped Carlito's hand firmly. "Don't let me down," he said.

Infa and Abdullah pulled up in front of the Caribbean restaurant with the music blaring from the stereo system of their Hummer. Infa was inhaling his daily dose of trees and was nodding his head back and forth to a rap remix. Erik's patience was getting the best of him, and he wanted to run outside and smack the shit out of them. It seemed that he only had their full cooperation when the table before them was covered with money. Since this meeting was for talking and not dividing any ends, Infa was in no hurry.

"Yo, come on! You know E is heated!" said Abdullah, passing the spliff back to Infa. The song "More Bounce to the Ounce" came on, and Infa just started rocking his head back and forth like Abdullah hadn't said a word. Infa began to snake his head from side to side with exaggeration, and upon making eye contact with his partner, Abdullah couldn't hold back the laughter and started snaking right along with him. Their heads and necks moved rhythmically back and forth, each of them snaking and rocking to the base of the vibrating speakers located in the trunk. The windows were up, but the thumping sounds could still be heard from inside the restaurant.

Infa and Abdullah were inseparable, and they knew that no matter what, they would still get money—even if they had to keep shining up their heaters and robbing. They had become stick-up kids. That was their little secret, so although Abdullah wanted to leave his buddy in the car, they had to honor their pact: One don't move unless the other one does. Infa continued to get stupid with his dancing as Roger Troutman's computerized voice sang, "More bounce to the ounce," over and over again. He started moving his legs like he was at the roller rink skating and he was as fine as he was entertaining.

Erik, having watched through the window the entire time, had had enough. He got up, went out to the street, picked up a stick and pounded on their windshield. "Motherfuckers, get out the car!" Startled and with their sanity regained, they exited their vehicle and went into the restaurant following a steaming Erik, barely controlling their laughter at the sight of how furious he was. Erik thought of fucking them up right there on the spot, but he wanted to believe that these guys were in his corner and that they were all stressed over the slow money that was coming in. Erik thought that this would all change if he could just get them organized. Then he could approach Dragos with a workable plan. He still couldn't get over how Dragos had worked with Carmen and how she had taken a plan that he had in mind for years and ran with it. That's how she got jacked, and she was lucky that she didn't get killed. If it wasn't for T-Love and his deep, buried feelings for her, she would have been stankin'.

After analyzing how that all went down, Erik realized his mistake was that he never came to Dragos with a plan. But since Carmen was now in jail it didn't matter anyway; he had outlasted the majority of money-gettin' niggas in Columbus. He knew the city, and it was his. Although Paul had cut his throat, he knew that there was still money to be got out there, and he was determined to get it.

They all sat down, and when Erik looked at what he had to work with he shook his head. The Three fuckin' Stooges crossed his mind. Nonetheless, these clowns would have to do. Despite their weaknesses, he could trust them with his life and knew that they were capable of much. He also knew that their MO was to keep their level of anxiety down by acting crazy and keeping shit funny. Some in the life took the unemotional route, and others, well, kept shit comical to keep their level of anxiety down.

Erik waved his hand to the waitress and called the meeting to order. They huddled around the table as a ceiling fan buzzed overhead. "Okay, we got to work this program. This is the only way we gon' make it and get money," he said, and T-Love nodded his head as he began to eat his dessert.

"Well, what we gon' do?" Infa said. Erik wanted to check his attitude, but continued to try and hold it together. He knew that everyone was on edge, and at the end of the day they wanted to see the benjamins.

"We gon' talk about some shit and move forward. Those that don't want to roll need to say something now." Erik looked around the table, and all eyes were focused on him. Infa and Abdullah were seriously listening now. Despite their silliness and somewhat lax attitudes, they both really admired Erik. He was the risk taker, and up until recently, his plans always brought a profit. Erik continued. "So I've been trying to get in contact with Dragos. I asked him to join us here today. I'm so glad that he didn't and wasn't able to witness the two of you being late and not about business."

The thought of Dragos witnessing the earlier episode in front of the restaurant made Abdullah feel badly for Erik, and it showed all over his face. After all, Erik was his brother and he wanted him to be a success. Infa felt badly as well and extended his hand in apology. "E, you know you my nigga. I'm sorry, man, I don't want to fuck up nothin' you puttin' together." Erik felt better, feeling like he had regained control, order and respect. He shook his head, rubbed his brow and continued to explain.

"Yeah, I want to get with Dragos and I want us to roll out to the Midwest to hustle, to put some work in." Everyone looked at each other, wondering exactly which city in the Midwest they'd hit. T-Love didn't say anything, as he knew Erik wanted to go back to Columbus, Ohio.

"What city, nigga? Stop beatin' 'round the bush. You trying to go back to Columbus, ain't you?" Infa said.

Abdullah chimed in. "What? You going back to where you know it's blazin' hot?"

"Wait!" Erik stopped the conversation. "Yeah, it's hot there and everywhere else you do shit that's illegal, but still, there's money out there that we can get. I want it. I'm talking about in and out in about six months until we all got something to retire on," he explained.

Infa spoke. "E, we didn't make n-o-o-o-o-o money out there—you did. It ain't worth it for me to go out there to Cow-Town, USA to hustle."

"Things are going to be different. We'll split everything four ways even," Erik said. No one could believe their ears, as Erik was always so unfair with splitting ends evenly and liked to ration out allowances instead. But after seeing how Carmen divided shit up and how that had such a profound effect on T-Love, he learned a thing or two about how to treat people.

"Okay, so what about Carmen? Did she tell? Is she telling? How do you know that we ain't got secret or hidden indictments waiting for our asses?" said Abdullah. Erik became furious.

"Look, I ain't no attorney and I ain't Miss Cleo. Either you want to hustle and take a chance and go out there and get that money, or you don't. I can't promise you shit ain't waiting out there for us. Yeah, there's prison out there and beef, but a baller's life is out there too, and all that comes with it, nigga. Either you wanna roll or you don't!"

"E, I got you. I'm in," T-Love said.

"Count two, I'm in," said Abdullah.

Infa was the last to commit, knowing that his word would be his bond. He had one more question. "How we movin' da product? Can you get dem vans?" Erik didn't even have the product, let alone the mode of transportation, but before he could answer the question, Carlito walked into the restaurant along with Capo, their driver.

Capo was one of the drivers that knew the route to

Columbus, Ohio, all too well. Erik began to think that Dragos had not forgotten him. They approached the table and Capo made the introductions. "Infa, T-Love, Abdullah, Erik, this is Carlito." They all said hello and sat silently, waiting for the next word to break the ice.

"Scoot over, fellas," Carlito said, making room for himself. "Dragos sent me. Let's talk," he added confidently.

They all looked at each other, and Erik wiped the sweat from his brow. "Fuck it, let's get dat money!" Infa said. "And if we have to dead dem bama motherfuckas then they just get deaded!"

Abdullah added, "It's easy to do them country-ass, Ohio muthafuckas." He and Infa gave each other some dap with a finger snap.

"I'll kill any of dem—dey hoes, dey mommas and dey kids," said Infa nonchalantly.

"*More bounce . . .*" Abudullah began to sing, snaking his head back and forth again, and Infa joined in.

MONTH EIGHT

I returned to the east side of the jail, and I got bombarded with a million questions from the girls. Mychala was still there, having not yet gone to court. She was on a probation hold and waiting for her probation officer to come see her. I explained to everyone who asked that I was fine; it was back to jail as usual. After all that drama—tears, counseling and wanting to die, I was still alive. But I was in jail. Why did living have to hurt so bad?

The *Wheel of Fortune* was about to come on, and I was called out of my dorm for a pro visit. It was the feds. I felt uncomfortable and vulnerable because my attorney was not present. Why did they keep doing illegal dirty shit like this? And I knew exactly what they were here for; they wanted answers, and they were going to squeeze me until I cooperated with them.

"Sit down, Ms. Xavier. You smoke?" the tight-ass agent asked. He looked like a Harvard Law School reject, which made me feel sheer contempt for his being in my face.

"No," I replied.

"Would you like some coffee?"

"Puh-leeze. No!" My indignation for the three white males was clearly visible in my demeanor.

"All right, then. Let's cut to the chase, Xavier. We arrested your boy, Chino, again. The prosecutor assigned to this case has a real hard-on for him. Turns out, they have some history; he prosecuted him three years back when he worked for the state. He feels that Chino got off light—that the state laws were too lenient. But Chino has fucked up. He's playing in the big league now. It seems to us that he is undeterred by your arrest. The prosecutor allowed for a low bond, and he's already out doing his thing." *He had Chino and let him out? What is he talking about?* "He continues a criminal lifestyle that leads us to believe that the onuses of the crimes are not all on you; his activity continues with you still behind bars. We thought you were orchestrating things from here, but, uh, people don't run enterprises from jail on suicide watch." The motherfucker began to laugh right in my face. "Do they, fellas? Yeah, we know all about your little break-down."

I thought of Delano's horrible death and defending my emotional state against this moron. "I was stressed over my . . ." Then I came to my senses. *Wait, dumb ass. Don't even claim that you knew Delano. He was murdered. Remember? Let these motherfuckas do their job. They're supposed to pick and break your ass until you tell them what they want to know.* It was about time Carmen showed the fuck back up again—at Pam's weakest moment. I hadn't heard her voice since my arrest and assumed she bailed on me like everyone else. And assuming her persona, one that was so unlike mine, was the reason I was in all this bullshit in the first place. Carmen made me believe that I could be a *baller*—that gettin' money was an equal opportunity for all men, women and children over twelve.

Although I had decided to keep my mouth shut, I ignored my alter ego and let the feds continue. "Hold on. What he's saying, Ms. Xavier, is that it doesn't have to be like this," the second agent chimed in. "Work with us, and this'll be all over in no time." As if on cue, the third agent dropped a piece of paper in my lap. I grabbed it like it was a life preserver, only to find out that it was loaded with incriminating evidence against Chino, and subsequently against me.

It read: "On or about May 19, 1994, knowing that $4,000 in U.S. currency used to lease a van, vehicle identification number 4m2dv11, represented proceeds of some for an unlawful activity, that is distribution of and conspiracy to distribute a scheduled II controlled substance, cocaine, in violation of 21 U.S. 841 (a)(c) and 8846, conduct did financial transaction using the proceeds of said specified unlawful activity knowing that the transaction was designed in whole or in part to conceal or disguise the nature of the location in the source, the ownership or the control of the proceeds of the specified unlawful activity." I looked up at the agents like what I had just read was written in Chinese. The second agent snatched the paper and continued. "In other words, Chino purchased another car with drug money. He also purchased a Lexus, Land Cruiser and Benz. And you, my pretty, in jailhouse wear, will receive a superseding indictment." Then he dropped a two-inch-thick stack of papers in my lap, smiled and continued flexing. "My pretty, meet your codefendants," he mocked. "Your attorney will have your new indictment in court when you're charged again as this conspiracy grows. Do you know these people? Do you have any information on their involvement? Do you want to make a statement?" he asked menacingly.

"No!" The Elavil was still in my system, but I was feeling anxious like a motherfucker.

He slid a chair beside me. "Wanna hear something funny? We snatched Chino's smug ass out of the Lexus. He thought it was a routine traffic stop, and trying to look innocent, he had his driver's license and insurance card ready for inspection. We told him to get out and walk. And you know what he did?" *Knowing Chino, he pulled up his pants and walked.*

"No, what did he do?" I asked to entertain him.

"He pulled up his pants and walked like it was nothing," he said, letting out a chuckle.

"I wanna go back to my dorm," I said.

"Do you know these people?" interrupted the Harvard reject, referring to the information in the stack of papers on my lap.

"No," I said solemnly.

"Do you have any information on their involvement?"

"No," I said again.

"Do you want to make a statement?" the second agent asked again.

"*I want to go back to my dorm,*" I emphasized, hoping that they could finally understand me.

"Go ahead. You'll call us before we call you. Oh yeah, and the prosecutor's office accepts collect calls," said the Harvard reject. Laughter broke out between the three clowns.

I was unable to sleep when I got back to the dorm and wondered why, or how, Chino continued his criminal activity after being arrested for the second time. Didn't he know that the feds would be watching him? He always said that the catching comes before the hanging. I figured he meant that. Didn't he know that the feds would be looking for a slipup? Or, I presumed, that since I was the head of this conspiracy and still on motherfuckin' lockdown, this shit was entirely my fault, and he felt like he was in the clear—scott free. I pondered my position.

What is going on? Superseding indictments, codefendants and evidence that I don't even know . . . Delano dead. Still hustling, that Chino—making our shit look like a cartel in addition to showing no fear to the feds. He knows that they're watching, but knowing him, he's still stacking that cheese.

We've gone from a fourteen-count indictment with five codefendants to twenty-nine indictments and nineteen codefendants and growing.

• • •

My nightmare continued. I would have never imagined this, ever.

"Xavier, get ready for court!" the CO yelled through the chute in the door. I stepped over a girl lying on the floor. She jerked her cover from underneath my flip-flops and caused me to stumble.

"Think you cute, bitch, you should have fell on your face." For the most part, I wanted to go and kick that tramp straight in her grill, but haters were everywhere and they came in every shape and form.

"Later for you, trick!" I said as I continued out the door for court.

"I got your trick. While you gone, practice sleeping with one eye open, bitch!"

Her words echoed out into the hallway, and I heard some voices in the dorm cheer with excitement. "Woo-hoo!" The anticipation of a fight in jail was like preparing for a sporting event.

I was escorted to the federal court building for my additional indictment, and I sat in a holding cell, behind the chambers, waiting for my court hearing to begin. My attorney came to speak with me. I looked up from my cement bench with tears in my eyes. He touched my hand and said, "Pamela, as I mentioned and will explain later, you are in court to answer additional charges. A conspiracy makes everyone responsible for the actions of each other. You have additional codefendants added to your case. And before it's over, you'll be in court again. As I previously mentioned, as deals are handed out, it'll mean more arrests. You're here in court today to respond to this indictment. When asked how do you plead, just respond *not guilty,* and the process will continue."

I couldn't say a word. All I could do was think about all of the bullshit I was facing, and this was just beginning. I had been locked down for eight months in the county jail, and the issues were nowhere near being resolved. And eight months later not one word from Chino, my baby's daddy, who still walked the streets a free man.

I was escorted, shackled, from my holding cell and led into federal court with a bunch of foreign mofos that I didn't even know. I heard the judge read the names of four new people. Chino was dressed in an Armani suit. I, on the other hand, wore khakis, flip-flops and footie socks and felt like a total idiot with my hair cornrowed straight back, looking like a dyke. As the court went through the procedures of digging my ass into a deeper hole, I stood numb, wondering how Chino could leave me for dead and not tell me what to do. And I surely didn't know what to do now. I only knew one thing for certain and two things for sure: I didn't want to go to jail a young woman and leave an old one. The court proceedings lasted approximately ten minutes.

I hadn't slept much the night before, and the unit seemed to be unusually noisy. The lesbos had been furiously rubbing pussies together like they were trying to start a brushfire, and the lone white girl in the unit had whimpered and cried all through the night. When I finally did fall off to sleep, I was jarred awake by someone calling my name. "Xavier, visit, get up!!" The guard sounded especially agitated. I had obviously been called several times already with no response.

"Yeah, I'm comin'!" I yelled back at her. By now I was sick of this shit—being treated like an animal. I wanted out of here more than ever now.

I stepped into the corridor to accompany the officer down to the visiting area. I pretty much knew who my visitor was. When I had spoken to my sister, Lori, the previous night, she had mentioned that my mom had read in the papers about my reindictment. She told her that she was coming down to see me on an emergency visit. She wanted to try and talk some sense into my head. I missed my mother, but I couldn't really say that I wanted to see her— at least not under these circumstances. She had made every sacrifice imaginable to ensure that I grew up to be, if not Miss America, then the runner up—I had failed her on both accounts. I knew that it would be humiliating for her to see me here. It would be equally humiliating for me, knowing the turmoil that she had to have been going through.

To face my mother behind bars would be an absolute disgrace, and I was scared to death. When I walked into the small visiting booth where she sat, I noticed that she had aged since my incarceration. I studied her, wearing a floral dress, seated on a stool on the other side of the glass. If this brief, eight-month bid had already worn her down so, what would she look like if I had to do twenty, or even thirty years? Would she even be alive when I came home?

I just sat there behind the glass as my mother wiped the tears from her eyes. She looked at me as if I was a caged animal. I wondered what it would feel like to see my son, Antonio, behind bars and be a helpless parent, unable to ease his pain.

"Hi, Mom. How are you?" I said, hoping to just have small talk with her.

She squirmed around on the stool, trying to compose herself and get comfortable. The shame and powerlessness that she felt was apparent, as it took her a few moments to look me in the face. "Pammy, this place brings back sad memories for me. I once visited my brother on a plantation farm in rural Florida when I was a young child. Your uncle, Jimmy, he's been imprisoned since before you were born. He's doing time for being accused of raping a white woman. It was in 1969." (She always had the longest stories, told in parables.) "They housed him in a barn on a huge plantation. During the visit, we sat at a picnic table, out in the open. The guard came over with his dusty nasty boot and propped it up on the table. He had a gun in his lap and kept it there the entire visit. I will never forget the prejudice, the outrage and injustice done to my brother who received a life sentence for the alleged rape of a white woman. Now, here my daughter is, in jail, locked up like an animal, and it makes me sick to my stomach. It was hell getting back here to see you, and I had to stand in line for hours waiting to visit."

"I know, Mom, they use scare and bully tactics to deter the families from visiting their loved ones. It's a divide-and-conquer strategy on their part, but it's not anything that we can't overcome." I tried to make the visit as positive as possible and let her know that we would be okay.

"Pammy, I will not beat around the bush. Antonio needs you. He is not talking. He simply refuses to talk, and I am worried about him. How much time are you about to get?"

"Mom, whatever happened to your *God will give you the time,* etc.?"

"Look, don't get smart, and yes there is a God, and God don't like ugly. We need to look at how much time you'll do to insure the best for your son. I still believe in God and do know that He is able, but you have a child out here depending on you. So, what's it going to be?" My mom gave me a stern look. She wanted the truth and the truth was what she came for. I got the message loud and clear.

"Mom, they want me to take a deal. They want me to become a snitch, roll on people and get others locked up," I confessed.

"Oh, so they want you to be a pawn. They want to use you?"

I felt relieved that she knew what time it was. She was on my side of the street code of *ride and die. Pick twelve, take-that-shit-to-the-box* type shit. That was my mom's dukes. "Yeah, Mom, and I just can't do it," I said, looking away.

"Put that phone to your ear and listen to what I have to say." Then, on her own side of the glass, she placed a phone to her ear and continued. "First of all, your *friends* left you for dead when Chino would not take care of his son. You played yourself when you laid down with a man other than your husband and had his baby. You don't owe anyone but Antonio. You put him in jeopardy when you left him, so don't tell me what you can't do. I'm gonna get off of you for a minute and tell you a story about your momma and what a real momma does. You have never seen a day hungry, cold or naked. You ain't never walked in the house and the lights didn't come on. And it wasn't because I had a husband or a good man in my life. That was because I was a momma first. I slept with many a man to provide for my children, and there were many jobs I took to feed them. I even stole from those jobs to make your lives better. The difference was I was old enough and wise enough to know not to do something that would take me away from my children. I would humble myself and date someone who liked me that I didn't like. Now, you have to be a woman, a grown woman, and do what you have to do for your son.

"Back in my day, when there was a case, the man took the time. I ain't never heard of no shit where the only female on a case takes the time. These kids thinkin' they *ballers*. They *crawlers*, and need to sit the fuck down! Back in your momma day, the men were men and they would never let a woman hustle. They would never let a woman go hungry, and if she had a child, some man, somewhere would help her. Choose life for your son and say a great big kiss my ass to them motherfuckers! And when they want to call you a snitch, say, and I mean loud: *Kiss my free, snitching, watching-my-baby-grow-up ass!*" I started to chuckle, peeping my mom's attempt at being cool. It lightened the mood for us to keep talking.

"Now, I'm not saying lie and I'm not saying create shit, just tell them a little truth, a little lie, and a lot of I don't know. If you act like you're cooperating, it will make it easier. You need to think about your son and not Chino or anyone else. You should have married Delano and let his ass go to jail."

"Mom, Delano got killed." She froze instantly. I wasn't surprised, because I knew that she really liked him. "I can't really talk about it though."

"Sorry, Pammy, I knew that you liked him and he loved you. What you could have done was let him try to provide for you instead of being afraid of love and trying to be a man and get your shit fucked up. They created visits for women to visit men behind bars, not the other way around. Don't get it wrong, missy."

"Five more minutes," a CO yelled from the intercom.

"Mom, it's almost time to go." My mother hung up the phone and placed her hand to the glass. I held my hand up opposite hers.

"I will always take care of Antonio and he will be fine. I promise you that on my life; I will do what I can for him, but I need you to promise me that you will do all that your lawyer asks of you, and you will do what you can to come home. You owe your child, Pammy. And I'm not getting any younger. I got about ten good years left in me; I won't be here forever. You need to be with your son."

My mother began to cry, and I knew what she was telling me I needed to do. It was time for me to commit to making a decision. The problem was how would I do it? I couldn't. I just needed to find a better way. I had learned that the obvious solution wasn't always the best one. In the meantime, I needed to tell my mom something that would ease her worrying. "Mom, I promise to come home as soon as I can."

She reached into her purse, pulled out a wrinkled tissue and wiped her wet face. Then she picked up the phone again and said, "It would make me proud to see you make decisions for the sake of your child. There could never be any shame in that, 'cause I'd pick trash for my children and suck a pig's dick to feed 'em. Thank God I never had to go there, but ain't a woman on the planet that doesn't understand that. Trust in God, for He will always offer a way."

The guards cut the sound off on the phones, signaling the end of our visit, and my mom and I waved and blew kisses to one another through the thickness of the glass. I watched her stand up, straighten out her dress and walk away. She left me feeling numb, but with a new resolve and strength to fight my Goliath.

I was happy to see my mom, but it made me sad that she had to stoop to such an unclean level of conversation to get me to understand her point. *Damn, suck a pig's dick?*

SKELETONS

Chino was sick and tired from the drive and the nonstop chatter of his latest trick, LaShone. He had met her in a strip club, and her body was bangin'. In addition to that, she gave him the best head that he had ever had. Just thinking about it had his dick on swell inside of his pants. Talk about the snapper! Girl had it goin' on! On the drive down to Kentucky, she leaned over and unzipped his shit on I-71. Chino pulled into a rest stop away from the other cars and allowed LaShone to handle her business.

"Mmmm . . . daddy, you got a big dick!" LaShone purred as she slurped. Chino didn't want to come too fast, and he tried to think of other things. It was no use; the sight of her head bobbing up and down and the slurping noises turned him on so much that he gave her a warning.

"Yo! I'm about to come. Slow down, hold up." This only urged her on all the more. Unbeknownst to most of the men in LaShone's life, she got her kicks off giving pleasure. It really had nothing to do with them, per se, but with the thrill in making a man come. It was a challenge, and when they moaned her name, she stuck her busty chest out like a proud peacock. She squealed with excitement as she felt the vein along the shaft of Chino's dick pulsate. She knew what was coming—lunch.

"Come in my mouth, baby." This was music to Chino's

ears; he was happy to find a chick that would swallow. LaShone swallowed so well that she could do a blowjob on the highway. She needed no after-sex face cloth, as her tongue lapped him dry. "Mmmm, you taste so good," she said.

"You *feel* so fuckin' good," Chino whispered as he thought of how to make an honest hoe out of her. But he knew from years of training that a hoe couldn't be turned into a housewife. *What a shame,* he thought. Chino never, ever kissed LaShone in the mouth as he thought of how many dicks she had probably sucked. But they were both cool with that. He tidied his clothes as she sat smugly in her seat like the cat that swallowed the canary. Chino continued to drive as LaShone began humming the song that was playing on the radio by Joe: "All the Things Your Man Won't Do."

That song always made him think of Pammy, his Pooh. He used the palm remote and changed the station as LaShone looked out of the corner of her eye and sucked her teeth. Chino didn't really give a damn. LaShone lifted her right leg and placed it on the dashboard. It was times like this, when he was thinking of Pammy and taking attitude from a female that could prove lethal. He was a chauvinist and proud of it. Chino picked and chose his women with a certain persona—sweet, docile and cooperative, and when they deviated from that mold he could be downright ugly.

Chino finally pulled into the valet circle in front of the Ritz Carlton hotel and turned over his vehicle to be parked. He tipped the attendant forty bucks and carried his bags into the lobby. Gliding through the plush entrance of the hotel and checking into a reserved suite, he watched LaShone as she took a seat at the lobby bar. He reminded himself to call Paul on his cell phone and tell him what time to report to dinner.

"Hello?" Paul answered his phone anxiously after awaiting the call for hours.

"Wuz up?" Chino asked.

"Nothin', waitin' on you. What's up?" Paul's impatience was clearly annoying to Chino, but he continued his efforts to fake it. It was almost like Paul couldn't relax, and this drove him mad. Chino preferred to work with those who were true to the hustle and not as new to it as Paul was. His motive for getting ends and getting out was too obvious. Chino knew that there was no way out for himself; he had gotten in way too deep. He had committed too many crimes, and furthermore, the clock was against him. Irritated by the thought of that reality, Chino gave Paul the instructions.

"Yeah, shorty, we gon' meet at the Ritz Carlton downtown tonight at nine sharp. Come dapper."

"What?"

"Come clean, on point, polished, yo. We goin' out on the town," Chino said.

"Oh, okay. I brought some gear," Paul informed.

"Nah, *gear* ain't gon' get it. You got a vine? A suit? A name on the collar or sleeve?" Chino asked.

"I can put something together." Paul felt a little anxious. Aside from the denim pieces he had with him, he could only put together a shirt and slack combo.

"Yeah, do that, and I'll see you later tonight to discuss *biz-ness*. See you in, say, about three hours." *Click!*

Chino gazed at LaShone as she lay across the bed, ass tooted up in the air. *Damn, she's pretty*, he thought. He examined the dress that she pulled out of her Gucci luggage and admitted to himself that she had some class. The dress was crimson red, and it had a scoop neck with spaghetti straps. It was backless, with a *V* design that stopped at the crack of her ass. Chino loved the selection. He couldn't wait to see how the soft fabric hugged her small waistline, the small arch of her back, bent to perfection. The dress really didn't allow for any underwear, and LaShone had the body to handle it. She also had the prettiest damn feet on the planet! She purchased a pair of sling-back, six-inch silver heels. As long as she didn't talk, she would be that dime piece for the evening.

Chino walked over to the side of the bed and removed his shirt, revealing a dark blue, bulletproof vest. He took the remainder of his clothes off and looked around the room to make certain everything was okay; he needed to feel safe. His safety had become an issue for him, and with Yellow not in town yet, he had felt a little alone these days. And he didn't know who wanted him more—the feds or the rival hustlers. Either way, he knew that someone somewhere wanted his demise.

Chino slid the bathroom door open in the oriental theme suite. He stepped onto hardwood floors that led to a shower adjacent to a garden whirlpool tub. The hot steamy water from the showerhead pounded against his skin. It was relaxing, peaceful times like this that he thought about his life and how he had come to this point. There was really no one that he could turn to or confide in. As the water rinsed the shampoo from his hair, he leaned back against the shower wall and wondered: *How do you turn back the hands of time?*

As soon as he was released on bond, following his first arrest, Chino drove to Atlanta, Georgia. He headed for the United States penitentiary to visit his father, who was serving a life sentence. Here was the man, the father and role model that he looked up to and wanted to understand. After Chino's parents caught a federal case, his life was never the same. Keyes, his father, got his moniker due to the amount of keys that he carried back in the day. He would carry keys to every house and bar establishment that he owned. He was frequently asked why he had so many keys. He would always proudly respond with, "These keys represent responsibility." Chino had two single keys tattooed on his forearm in memory of his parents. His mother's name, *Lala*, was written on one key, and his father's name was inscribed on the other one.

While Chino was growing up, the details of his family were generally not discussed and kept on the hush. His mother, God rest her soul, didn't really have a chance to pass anything down to her children. She had the opportunity for a second chance but she chose to remain in the streets, and it was the streets that eventually took her life. The murderer was never found. Being left without a mother at age twelve, Chino had to struggle to survive along with his siblings.

Chino was second to the youngest and was the spitting image of his mom. They shared the exact same birthday and spent Sundays lying in bed watching old movies. It was then that Chino became obsessed with some of the old school gangsters like Humphrey Bogart and Al Capone. As he grew older, it was the likes of the modern day gangstas, such as John Gotti and Al Pacino, who turned him on. It was during this time that he met Pamela. He believed in her, but when he began to see her as less than perfect, he gave up on females and looked to the streets to affirm and praise him.

Walking into the visiting room made him feel edgy and apprehensive all at once. It had been nine years since he had seen his father face-to-face. Aside from the infrequent phone calls and the constant money orders, there was not really much of a relationship between them. Chino never understood how his father had his mother in the streets hustling alongside him with six children to raise. But, then again, to understand his father would mean to understand himself.

The older Chino became, the more he knew he was his father's seed by the compassion he began to feel regarding his mistakes. Chino actually understood why a man chose to be unfaithful and how responsibility was a choice and not a gender requirement. During quiet moments, when he claimed his son with Pamela, he secretly thought he was doing the child a favor. Chino wondered what he would actually give to the child he fathered with Pammy. What could he pass down? Would his son grow up and follow in his footsteps? Would the boy become a little him, or could he give him something other than the life? No matter how deeply he searched his inner self to find something different other than the monster that society had said he'd become, the more he found what was said about him to be true. This truth frightened him. The thought of being a father made him feel inadequate. But rather than just admitting it, he acted indifferently to the entire situation.

Sitting at the table waiting for his father to come into the visiting hall made Chino feel like a child again, and all his fears were present. His father was revered as a stand-up guy, both on the streets and behind the wall. He didn't tell. He was a don with much respect—doing life for the cause and what he believed in.

Chino's father had taken his bid on the chin. In the jailhouse culture, he was a trouper. He was serving life with no parole, but he was handling it. He was respected by the general convict population and had a speaking and/or nodding relationship with many of the street legends and luminaries that were housed in USP Atlanta. He had met and somewhat befriended the political prisoner Mutula Shakur, had a fair relationship with Big E from the West Coast and had walked and talked once or twice with Noah from Chicago. He played several hands of poker with Underwood from New York, Rudy from Baltimore was his workout partner and the urban legend himself, Big Akbar, was his jailhouse lawyer. Even for the incarcerated, the cream still rose to the top, and he was among the crème de la crème.

The officer working Keyes's tier had told him that he had a visitor. Although he wasn't totally sure who it was, he was pretty certain that it was his son, Chino. In jail, inmates sometimes got news as fast as they would get it in the streets. Some time back, he heard a rumor that his son had taken a bust. Chino had not come to see him in over nine years. Keyes thought that if that indeed was him in the visiting room, as he suspected, then he was probably looking for advice.

As he walked from B-House across the compound to the visiting room, Keyes felt a cool breeze on his face and thought of his deceased wife. He reminisced on how their life together had started and her dreams of becoming a nurse. *What would their life have been had he taken that job at the Chrysler Motor plant?* Shaking the thought, he strolled up the stairs to the administration building's third-floor visiting room.

In the search and dressing room, Chino Senior went through the standard procedures. "Take everything off, open your mouth, lift your tongue, bend over and spread your cheeks. Perhaps you've got a grenade launcher in your ass," laughed the cynical correction officer. "Now get dressed!" he ordered.

Chino was proud of a man that he didn't much know or understand. And this day, he prayed as he waited, that the man be his father.

About twenty minutes later, in walked a well-groomed, handsome man who was a replica of Chino with twenty more years on his face. His build was athletic, and his skin glowed, revealing good health, clean air and fresh foods.

Keyes sat at the table and left his son standing before him. Chino had wished for a hug, but instead he was given an ol' G handshake. He sighed from disappointment and sat across from his father.

With snacks laid before them and the air filled with silence, Keyes searched the room, scanning it like a freed bird released from its cage. It seemed, for a moment, that he was more concerned about his new surroundings than the visit from his son.

Chino wore a short-sleeved shirt, hoping that his father would notice his tattoo. "I like dem dere tattoos." Keyes raised his sleeve to reveal some of his own penitentiary tats. They revealed the names of his children who Chino thought were only rumors. There was no tattoo for Chino. "This one here is for your younger sister, Tarsha." He pointed to another tattoo and added, "And this is for an older brother you got that I never told you about. He's with my bottom whore. You remember Stacey, don't you?" Chino shook his head no, not understanding how his father, after all this time, with everything going on and the passing of his mother, could talk about another woman in his face. "Well, Stacey still around and she takes care of me. Shit, I don't even know if I'm the daddy, but when you accept a woman, you gotta accept her children. You know that, right?"

"Yeah, Dad. I do," Chino responded, nodding his head.

"So, what's on your mind that you came down here to see me? I heard you caught a case—a fed one this time." Keyes extended his hand to give him five as if this was an accomplishment. Chino was confused by the gesture. He expected a father to say, "What in the fuck did you do?" or "Why in the fuck did you do this?" or "What happened?" But instead, he got the same shit the niggas gave him in the street—bullshit.

"Yeah, Dad. My shit looks fucked up." Chino wanted to know: *How do you go on from here? How do you salvage your life after making so many mistakes, or do you keep spiraling downhill from there?* He looked into his father's eyes for answers.

"Look, you chose the game," Keyes said and moved closer to his son. "The game didn't choose you and you gots to hold it down. Ain't no whole lot to that. Do like me; don't ever snitch. Take what they got to give you. Press that bunk and do that muthufuckin' time. I don't want to hear my son snitched. Your ass will be disowned. Hold ya head.

Hold your water. I am certainly not going to take you by
the hand and tell you to 'do you' as the snitches and the hot
niggas now say. If that was what you came here for, you
came to the wrong nigga. I *will* tell you this, though: Trust
no one, and if you think they can do you . . ." Keyes said,
leaning in close to whisper into Chino's ear. "Dead men tell
no tales," he added, and leaned back into his seat as if he
hadn't just endorsed murder to his son. He continued.
"Enough said on that. Let me school you. Back in my day,
there were soldiers and things were different—a lot different. Never in my life have I seen so many snitches, and live
ones at that. The game, as I knew it, is dead. See, when I
was your age, I had bitches on every corner . . ." Chino sat
through three hours of shoulda, woulda, coulda stories
from his father—at a time when he was there to discuss *his*
life. He began to contemplate, as words that he had already
heard so many times over the past nine years went into one
ear and out the other.

"This my son. Yeah, he that nigga on the streets. He
takes care of me," Keyes said, finally bringing his stories to
a halt to say hello to some other inmates visiting with family. They all knew Keyes was being taken care of like a king,
and it was a source of pride for him behind that dismal
wall. Chino looked away from his father and sucked up
tears of frustration and disappointment. He bit his bottom
lip, refusing to fold like a card table and thought: *Didn't my
father know that I needed him? Didn't he know that I was
here about my life? Didn't he know that even though he's
already doin' life that maybe I need hope? The first time in
my life I needed my father, and he still wasn't there. I wonder
why God took my mother and not him. Who can I turn to?*

"Visiting hours over!" the white officer snarled.
"Inmates to the back of the room, visitors to the front. Visitors, when you hear your name called, step forward
together and follow the officer standing at the door. Ms.
Smith; Ms. Culpepper; Ms. Jones; Mr. and Mrs. Muham-

mad; Mrs. Stefan; Mr. Reiter . . . Mr. Cruz, would you please stop your children from running around the visiting area? Ms. Robinson and Ms. Bozeman . . . all right, the rest of you remain seated until your name is called," the officer sharply instructed. Chino was in the second group, standing with a young black mother whose twin girls were crying uncontrollably as they waved good-bye to their dad.

The staff continued to give notice that visiting hours had come to an end, and Chino was at least saved from the torture of his father's street tales. As Keyes turned to walk away, Chino reached out and gave him a big bear hug. He was pleased and a little surprised that his father didn't resist him. He didn't embrace him back, either, but this would have to do. Chino couldn't remember the last time he was this close and open with a man. He inhaled his father's scent deeply into his nostrils and figured that this was the last time he would see him. But then again, he knew that he would probably end up in either this jail with his father, or another one, with some butt-head fuckin' CO looking up his ass for dope the rest of his life. Then they could be pen pals and swap shoulda, woulda, coulda stories for eternity.

Chino very well knew that death could also be his fate. Then Keyes would just have to mourn him—or would he?

During the walk back to B-house, Keyes thought long and hard about his son's problem. He couldn't help but see his wife, Lala, God rest her soul, in his eyes. He wished that he had done things differently. He missed his son. He missed all of his children, but there wasn't a lot to discuss regarding a criminal case. If a nigga had a case, then he should stand up, be a man and deal with it without all the bullshit. Every tub had to stand on its own bottom. Chino was going to have to stand on his.

Chino walked between the cars in the parking lot leading to his vehicle. When he reached it, he opened the door, sat in the driver's seat and cried in the privacy of his custom Suburban. As he felt his tears creeping down his face, he wasn't exactly sure of why he was crying. Was it for the lack of reassurance from his father? Both men were born and bred in the game, with the belief that any display of emotion was a sign of weakness. Here he was with silver rims on his ride, Play Stations in the headrests, guns under the seat and a pocket full of dough. But all of this was nowhere near enough. All Chino wanted was some answers, and if he didn't get the answers he needed, some unconditional love, for just one day, would have been nice.

Because no one loved Chino, it was virtually impossible for him to return love, so he decided to dish out what he had received his entire life—the short end of the stick and a lousy dealt hand. If he had to play, others would have to pay. It's was as simple as first-grade math.

TIP YOUR HAT

Yellow pulled into the circle drive of the Ritz Carlton behind Paul's Land Cruiser for valet parking. He felt his girl Jewel's leg and smiled. They had been together for five years and he was still as in love with her today as he was the first time that he laid eyes on her. They were both from Compton, California, and she had joined her sweetheart to come to the Midwest to get paid. Jewel was sort of on the plain looking side, and it seemed that no matter how much money he spent on fixing her up and buying her the latest gear, it never made a difference; she just was the Plain-Jane type of girl—the girl next door. They grew up two houses from each other, and if anybody understood Yellow, it was Jewel. They both were members of the Crips and held each other down when no one else would. Although there were times when Yellow thought of trading Jewel in for a show-piece, he knew that that would be a mistake; Jewel had stood by him through two bids and about four bodies in addition to thousands of dollars. Yeah, Yellow knew she was wife material.

It was one of the coolest weekends. The Kentucky Derby was always a spectacular event and drew thousands from all over. It was a tradition of both the legal rich of the Midwest and the upcoming hustlers in the area. One of the most exciting parts of the event was when the victor was allowed to enter the circle and get the Triple Crown Win. Chino especially loved this part of the event, when the announcer would ask the audience to "Tip your hats!" Everyone would tip their derby, the hat worn by the attendees.

Chino had been planning for the Kentucky Derby for three weeks. The Derby wasn't simply a horse race; it was the first leg of the Triple Crown. The horse that won this event, and went on to win the next, would, at the last event, be named one of the rare Triple Crown winners in the world. People in the racing crowd still spoke in awe of the legendary Secretariat, a past Triple Crown winner. This was a major social gathering, and like all social gatherings of such magnitude, players, hustlers, ballers and pimps from across the country would be in attendance.

LaShone, dressed in a red outfit that would give J-Lo a run for her money, answered the door of the hotel suite. She decided against a hat, but instead, placed a red ribbon on the left side of her head. After spending three hundred dollars on a hair weave, there was no way that she was about to hide it under a hat.

Yellow, Jewel and Paul made themselves comfortable in the living room area of the suite while Chino was still in the bathroom dressing. "P, why didn't you bring your girl?" Yellow asked. Paul knew he didn't want his girl around his work, but he didn't want to tell this, for fear they would think that she felt she was too good to hang with them—so he lied.

"She had to watch the kids. Her mom backed out on the babysitting, and my girl is crazy about those kids—won't let anyone else watch them."

Jewel smiled, as she understood. "P, I'm the same way about our kids and Yellow knows that." Yellow nodded his head and took an appetizer off the platter from room service that was left in the lounge area of the suite.

LaShone asked the men if they wanted anything to drink as she stood at the bar. Yellow responded, "Yeah, pass the Courvoisier."

"I'll take a Heineken if they got one in there," Paul replied. Jewel walked over to assist LaShone. She wasn't having any other woman serve her man, and Yellow smiled as he peeped her move. As Jewel approached LaShone, she felt a little envious about her curves. Jewel wore a white linen pantsuit that matched Yellow's, a straw hat with navy blue piping, and white shoes with blue detail. She was clean, but not as sexy as she now wished she was. She uneasily eyed LaShone's shoes.

LaShone felt someone walking up on her and turned to give her gold-digging smile to one of the men. LaShone was always thinking of who had the biggest bank, and although she was perfectly determined to keep Chino—with his impending legal issues—she knew that eventually, she would have to work on a backup.

LaShone met Chino at the club, and although he thought it happened by chance, she had been going to that club every night for thirteen days straight waiting for him to come into the spot. Thanks to her former lover, T-Love, she had heard so much about Chino that she was like, "I need to be doin' that nigga," and eventually, she was.

LaShone looked at Jewel as she made the drinks and thought to herself that she would never go anywhere and not show cleavage. But LaShone decided to be nice and try to befriend this girl. *Who knows, maybe she can introduce me to someone, after Chino's ass is gone.*

LaShone also secretly wondered who Chino's wife was. He always wore a wedding band, and inquiring minds wanted to know. But that would make her have to care, and if Chino wasn't facing a federal drug case, maybe she would. But since he was, LaShone figured he was a waste of emotional energy, but not her time as he treated her just fine.

"Damn, nigga! You take as long as a woman." Yellow stood to embrace his partner as Chino finally came into the room.

"Don't wrinkle me, crab!" The men both enjoyed a laugh, and Chino was really glad to see his friend. Yellow was the one last comfort in Chino's life; they went way back. LaShone handed Chino a glass of cranberry juice with lime, as she knew that he didn't drink or smoke. He had taken a vow of sobriety after growing up with a heroine-addicted grandmother. The memories were horrific. Although Chino had mad love for his grandmother and respect for how she made a sincere effort to step up to the plate and help raise her daughter's children, he still never understood the addiction, which kept her off the scene most of the time. His determination to stay drug free came as a result of witnessing the profits made from the weakness of others. He vowed to be strong.

Chino pulled up a chair and sat down. He eyed Paul, who appeared nervous. "Damn, P! What the fuck is your problem? Do you need your dick sucked before we leave?" he asked.

Paul shook his head no and almost spit out his drink from embarrassment. "Nah, I'm straight," he replied.

"No, LaShone, take that nigga into da bedroom and give him a straightener," Chino demanded.

Like an obedient slave, LaShone walked over to Paul, who was sitting in a chair with his legs crossed, trying to conceal his rock hard dick. "Come on, baby, let's do this," she whispered into his ear while caressing his left inner thigh with her right hand. She began making cooing and slurping sounds, and licking her lips, giving him clear indication of the treat he would get if she stuck his dick in her mouth.

"N-n-n-no . . . thanks," Paul stuttered, as he was obviously tempted by the beauty before him. He continued to dismiss the idea as he was urged on by Yellow and Chino.

Chino glanced at his diamond-studded watch. "Let's roll. The limo should be downstairs any minute," he said. They all left the suite and headed for the downstairs lobby.

Everyone piled into the white custom Cadillac limousine. The first stop was a black-owned downtown restaurant called the Brownstone. This spot was a legend in Lexington, owned by two brothers who left the corporate world to go for their entrepreneurial dreams.

Lance and Rashim Johnson were identical twins, born to a seventeen-year-old Tkessa Johnson on Christmas day. As kids, the boys drew prolonged stares from anyone seeing them for the first time; they had heads full of wavy hair, high cheekbones, skin that looked like polished black mahogany and emerald green eyes. Unlike many sets of twins—growing older and going their separate ways, Lance and Rashim seemed to only grow closer with time. The brothers were inseparable. And like most young boys growing up in the inner cities, the Johnson brothers had had their share of run-ins with the law. However, their mother, although a young high school dropout, knew the value of an education. Both brothers finished high school and enrolled in the School of Culinary Arts. Three years later, they returned to their old neighborhood with a small business loan from the local bank and opened up an elegant restaurant in the heart of their old neighborhood. Less than thirteen months later, the restaurant would fold. It proved too extravagant and pricey to survive in an inner city, working-class hood in Cleveland.

Having no money and licking their wounds, the brothers would eventually run into their old high school friend, Christonos, better known as Chino. One day during a pick-up game of basketball at St. Adelbert Park, Chino and Stutterman, the neighborhood ol' G, were playing two-on-two against Lance and Rashim, and a conversation arose about their failed business venture.

"Man, it was a good idea. It was just the wrong location," Rashim reasoned. "If I ever had an opportunity to do it all over again, I know exactly what I'd do and where I'd open it," he casually continued.

"How much would you need, and where would you open it?" countered Chino, as a light went off in his head.

"Probably between two hundred and two hundred fifty thousand dollars," interrupted Lance.

"Lou-Lou-Louisville, Kentucky, home of the Derby would be the spot," suggested Stutterman.

"You guys looking for a partner?" Chino said with a smile. "If you are, then I think we can hook it up." Chino let off a three-pointer from behind the foul line. "Game," he said, as he walked over to the twins and gave each of them a pound. The three of them stood there grinning. It was understood that Chino had the cheddar and they had the know-how. The rest, as they say, is history.

Lance and Rashim Johnson became two of Kentucky's wealthiest and handsomest restaurateurs. Aside from the normal operational issues, they got no complaints from the patrons. The restaurant was a restored brownstone building in the heart of downtown Louisville, hence its name. Upon entering the exquisite Brownstone, the first thing one would think was that they'd left Louisville. The artful, eclectic interior design could hold its own in any city, though, and it never failed to grab the attention of the patrons. The ceilings were approximately twenty to thirty feet high. The restaurant's colors, predominately earth tones, intermingled with dramatic hues of red overtones, and they made the space feel cozy yet elegant. The entire second level was reserved for VIP clientele, of which, naturally, Chino and his group were a part.

Chino, LaShone, Paul, Yellow and Jewel pulled up to the front of the restaurant, and they entered the place like they owned it. "Chino, long time, no see," Lance said, greeting Chino and nodding toward his guests.

"Lance, my man. How's it going?" They embraced. Lance was someone that Chino was proud of, and he was too much of a man to show envy. And truth be told, Chino was more than happy to finance the restaurant. A grateful Lance paid him back—with interest. Chino wanted the best for his friend.

They settled in and ordered bubbly. Seeing businesses that were made good from bad money, made Chino think of what he could have become in the legal world, if only he had believed in himself.

The waitress approached the table, and LaShone immediately went into her routine. "Yes, I will have a bottle of Clos du Bois or Jordan, whichever you have. I will have the shrimp cocktail appetizer, the filet mignon, salad and crème brulee for dessert with coffee."

"Damn, yo! Slow that shit up!" Yellow screamed, instantly disliking LaShone's obvious gold-digging ways. "Trick, you ain't got one nickel in this here quarter and you spending like you got a job," he added, sucking his teeth in disgust. If not for his wifey being present, he would have wiled out on her. LaShone opened her purse, wrapped her French-manicured nails around a tube of lipstick and pulled out a compact mirror. Something shiny and silver quickly flew out of her purse, and a thump and rattle was heard underneath the table. Instead of bending down, LaShone simply looked straight ahead like she had heard nothing. Her eyes looked like those of a deer before flashing headlights. Yellow glanced under the table and discovered the object that had created the noise. "What in da fuck are those?" he asked.

"What?" LaShone replied.

Yellow reached down on the floor and said, "Bitch, these." He dangled a set of silver handcuffs from his left index finger. Jewel looked at Yellow, and then they both looked at LaShone.

Sipping on her drink, LaShone began to stutter. "W-w-what? Oh, those handcuffs . . . w-w-well . . ."

"Well, what?" Jewel asked impatiently, and then turned to Yellow to judge his reaction.

"Okay, you guys got me. I was planning to get freaky in the bedroom." LaShone turned to give Chino a devilish smile.

"Not wit' me. Ain't nobody puttin' no muthafuckin' handcuffs on me!" Chino said heated. *Trick bitch*, Yellow thought.

"My fault, boo—just wanted to try something new," LaShone replied.

Chino asked the ladies to dine together so that the men could discuss business. As they got up to move to another section Yellow lit a cigar, and an Asian waitress approached the table. "Steaks for everyone, medium-well and whatever goes on the side," Yellow instructed. Paul didn't even eat red meat, but at this point he was happy to finally be discussing business and really wasn't concerned about the meal.

The ladies had moved to the lounge area of the restaurant and seemed to be engrossed in light chatter while the men discussed their next intricate move. Chino eased in closer to the table and laid his cards down. "Yellow, I need you to get me one of them Latino brothers from Compton to come out to Columbus." Yellow nodded his head in agreement. "Now, don't get one that looks like a Mexican or nothin'; I need one that looks Latin and is well versed in the lingo of the Dominicans and Colombians. And we need to take a little trip to get money," he said.

"Why? Where we goin'?" Paul asked curiously.

"Hold up, P, I'm gettin' 'ere." Chino held his hand up like a stop sign directing traffic. "Now, we have been moving weight and taking care of the demand in Columbus. We need to branch out our territories and move a little further abroad. Yellow, you got Cleveland covered and you're working well with the shorties up that way. Have you had any problems?" he asked.

"Nah, my problem is mostly supply. We got the demand and the loyalty, and we got the blocks locked and turf covered, but the demand is outweighing the supply," Yellow said taking a bite out of his steak.

"Any people on your team having any problems lately?" Chino asked.

"None that we need to worry about," Yellow stated.

Chino, with a mouth full of salad, then turned to Paul and asked, "What about you, P, what yo' people doin'?"

"They're straight—a little worried and waiting to see what happens with Carmen's federal case. Otherwise it's still good. Do ya'll think she gon' tell?" Paul asked.

Chino wanted to tell him that there was always a possibility of someone telling. He had seen enough, and especially with the details of his father's case, to know that people would tell on anybody, regardless of the relation, when they wanted out; the days of the stand-up person was long gone. Chino knew that Paul wanted to hear a lie, but he knew that nothing soothed the soul like the truth. He sat silently for a while, appearing to give this major thought.

"P, the game done changed, nigga. It's always a possibility that she will tell. But what she don't know can't hurt you. She don't know about this here. I can tell you that you straight with what we do, but what you did with Carmen, hey, that's on you. We just need to keep your shit tight and get out." Everyone nodded in agreement; at least that was one thing they all felt the same about. Chino decided that he would get rich or die tryin'.

"Chino, so what's up? Don't you think Columbus is too hot?" Paul asked.

Chino shrugged his shoulders and said, "Shit, nigga, I'm a Southern boy at heart. I like it hot. It's no hotter than any other city where you do dirt. It's hot for me 'cause I caught two cases there. Shit, I'm in it to win it, and I gots to get mine. There is too much fuckin' money in Columbus to let it go unclaimed. That's it and that's all. I'm not going to pioneer another new city, and I damn sure ain't gonna let that city go just because people get scared. That city is mine. It's no different than a man courting a lady. I courted that city for the purpose of busting that cherry, and I am going to fuck the shit out of Columbus."

Yellow began to smile, as he loved to see his partner throw his heart into it. Lately, Chino was a little soft about things, and Yellow knew that that was about the pending fed case. This was the time when a real baller showed his true colors—be true, stay down, get yours no matter what, or you fold them and punk out of the game.

"Chino, I'm wit' you, and ain't no turning back, yo," said Yellow wholeheartedly.

"Good, I need a Spanish-speaking, trustworthy moth-erfucker, and I'm going to let you pick him. You know, we need a translator, someone to help us negotiate. Get your peeps to fly out to Columbus and join the team."

"I got the right person in mind, too. His name is Julio. He's Dominican and a thoroughbred. Julio and I had met when he and his family first moved from the Dominican Republic to California," Yellow explained. Chino began to smile. He even liked the name Julio. Yellow flipped open his Nextel cellular and hit the code for Julio's number. He waited confidently for Julio to pick up as the phone rang.

"*¿Qué pasa?*" Julio said as he picked up the phone by the side of his bed.

"What's up with you, my nigga?" responded Yellow cheerfully with a smile.

"Crippin' ain't easy," responded Julio.

"Sometimes it's low down and greasy," added Yellow.

"So, what up wit' you, Y, why ain't you been hollering at a nigga?"

"I'm hollering now, homie. And I need a name out East," Yellow said.

"I'm all ears," said Julio.

Yellow could always depend on Julio. They were cool

from the first time they met. When they would go into the Mexican area to cop bud, Julio was the interpreter, and Yellow jumped Julio into his crew, the Rolling Thirty Harlem Crips. Julio put in work and could gangbang with the best of them. Some members of the crew seemed to rethink gangbanging when long-time triggermen, Jim and Baby Brother, got snuffed, but Julio, Yellow and Little Bandit, another member, stayed true to their code. *Crippin ain't easy*, for them, was an understatement.

When Yellow left LA several years later to go East to hustle, Little Bandit and Julio would continue to swing out and hold it down. However, in the third year of Yellow's absence, an incident would happen that would change Julio's page from gangbanging to contracting. One night, Julio's brother, Rafael, was mistakenly identified as a member of an Inglewood Blood crew. Some members of a rival gang, The Rolling Sixties, sprayed him as he was leaving from the Fox Hill Mall in Culver City. It was his sixteenth birthday. Rafael was left paralyzed for life. That incident flipped the script for Julio; he hunted down and murdered each member of the Rolling Sixties. From that point on, Julio swore that if he was going to bust heads again, it would be for scrilla; the gangbang shit and drive-bys were dead. The new philosophy became "Murder and money, money and murder."

Julio listened with great interest as his man gave him the 4-1-1 on the situation in Ohio, and his handsome face broke into a satisfied smile. He could grind himself up a bankroll with the coca and pick up extra cheddar for some easy contract work. "Yeah, drop that plane ticket and I'm down for whatever!" he confirmed.

Yellow snapped his phone shut and turned to Chino and said, "It's a done deal."

Julio looked at the clock as he hung up the phone. Ohio was three hours ahead of him and he still had time to catch a little more sleep. He reached in his drawer and retrieved a blunt. Julio lit the cigar, inhaled deeply and closed his eyes. He had been in a bit of a slump and had a feeling that this was his lucky day. *Indeed, the sun rises again,* he thought.

Chino continued with his dinner discussion. "We have about forty kilos left to distribute, and then we out. We need a new connect, new contacts. Anyone got any other ideas?"

Yellow spoke up. "Well, you know, they robbin', they pullin' them stick-up moves and reselling the products. It ain't nobody but Ducky and Benzo doing that shit. We could buy from them."

"Well, I don't do stick-up moves. I am far from a thief, and them niggas ain't got no ethics. I ain't gon' fuck with them and mess around and buy back my own dope. That shit is no good. We need a connect, a supplier. We gon' hustle and make our money the old fashioned way—we gon' grind and earn it," Chino said. He turned to Paul and asked him what he had wanted to know all this time. "P, who moves your dope? We need to meet with your number one and two lieutenants. This will give me a feel of what they can do." Paul instantly thought of being cut out as the middleman, but he didn't really know how to say no to Chino. Chino sensed his hesitation. "You still gon' be the man and in charge," he assured him, calming him down. "I just need to see how we can unite and get maximum on what we move. I have some ideas. You still the contact. I just want to know who they are. I don't want to meet them; Yellow will hang with you and meet them, to see if we can work on territory. Yellow didn't show his surprise. Instead, he nodded in agreement with whatever Chino said, be it truth or lie. Yellow was with his nigga. Paul wanted to protest and tell what was on his mind: *This is my business, and I will keep supplying them. Get your own shit! I see what you're trying to do.* But rather than protesting, Paul agreed to allow Yellow to meet his best two customers as soon as they got back to Columbus.

"Not a problem. So we gon' make some last deliveries, right?" said Paul. Paul was thinking that to serve these last deliveries would bring him about sixty thousand, and he would just have to get out of the game. It didn't feel right to him that all this time Chino never asked to meet his people, and now he needed to meet them. It didn't feel right. He remembered how Carmen did the same thing—cut a side deal, leaving Erik and T-Love out. He wasn't going out like that—again. *Ah, so what if they take them! They can have them!* Paul was truly tired, and this would be his last delivery.

Chino sipped his glass of water with extra lemons. He placed both his forefinger and middle finger inside of the glass and removed the floating lemon. He raised it to his mouth and sucked the bitter pulp, tearing it from the rind. Smacking his lips he said, "Okay, we head back to Columbus after tonight's festivities and we make our runs. In the meantime, Yellow, get Julio on a plane. We work out in Columbus, and in three days, we rollin' the country lookin' for a connect.

"What's the first stop—Cali, Florida, Texas or New York?" Yellow asked.

"Nigga, we goin' to New York. The place where stars are born!"

MONTH NINE

"Xavier, you got a pro visit. I'll be back to get you in five minutes." I bounced up off the floor and ran to the sink with toothbrush and toothpaste in hand. I wanted my breath fresh, so I could be all up in my attorney's face with questions. I grabbed my notepad and stood by the door awaiting the guard's return. I was escorted down the hall and around the bend to the pro visiting booth. My attorney, Myer, looked casual, wearing a yellow oxford shirt and blue jeans. He didn't look like he was dressed for work.

Wanting to relax the mood and my anxiety, I asked him a question. "So, this is how you dress for work?"

"Nah, when I take a day to visit, I dress down so that everyone is relaxed." *How does he dress for court?* I thought. "No, I won't walk up in court looking like this, if that's your thought." Myer reached underneath the table and grabbed a box. He plopped the box on top of the table. He lifted a three-ring-binder notebook from the box and pushed it in front of me. "This is your discovery package. The prosecutor turned it over to us yesterday afternoon."

I looked at Myer, a bit annoyed. "So, what is this stuff? I've never seen it." He didn't need to answer my question. I flipped through the pages and started noticing some of the recognizable items. I picked up my monthly planner. I noticed some figures that I had written down and circled and appointments and phone numbers—nothing that looked incriminating to me. "So, what does this mean?" I snapped. He raised his hand to calm me.

"Listen, Pamela, calm down. If we're going to work together, then you're going to have to trust that I know what the hell I'm doing and extend some common courtesy. Do we understand one another?"

"Yeah, listen, I'm sorry, I'm just a bit uptight. Bear with me, will you?" I forced a smile that I certainly wasn't feeling. *Why would I bite the hand that was defending me?*

"Basically, the motion of discovery hasn't uncovered anything that could be detrimental to you—hotel receipts, car receipts, jewelry purchases and the cars that were confiscated. Well, all that's not debatable. You're in the position that you need to be in to see the motion of discovery—to see the depth of the case against you and see how, and if, it could be defended. Pam, this is where we are. This case won't rise or fall on what's in the discovery motion. But we do have a five-hundred-pound gorilla sitting on our laps here, and that gorilla is your direct sale of narcotics to a CI, aka confidential informant. Pamela, listen, you have a direct sale to a confidential informant with prerecorded marked bills. They uncovered and detected your *stash boxes,* or hidden compartments in the vans driven by your codefendant, Diaz. They have that on display in the evidence garage. That won't help us, but it won't kill us either, sweetie." I hated it when people called me "sweetie." "They recovered the fake identification from your billfold and want to add a fraud case to your file. The authenticity is a curiosity to them. I'd like to personally know, myself, how you got a passport with an almost perfect watermark contained on the document."

Why was he going there? I wasn't even trying to talk about where I copped that fake ID. Damn attorney. I kept a blank look on my face, and Myer continued yapping. "It was also featured on the news. Therefore, your motion of discovery folder could be empty, and you would still be in trouble. I also have a folder, which is a part of your discovery and it's full of statements from your CI, your informant. I believe you know him, right?"

"Yes, Mr. Myer, the CI is Greg or G-Money." *OOOOHH-HHHHH, I HATE THAT NIGGA!*

"Your, uh, *buddy*, for lack of a better term, G-Money, has been working with the government for some time now. He's going to implicate you. But on cross-examination, we'll probably be able to impeach his credibility. He's satisfying for the government in order to reduce his sentence, so his credibility and testimony is automatically suspect. But that direct sale is not going anywhere, and the conspiracy count may be difficult because of the cooperators—"

"Are you saying that every time someone comes in to testify against me that they can have their sentence reduced?" He shushed me. I obviously had raised my voice loud enough, because a guard passing by peeked through the glass window.

"We are not in state court, municipal court or traffic court. In federal court under a federal provision, a judge can offer a reduction in sentence based on cooperation. It's called substantial assistance. That's the nature of the beast, sweetie. That's what we're working with here."

The more of this shit I heard, the more I became convinced that I was ass out. I was thinking about my mother and the last time I saw her when my lawyer nudged me and asked, "Do you understand what I just said?"

"Yes!" I said.

"But there's also a statement from another related case implicating you. Let me break down the terms used for the various sources that can provide information against you. A cooperating witness is a person that may live where the crime was committed, they know what happened and they are willing to testify. They're listed in the paperwork as a 'CW.' Now, some of your neighbors have given statements to the federal investigators. A confidential source or 'CS' is a person that says, 'I'll tell you what I know, but you can't use my name and I am not testifying.' They're also in your paperwork. These can be rival drug dealers. Lastly, the most damaging is the confidential informer; this person signs up to do the work. Part of his deal is he can't continue any illegal activity except what is required of him or her by the government to set up the next person. Now, there is only one statement that I see as relevant, which is from Joseph Jamison. He caught his case two years before yours and named you and Chino as his suppliers. He wants to use this current arrest to further support his 5k1 motion of downward departure from the guidelines or reduction of sentence."

"What is a 5k1?" I asked.

"The name of the motion that allows for a downward departure reduction in sentence," Myer explained. I stared blankly as my stomach began to feel sick. He continued. "Next, there is G-Money's statement and his actions with the direct sales, so the prosecution's case would include the testimony of G-Money and Joseph Jamison. They would become government witnesses against you. In Joseph's case, a further reduction in sentence could be the result, and in Greg's case, immunity."

I stopped him before he could continue, as I could not understand how someone could get a reduction after being sentenced. I slid back from the table and said, "What do you mean a *reduction* in his sentence . . . so people can just tell and keep gettin' time taken off?"

He waved me silent and continued. "And with the evidence including, but not limited to, the forfeited home, condo, cars and money found in your car, which they want to convert to drugs, and according to the law, they can, this would put you in a guilty verdict range, no doubt. Now the composition of the jury: A federal jury will consist of selected persons from within the surrounding communities and counties—meaning, there will be, say, two from Franklin, two from Boone, two from London, etc. . . . And they will more than likely be white—white people who have no understanding of all that money and you never ever working a job in your life. You have no income tax return on file and you're twenty-four years old. Pamela, listen—"

"Are you saying that there won't be any blacks on my jury?" I asked, cutting him off.

"In all probability, Pam, no, there won't be any. It's fairly common knowledge that blacks don't often vote to be eligible for jury selection, and they're not as trusting as whites when it comes to the conduct of police officers. I guess Rodney King, Abner Louima and Amadou Diallo had a lot to do with that. At any extent, Pam, although we certainly want blacks on the jury, it's doubtful that we will get any."

I began to cry again and wiped my tears with my sleeve. "See, that's why I know you're different. Most criminals, for lack of a better word, that I defend, will still sit here in my face, their attorney, and proclaim their innocence and demand that I go to trial even when the deck is stacked against them. They'll yell and scream and call the CI a snitch and even threaten to kill him. You just want to go home and you appear sorry for your mistake. I think I'm reading you correctly. As your attorney, I must give you your options and advise you of the best route to choose; so in summary, you have three choices. One, go to trial and defend yourself against the numerous counts of the indictment that the government has against you; two, plead guilty to the offenses as they read; or three, take a deal and plead for less time," Myer said caressing my hand.

I shook my head no and naively asked, "A deal is like being a snitch, right?"

"It depends on how you look at it. The risk of this life never outweighs the rewards. Moreover, when my clients survive prison, they thank God. Whether they get a lot of time or not, they blame me. I want to help you."

"No, I won't be a snitch. Can I plead guilty and just do my time?"

"Well, let's see, you're at the guidelines which could bring your sentence to twenty-six years. I'm leaving you a copy of the *Federal Sentencing Guidelines* for your review. You can have law books in here, right?" Myer asked.

"Yes, I think I can, but what am I reading and what am I trying to understand?" I asked again, trying to make sense of it all.

"Pamela, the feds want you to become a government witness, which is a cooperating witness on behalf of the government. You'll be a pawn to get others, or bait to trap others, or a tool to bluff others. It's like, depending on the information that you hold, and they believe it to be substantial due to your position in this organization, as well as valuable, you can be an ace or a joker. I know you've been playing cards in here." He gave me a wink and tried to make me understand. "When you play, think of yourself as an ace or the highest trump. It's not about your pleading guilty. They can get a guilty verdict, so that is no problem to them. They will squeeze you until you cooperate with them and become a government witness, and this is the only way you can get a reduction in your sentence."

I tried to put on my gangsta look, as I felt I was being sized up, and gave him my Ice Cube frowned-up eyebrow impression. Myer continued. "Pamela, I'm losing you. Don't do this. Listen." He leaned in close, and I felt his breath on my tears. "Imagine this: Your son is what, two going on three? Imagine seeing him when he is seventeen or twenty-eight years old for the first time. Imagine not being a part of his formative years. Imagine him calling you Pamela after all this time. Imagine others coming forth to save themselves, and you getting a Rico charge or Queen Pen status as the leader of this damn thing. You are the only female on this case and all the fingers are pointing towards you. There will be deals, trust me, there always are—especially on drug cases. Hell, John Gotti's people rolled on him. Keep in mind that I am very good friends with your codefendant Diaz's attorney, and he will take a deal. Diaz wants to get 'mule status' that says he was just a transporter, and in order for him to get that, he must become a government witness and tell what happened, and they'll make him a 'mule' with a 5k1 reduction. Along with that, he will implement you in more offenses, and his word will bring forth charges. The feds go by he-say, she-say, and they will charge you. Now, whoever flips first, gets the best deal. The last to come forth will bring already discovered information that will be of no use. You need to come forth." I shook my head no and wondered why he wasn't telling me any trial success stories. It seemed that the feds plus drugs was synonymous with doomed.

"Now, if you want to go to trial, I will take you. If you want to plead guilty to the offenses as they read, I will do that also. If you want to save your life and be with your son, listen to me and trust me. This process will take many, many years off your sentence. Imagine this: A second chance at life. Now imagine this: life behind bars without your son. It really is as simple as that. Do all this time and go down as a hero or help yourself and raise your son." I stood up and walked around the tiny square room.

Myer continued talking as I paced the floor. "Will you have to do time? Yes, but probably only half the time you're facing now—like about thirteen years." The thought of doing twenty-six years as a first-time offender was unreal. All I was trying to do was eat and bling-bling a little bit. When I sat back down, he patted my hand to comfort me. *Fuck all this drama, how can I break out of this mother-fucka!* Myer shuffled the papers and began to stuff them back into his briefcase.

"I know that you can't conceive all of this, but please try to imagine it and let it sink in. Then make a decision as to how we will proceed. Like I said earlier, I'm going to represent you to the fullest. The choice is yours, Pam. No one can make it for you. I'll be back next week."

I jumped up out of frustration and the feeling of sheer powerlessness. I kicked the chair beside me and screamed. "You can have it today! Fuck the feds! They can't do that, they can't make up shit, they can't take money and turn it into drug sales, they can't take a snitch's word, they can't send me," I said pointing to my chest. "A first-time offender, to jail for life, they can't do this, they can't do this, they *CANNOT* do this! Call the NAACP!" The screams caused the guard to come to the door and my attorney waved them off, signaling that he was okay. He reached over the table and grabbed my flailing arms, not fearing me, and looked into my eyes.

"Pamela, I have been practicing law for twenty-seven years, and, yes, they can and will. They do it all the time. My first federal case with the inclusion of the guidelines cost my client his life; they gave him a life sentence. I, too, sat in disbelief that they could send someone away forever with no murder involved for the offense. From that day on, I, an attorney, who graduated with honors, became a believer. I vowed to never again allow a client to be ignorant of his or her choices and the reality of the outcomes. I've given you the law of the land, now you can choose. It's my job and I must advise you. I'll have my assistant send you articles and cases where clients had less than what you have; you can see what they got. Like I said, I'll be back next week to talk to you. In the meantime, I'll call the prosecutor's office and ask them to give me a week before I give them my answer on the court proceedings. Your mandatory minimum sentence is at twenty-six years. Imagine doing all that time and give me your answer next week."

Myer left and I was escorted back to my cell where I took a shower and cried like a bitch. I called my sister and told her of the time I was facing. I still could not believe it—losing custody of my son as if I was unfit and negligent.

This was just too painful. I had lost the chance to parent my son, and there was nothing I could do. Never in a million years could I have ever imagined this.

I called Meyer, and three days later he was back in the visiting room, pacing back and forth. "Pammy, I know you're doing the right thing," he said.

"What will they ask me?" I said.

"They'll ask questions about your case and then they'll ask questions about related cases. It's an information-gathering session; they'll collect information to see how they can use it. Then you may have to testify in front of a grand jury for subsequent indictments. The more indictments that come from your information, the better the reduction looks. If you can give them the supplier, you can go home."

"Hell no, I ain't fuckin' with my supplier, or any information about him," I stated.

"You can't be selective with your information. If it's something that you don't want to answer at that time and want us to discuss privately, then we will. Just take your time and answer the questions to the best of your knowledge. The sessions are called 'proffering,' and there will be either a videotape or camera to record your testimony in the event you die or recant what you said."

"I'm afraid and nervous and don't want to be a snitch," I said, and couldn't believe that the feds were so grimy that they would let dead men tell tales.

"Well, it's normal to be afraid, and they'll keep it as confidential as possible. Will people find out that you're taking a deal? Yes. What type or what form? No."

"If I do this, how much time will I get?"

"I don't know, but the prosecutor files a 5k1 motion with a downward reduction departure in your sentence. For example, if you are at level twenty-six, then the prosecutor will suggest a departure of, say, five points and bring you down to twenty-one, and whatever that sentence is, then that's what the judge will agree with. The guidelines have taken all control away from the judge; it's all in the prosecutor's hands now. And if you get the prosecutor on your side, whatever he wants your sentence to be, it will be." He shifted his weight and removed his glasses. "There are no guarantees, no promises in writing, and we can make a deal, but trust me regarding the credibility of the prosecutor to keep his word," Myer added.

"So, I got to trust the motherfucker that got me on lockdown with my life and believe that he wants me out, the same asshole that got me held without bond, away from my child?"

"Wait, Pamela, you put yourself here and you can't go in there blaming him for doing his job, and if you do, then you'll build a horrible rapport with him and all of this will end in disaster for you. Attitude is everything. Let's go over your options of defense again so that you can get cleared: You had a direct sell to a confidential informant with pre-recorded marked funds, monies that had the serial numbers documented and written down for verification and later used as evidence. You were then apprehended, video-taped with the prerecorded funds, and had, along with twelve grand in your purse, an additional five-hundred-sixty thousand in the trunk of your car—no job and were then set up by an informant. Ms. Xavier, aka Carmen, not only did your serial numbers match, they will say, but the exact color rubber bands were still in place. There is no out with the deck stacked against you, and you are fortunate they offered you a deal. The best thing your son's father did for you was to continue illegal activity while you were locked up. This lets them know that he was possibly the lead or partner in the cartel. This took the light off you, so thank him for your deal opportunity 'cause they know that you know what he's doing and they *will* want to know more about that. You are now said to be the ringleader, but we must raise doubt about that. We must make this accusation a debate. It's helpful that you're a first-time offender with no criminal past and a female. This puts you in a good position for bargaining."

The weight that I already felt on my shoulders got heavier and heavier with every word that came out of Myer's mouth. I leaned in toward the table.

"I *will* do it! I *will* do it! I want to see my son. Fuck dat! I can't do twenty-six years. I just can't do it." Like a lame, I forgot my pride and begged for the light of day. "I wanna go home."

Myer's pale face was a picture of sadness, compassion and relief. He patted my shoulder and said, "I know you do. Now listen to these words: You made the best choice. I need you to sign these papers."

"What do they say?"

He pushed the papers forward and showed me the place to sign as he began to explain the last paragraph, located way below tons of legal mumbo jumbo. "You have agreed to become a government witness. You are a witness for the government against your codefendants, including your son's father and your brother, and anyone who comes along later. And, Pamela, believe me, they will come. You are no longer a codefendant, actually, but a separate tool for the prosecutor's case."

I read the last line aloud, hoping to understand what I was about to do. "Pamela Xavier, government witness for the United States of America in exchange for a 5k1 downward departure motion." The teardrops fell from my eyes and my heart sank. My mind went back to the times that I saw snitches get talked about and beat down in the streets, and the conversations I had with Chino about doing time came rushing into my mind.

Lying in bed listening to the raindrops fall onto the sky-lights above, I once asked Chino a question about the consequences of our lifestyle. *"Are you afraid to go to jail?"*

"Pooh you can't be. When you choose the game, you

must take the life and all that comes with it. I ain't worried about niggas in the streets. A snitch gon' do what he do best and that is snitch. If you don't got heart, stay out the streets. Motherfuckers throw bricks at the penitentiary and then get mad when they make a cell and stack his ass in. I won't ever let anyone get that close to me. The streets is biblical. They got Jesus through a snitch—pointed him out, somebody from his crew. The enemy will always use someone close. I guess if I ever do time, it will be by your hand. Shit, if the feds ever get me, they gon' have to get me through my Pooh. Don't nobody know me like you do. You the only person in this entire world that knows me. It's like in God we trust. But in my Pooh I trust. In my Pooh, I trust my life.

You gon' get murdered; if you don't ride, you die. Don't be weak. Watch your back, snitch-bitch. Watch your mother- fuckin' back.

"Maaaiil Call!"

I got a letter with no return address. It said: "*¡Cállate la boca!*" (Shut your mouth!)

ON THE ROAD AGAIN!

Infa and Abdullah cut the fool in the back seat of the Mazda MPV van, smoking indo and singing a Willie Nelson song, while T-Love heartily ate a bucket of Kentucky Fried Chicken. Erik pulled the black van into the center lane of the Pennsylvania Turnpike.

"On the road again, feels so good to be on the road again . . ." Infa and Abdullah sang, ecstatic about sitting on twenty kilos of cocaine, one kilo of heroine, bulletproof vests, burnt out cell phones with unlimited use, chrome-laced burners and bullets with hollow points. The singing was getting on Erik's nerves, but there was an empty row of seats between himself and the Three Stooges; he couldn't drive and reach back to smack either one of them.

Slowly but certainly, they were inching toward Columbus, Ohio. Abiding by the speed limit put them hours behind schedule. It took everything Erik had in him to obey the speed limit and not exceed it. He loved to race all of his rides, and he quite often pushed his M5, silver Jag and his pride and joy, the Mercedes two-seater convertible over the limit regularly.

Erik was clearly on a mission. He had no customers, per se, lined up, but he knew that with supply, demand would not be hard to acquire. At first Paul's decision to work with someone else, made him heated. Eventually, he got over it and knew he had to show what he was made of. He had pioneered Columbus, and besides, he was from New York, and nobody could do it better than an East Coast playa. And above all else, the new tickets that were given to them by Carlito made it all the better. At those new low prices, shorties would be *chasing* the vans, let alone wanting to get served out of them.

A view from above could not have shown a better picture. As fate would have it and the dice continued to roll, the Mazda van glided off exit I-71 Hudson Street and screeched to a stop at the light. At the same exit was a Shell gas station. A green Land Cruiser was at the pump getting gassed up by no other than the one and only Paul.

"Hey, check out that former customer over at the gas station," said Infa. "It's P!" He rushed toward the middle seat for a clearer view.

"Where? Where he at?" asked Abdullah. Erik raised his fingers, holding them like a mock gun and pointed it at Paul. "Let's do that nigga!" screamed Abdullah. As the light turned green, Erik made a right turn and parked on the far left side of the station out of Paul's view.

"Hey, later for homeboy," said T-Love. "We can't do no *Wild Bill* shit in this van. P ain't nothin' to worry 'bout. Besides, we may need his customers to unload this shit. Let me go scream at him." It was more like a question than a comment. Erik glared at Paul—the person he had grown to hate—with contempt. Erik put the van in park and put his foot on the brake. He turned on the emergency flasher, lifted the rear window and released a hidden compartment just below the rear floorboard. From there, Infa lifted two Glock 9s, an MP7 with fifty rounds, a magazine and a WSP from underneath the seat compartment.

"Who in the fuck put this little shit in here?" asked Infa, amused by the WSP, the smallest handgun on the planet.

"Oh, I put that in there," said T-Love. "I like those little shits. I hide it between my balls, yo. The WSP is the smallest handgun, but it's very easy to conceal. Most think it can't kill—it can," T-Love explained. Infa looked at the small gun that fit in the palm of his hand over and over again, as T continued to educate the crew. "Now, it won't stop a motherfucka, but if you hit a nig' up close in the eye or temple, he's as good as gone. And basically you can try and shoot a person's dick off. It's nothin' more than backup." Erik looked back at them as Paul got in his SUV to leave. T-love looked at Paul making his exit and screamed out loud. "He's getting away!"

Erik smacked T-Love on his arm. "Put that shit up. We ain't chasin' him, yo. Later for that punk. He can get did anytime anyplace—just not now. We gotta find a spot to crash at. T, call LaShone and see if we can headquarter her pad."

"Man, I ain't talked to her since we split over a year ago," T said, handing the arsenal to Abdullah for concealment.

"Well, you know she still chasing money and will put us up. Hit her off with some dick," Infa said.

"You have to hit that bitch off with some loot. She don't need no mo' dick," Erik advised.

T-Love squirmed in his seat. "Yeah, she's cool, but if my wife found out . . ."

Abdullah cut him off. "Man, if your wife . . . if da police find us sittin' on top of dis shit, especially wit' New York plates, we gon' be ass out. Now, before we go anywhere away from the interstate, we need to be going to someone's garage and switching our cars or tags and getting this shit moved."

"Don't LaShone have a garage at that loft she lives in?" Erik quizzed.

"Still ain't figured out how she got that place," Abdullah added, poking Infa in the side, as they both knew that T tricked out of control with that whore. T-Love remembered the time they jacked Carmen for some of them thangs, and how the night before, he had left LaShone with a good-bye gift of twenty-five thousand dollars. Somehow, he had hoped that she would get her life together and stop trickin'. But instead, LaShone just used the money to invest in herself. This allowed for her to keep her scam of lightweight pimpin' going and catch the next baller on her hook.

Infa placed the arsenal back in its place and asked, "Yo, where are the vests? We got this entire arsenal, but no vests. What if we go to battle with that motherfucker? What's his name, Carmen's baby daddy?"

"Chino! Yeah, he's gon' be a problem," Erik answered, pointing toward the stack of bulletproof vests.

"How did he get out of jail and Carmen stayed in, what's up with that shit?" Infa asked. "On a federal case, too? Did that nigga tell or what? Is he hot like dat?"

Adbullah chimed in and said, "Yeah, I thought he was that stand-up nigga out here—got caught up with a bitch hustlin'—"

"Hey! I am not gon' let you call Carmen no bitch, not up in here. She had that little baby, yo. She left a son out here, and for what? Trying to get money to live. That shit ain't right," T-Love interrupted.

"Yo, she was greedy!" Erik said. The others shook their heads in agreement. T-Love was heated, and when he got mad, everyone feared him because it didn't happen often. They had only seen him mad like three times since they were kids.

"She ain't no greedier than we are. That shit is foul," T-Love blurted out and shook his head in disbelief. "After all the stuff she did for us and all the times we headquartered her pad and used her shit. Now she on lockdown, y'all gone say some shit like dat. That is some foul-ass shit!" T-Love said, jumping out the van and walking into the gas station mini mart. They all knew that he was pissed, and Erik knew that he was right. As quiet as it was kept, he planned to go see Carmen or put some money on her books. Carmen violated the code when she stepped to Dragos, but wasn't nobody really tryin' to look out for her. What else could she do? Erik knew that he could have taken care of her or helped her out. But she was being so tight with the pussy, so he just played her and tried to convince himself that he just didn't give a fuck. T-Love returned to the van and was still fuming, evident by the way he violently shoved the potato chips that he had bought into his mouth.

"All the niggas in the street that Carmen knew, she shouldn't have had to live like that—selling pussy. You *know* she had to sell her pussy! We all just acted like she up and opened an escort service. How in the fuck you think she found out about that shit? We *knew* she was selling *her* pussy, too. We knew that nigga faded her, and what? We still bum rushed her pad and didn't help her. That shit was wrong." T-Love turned to the rear. " Infa, where your baby momma at?" T-Love turned to the left. "Erik, where your wife at? Yo, some people gon' pay for that. Carmen was good peeps, and I can't believe you gon' call her a bitch!" T-Love was about to wile out, and the more he thought of the audacity of Erik and the others to disrespect Carmen, his friend, the more he got mad at himself for the role he played in setting her up for the robbery. If only he could turn back the hands of time, he would have represented. Now he was ready to kick some ass about the bullshit. He asked again, "How in the fuck you just gon' up and call her a bitch? Why she gotta be a bitch?" Erik placed the car in drive and slowly pulled out of the gas station back onto the highway. Everyone was silent except T-Love, continuing to ask questions. He was on a roll.

"What about her two-year-old son, left out here for dead with no mom and no dad, but now, she a bitch for feeding her son? Really? Speak! Don't get silent, how?"

"Nigga hold that noise down." Infa said as he exhaled heavily. He was two minutes away from smacking T-Love in the back of the head. Still, it didn't deter T-Love.

After Carmen's arrest, he had had many sleepless nights and bouts of shame. He couldn't believe the choices he made out of greed and pride. He allowed a special friend to fall victim to the system. Shit, he could have taken care of her. When he looked back on all the money he gave to LaShone and thought back to all the times he tricked with sack chasers, he knew he could have kicked Carmen some money. He could have paid her rent up for several months. He could have made things easier for her. He could have looked out so she didn't have to take it to the streets. But how many times does a man equate help with pussy? And since he wasn't fucking Carmen, he felt no obligation to help. The booty was what kept him from helping a friend. He asked again for an answer to the question that he struggled so hard with.

"No, really, how you gon' call her a bitch? Why she gotta be a bitch?" The van was so quiet you could have heard a mouse piss on cotton—for a minute, anyway. The silence only egged T-Love on more. "Won't one of you bitch-ass niggas step out da car and explain to me why y'all gotta call her a bitch?"

PIMPIN' AIN'T EASY!

The speed bag moved back and forth with force as Chino's knuckles hit it with the skill of a seasoned fighter. The gym had the pungent smell of funk in the air. Thoughts ran through his mind as the sweat rolled down the back of his thick chiseled frame. Chino and the fellas had arrived safely back to Columbus to make the last deliveries before they depleted their supply of cocaine and heroine. The gym, where the boxers trained, was a place of solace for Chino. He and Young Ty, Pammy's younger brother, came here often. It gave Chino a sense of pride to watch Young Ty train for his bouts and tournaments. Young Ty was like a son to Pammy and Chino, who gained custody of him when he was a juvenile delinquent. Pammy encouraged Ty to box in order to keep him out of trouble, but it was Young Ty who influenced Chino to try the speed bag and some of the other training techniques that boxers used.

"Chino, if you want to get cut up, check out my schedule. Pure cardio will burn the fat away," Ty had encouraged. Ty stood 5'11" and 160 pounds. The body was right, and with its ribbed midsection, the only thing that came to mind from looking at his body was pain. Upon stepping into the ring, his opponents often underestimated his strength due to his size. When all else failed, his stamina kicked in and he crushed his opponents with two to the body and one to the head, sending them to bed.

Chino continued to come to the gym, though his younger mentor was on lockdown. Chino rose early with the birds and ran six miles a day, jumped rope, hit the speed bag and finished by sparring with others. He couldn't help but resort to the dirty street fighter that lurked within him. Chino understood, for example, why Mike Tyson bit the ear of his opponent; as a younger child, biting was something that he did often if the fight went the wrong way. However, he admired the discipline that boxing called for. Although this was the day and age of shoot-'em-up, bang-bang, Chino still preferred hand-to-hand combat. It was something about physically punishing your opponent that thrilled him more than merely shooting someone dead. A fight was a person's merit, a shooting was simply the draw. The bigger the gun, the harder they fell.

Yellow entered the gym, and Chino motioned him over to the heavy bag for assistance as he punched it. Yellow gave his partner some dap as he leaned in to hold the bag as Chino punched it with force, adding some kicks to his moves. "Kentucky was pretty nice." Yellow started off the small talk.

"Whew!" Chino sighed, twisting his head from side to side to loosen up as he continued his workout. "Yeah, I love the Derby and I had a nice time. What you think about P?" Chino asked, baiting his partner for an opinion.

"He seems a little distant. Are you sure he's okay?"

"Yeah, he's okay," Chino replied. "He's just a little scared. Times in the life are changing."

Yellow nodded in agreement as Chino continued to punch the bag. "Yellow, when you go with P to meet his two people, I'm going to turn his peeps over to you. They'll be your customers to take care of. You'll have what you got in Cleveland and you can have this in Columbus to share with Julio, if he wants to stay out here and hustle. I'm hoping he'll want to get down for his crown."

Chino left the bag to get his water bottle. Yellow followed his friend to a bench to rest. Chino had thought of running game on Yellow, but he then decided against it; Yellow had been tried, tested and proved to be a loyal friend. Besides, the street code called for no con between comrades. The worst type of person was someone who used drag on their own team. Chino knew honesty was what their friendship was made of. Since they both had similar hearts and intelligence levels, why try and play Yellow close? It was not so much that Yellow was a follower, it was just that his years of gangbanging and being down for his set qualified him to be a soldier for the cause. He loved to be the strength in the crew. Both men knew that either could lead or follow at any given moment. Yellow leaned over to his friend and asked him the question that had been on his mind.

"Chino, you know you been my nigga since we met in the pen on both of our first bids, right?"

"Right, right," Chino replied.

"Well, all you talked about then was Pamela. What's up with her, with ya'll? Is she gon' tell? I need to know before I bring Julio out here. I don't wanna put him in a trick bag."

"Yellow, man, if she tells, she will only tell on me. She ain't just gon' implement motherfuckers just because. Otherwise, she would be out by now. I know her to be a stand-up girl. Do you know how many secrets we got between us?" Chino replied with a grin thinking of the body and gun secret he and Pammy shared.

Chino and Yellow met at Orient prison, and all Yellow could remember was Chino being in love with Pammy and her coming to see him every week, twice a week. Yellow remembered all the food and boxes of clothes he would get from Pammy, and how he was grateful for her. The endless three-way phone calls and how she would even pick his girl up from the bus station and drive her to the prison with her to visit. Had it not been for Pammy, his time would have been much harder on him. However, this new drama between the two of them seemed very unnatural and confusing to him at times. Although he was determined to ride and die with his partner, he had to have some answers for peace of mind.

"Come clean, what's up with your wife? You two still together or what?" Yellow asked.

"Man, that's my wife and we gon' be together until she leaves me. But she wants me to be something that I can't be. She wants me out of the streets, and you know how that is. Her job can't feed us and our two kids, so I'm doing what I gotta do. I love my wife and my children." Yellow looked at his friend when he said this, and wondered about the child that he had with Pammy, his Pooh.

"Chino, so what happened with you and Pammy?" Yellow asked.

"Nothing, nigga, she wanted to be a big baller and got out here in a league she couldn't handle. That's it and that's all."

"So, it's like that, fuck her, huh?" Yellow said staring at Chino. Chino sat silently looking at the floor. He was hit by the reality of saying fuck to a woman that he once bragged to the world about. It didn't make sense, and he was tired of everyone quizzing him about the shit. "Look man, just let that shit go. I don't want to discuss her. When and if I need to talk, I know where you at. We got business to handle." Enough was said, and Yellow was ready to move on to the next episode. Chino's demons and decisions regarding Pammy were his and his alone. He just knew that he didn't want to get caught up in the drama.

"So what's up with P?" Chino was waiting for his friend to bring up the issue, as they both had an instinct as to what needed to be done.

"Partna, he got to get stopped. He was soft on the Delano thing, and we need him out of the way. I want Julio to do it. I know you know him, but I need peace of mind. When Julio comes out here, you guys go meet his peeps and have Julio drop him like he hot. This will let me know he not the police and we can go for the crown."

"Not a problem. I can get Julio on the red-eye out here tonight."

"Right, right. Handle it. Let's do this shit. I can't take no shorts this go 'round and I damn sho can't take no more chances on getting caught up with the police." Yellow understood perfectly what Chino meant, as they both vowed to not go back to prison.

MONTH TEN

Again, I was swamped with a million questions from the girls when I returned from my visit with my lawyer. Mychala was there, and I assumed that she still hadn't gone to court yet. Her shit was moving slow like a fed case, only she had an orange, state case band on her arm.

I saw the look of relief on her face when I came in, but she was keeping her distance. I figured she was just trying to give me my space. We would talk later when everybody wasn't in my face. I told the rest of the inquiring minds that I was fine, again. I began to think of my case and what was and was not in my favor. I had to get out of this jam. There had to be a loophole. There had to be an out. I felt like a mouse in a trap.

I pulled out my legal pad and pencil and began to write Young Ty a letter.

Dear Ty,

My attorney Myer's concern was that I had a direct sale to a confidential informant with pre-recorded marked bills. They uncovered the hidden compartments in the vans driven by Diaz, which they had on display in the evidence garage and the fake identification and passport with an almost perfect watermark found in my billfold. Myer keeps threatening that that could be a whole new set of charges for me.

With G-Money seeking immunity for his statements as the Confidential Informant, Diaz trying to get a sentence reduction, not to mention the forfeiture of my home, condo, cars and the cash found in the trunk, which they want to convert to drugs, the likelihood of the government to get a guilty verdict is phenomenally in their favor. I have two options: proclaim my innocence and demand that I go to trial, or I could take a deal and plead out for less time. I can accept responsibility for my mistakes and eventually go home.

The government wants me to become a cooperating witness. They feel that the knowledge I hold is key in helping them win the war. I can be their pawn to be sacrificed at will. What do you think?

When my attorney first brought this to my attention I could not believe this shit. Okay, imagine this: My son is two now and I will not see him again until he is like twenty-eight years old. I try to imagine seeing him when he is seventeen or twenty-eight years old and not having been a part of his formative years. He calls me Pamela instead of mom because I am nothing more than a name that has been kicked around at Thanksgiving dinners at best. Imagine others coming forth to save themselves while I get a "Rico" charge or "Queen Pen" status as the leader of this damn thing.

Ty, I am the only female on this case and all fingers are pointing to me. I'll become a martyr to the almighty dollar and a joke in the face of loyalty.

Baby bro, this is what I am dealing with over here. You said you wanted to hear it from me first. Yes, I am considering takin' a deal. I need to be with my son.

I love you, and I am so sorry that I was this sort of influence in your life. Had I known better, I would have done better. Please don't hate me. I just can't hold this down.

Pammy

I lay on my bunk and tried to find sleep and stop my brain from racing against all the possibilities. I had to deal with the flip side of the game. The "getting down first." Could I trust those niggas I was grindin' with? Were they true blue, ride or die? Would they roll on me in order to get some love from the courts? Would we stand united . . . fall divided? Or is my decision based on my own merit, the characteristics of a female baller or the responsibilities of a mom?

HOLD ME DOWN, BABY!

As Erik pulled the van into the parking lot of the federal detention center, his passengers remained silent, fearing to say anything that might start T-Love up again. No one wanted to hear a repeat of his tirade. They were occupied with their thoughts: "Why Carmen had to be a bitch?"

The parking lot seemed to spin in slow motion as they sat staring at the secured building. None of them ever wanted to be on the inside. They all knew that being here now was the right thing to do, but no one was anxious to get out of the van.

"So, who gon' go in there?" asked Infa. "I don't visit and I ain't goin' up in there. I might have a warrant or something."

"We ain't gon' visit. We just gon' drop her some loot on her books. That's it," Erik said.

"Yo, I'll take it in there," T-Love said. He wasn't going to let his partner put himself out there like that, not knowing what was waiting on him. A lady passed by the van with two small children, and Erik called her to the car.

"Excuse me, but can you help us?" The lady smiled at Erik, thinking it was a pickup or perhaps he was lost. "I'm here to visit my sister, but I think I may have a warrant. Is there any way that I can give you some money to put on her books, please?" The lady paused for a minute, showing her hesitancy. "If you just put the money on her books and bring me the receipt I'll make it worth your while," he said.

She took a deep breath and smiled again. "Okay."

T-Love reached in his pocket and pulled out five hundred dollars. "Hmmm . . . what's the limit on the books?" he asked out the side window, trying to get a peek at the lady.

"I think about one thousand dollars or something like that," she replied.

"Well, okay, give it up. Let's leave her a grand," T said. Infa dropped two hundred in T's lap and Abdullah did the same. Erik contributed three hundred, bringing the total to twelve hundred dollars. T-Love handed the lady the cash with interest.

"Put one thousand on the book of Pamela Xavier and you can keep the rest. But bring us the receipt."

"Thank you! Pamela, Pamela Xavier, right?"

Erik nodded. "Right, we'll be waiting right here for the receipt." The lady turned and was on her way. "Infa, go check to see if she goes to the window," Erik said. "And then we'll bounce."

Infa jumped out the side of the van and hoisted up his oversized pants. He walked across the parking lot to the left side of the building and eyed the visiting entrance. Standing on a bench used for a smoking area, he peered into the window and watched the woman standing in line with the money held tightly in her hand. Infa walked back to the van and Erik sped off, not bothering to wait for the receipt.

"Hell, if she did it, fine, if she didn't, we tried," said T-Love as he looked at his partners and slowly nodded his head in approval. "We did the right thing. Now I can rest."

"T, you right," Erik said and pulled to the side of the road as they looked back at the federal detention center.

T-Love took the soda that he was drinking and poured out a little bit in Carmen's memory. "It ain't liquor, but Carmen, hold ya head up. If anyone can survive this, you can."

Erik thought his mind was playing tricks on him, because he could have sworn he saw a silhouette of what could have been Carmen. And really, it could have been any male or female in the building. He was hoping, that for just one minute, she could see him for what he really was—a man in love with her.

T-Love dialed the number on his cell phone as Erik aimed the van toward downtown Columbus's German Village. German Village was a section in town for the wealthy and elite. The proximity to downtown made the area ideal for attorneys and doctors to live in the historic refurbished lofts and condos. Cobblestone streets and exposed brick walls graced the area. The rich landscape and culture added to the ambiance of the community, richly decorated with Rolls-Royces, convertibles and sports cars. *Ring, ring, ring . . .*

"Hello?" LaShone answered the phone half asleep; the weekend had worn her out.

"What's up, baby?" Instantly, LaShone recognized the voice and couldn't fake her excitement. Although it was a trick, freak-daddy relationship, she liked her some T-Love.

"What's up T, where are you? Are you in Columbus?" she asked, sitting straight up in bed. Moving her weave to the right side of her head, she listened for his response.

"Yeah, and we need to come through." It was more of a question than a demand. T-Love hoped he still had pull with her.

"Come on, daddy! I'm still in the same spot you left me. I just need about thirty minutes to get ready."

"Thirty? Why thirty minutes?" T quizzed.

"To freshen up for you and your boys. I got in late last night and need to take care of something. Besides, my brother is in town . . ." LaShone eyed the figure standing in her doorway as she rattled off the word *"brother"* to his surprise.

"And I need to tidy up a bit, but you know you are welcome, baby. I miss your kisses." That was all she needed to say before T-Love's dick began to get hard in his pants. She did it for him, whatever it was.

"A'ight, I need your car also. We putting in some work and we'll be here for about three days or until—"

Erik shot him a look, shutting him up. He knew T-Love talked too damn much, but what other choice did they have? They needed a place to crash, and under different circumstances, they would call on Carmen. But considering her whereabouts, the next person in line that they could trust was LaShone. Noticing Erik's expression, T-Love ended his phone call.

"Okay, we'll be there in thirty minutes," T-Love confirmed. *Snap!* He folded the cell phone and placed it in his side pocket.

"Yo, you be telling that bitch!" Everyone in the car froze at the use of the word "bitch." *Here we go again with the bitch shit,* they all thought. Erik stopped the van in the middle of the street and threw his hands up into a posture of surrender.

"Okay, before you go ballistic, let me correct myself. Do you be telling that whore our business? And I can tell you why she gotta be a whore!" Erik said. Everyone burst out laughing, including T-Love.

"Let's stop and blow some trees since we got time to kill," Abdullah instructed. There was a certain little spot in Columbus that provided them with the absolute best weed. Erik was all in for this detour. "Sounds good. Besides, I need to stretch my legs," he said. T-Love looked at his partner and smiled. *How do you stretch your legs from the bar stool inside a titty bar?*

The Bottoms Up lounge and titty bar was the spot for the best weed in the Midwest. The job of the girls in the place was to sell drinks, ten- and twenty-dollar bags of weed, and of course, their asses. The Mazda van pulled into the crowded parking lot of the club and it was on jam. Entering the front door, and getting a pat-down, they hit the bar stools. As the girls entered the stage area, Abdullah was whispering into the ear of a busty dancer wiggling her ass and rubbing the top of his head. She leaned down to wiggle her titties in his face. "Wanna meet afterwards?" He shook his head no and asked, "Can you get me a twenty bag, yo? Like immediately!" He slipped forty bucks into the side of her G-string while simultaneously getting a quick squeeze of her left nipple.

"I love these topless joints—titties fa days!!!" T-Love screamed as the girls moved back and forth in front of the gazing men.

It was ten minutes into the next girlie show, and in walked Chino. Chino scanned the room and his eyes met the back of Erik's head. Sipping on a Heineken and sensing someone staring at him, Erik turned slowly, his peripheral vision spotting Chino.

What in the fuck is this nigga doin' in town? Chino thought. And Erik thought, *Him or me.* Erik hit the deck. Seeing him dropping to the floor caused his boys to do the same. Infa looked around for the possible cause, thinking that it was someone else having beef up in the place, before realizing it was his crew. T-Love pulled the small handgun from his crotch and held it tightly. Chino was at ease as he rushed to where Erik was crouching. He just wanted to grab and ultimately beat the shit out of him. Doing him wasn't an option as the security was very tight up in the place. Bumping into yelling and screaming patrons, the group was rushed by the security squad and tossed into the parking lot. Outside was exactly where Chino wanted them, as he ran to his charcoal gray Explorer truck and snatched open the passenger side rear door. From behind the seat, Chino removed an AK-47 with a 33-round clip. He took aim at the four men who now ran, making an attempt to spray them as they scrambled for their van.

Yellow rushed to his partner's side and snatched the gun from his hands.

"Yo, get in the fuckin' car!" Yellow screamed. Chino stood there fuming as Julio jumped into the back of the truck. "Chino, get in!" Julio said in his Latin accent. Chino snapped out of his trance as the Mazda van screeched off.

Infa was screaming inside the van. "Hit them switches, let's pull out our shit!"

"Turn around, don't run from them niggas!" screamed Abdullah. Erik continued to speed the van down Livingston Avenue toward downtown.

"They tryin' to kill us. Fuck this shit, let's go home!" T-Love demanded. Erik drove on. He weighed the risk of having a shootout in broad daylight sitting on top of kilos of cocaine, or fleeing to fight another day.

The van took a couple of hits, but it was still running. "That motherfucker was trying to tear some shit up back there!" Erik said.

"Just head to LaShone's. Switch out of this van, move this shit and let's get the fuck out of Dodge. That motherfucker is crazy," T-Love said.

"Didn't I tell you that motherfucker would be a problem?" Erik said. "Now, T, don't ask me why he gotta be a motherfucker."

Yellow wheeled the SUV in the opposite direction, not even thinking about Erik and his crew. He knew he would get them later rather than sooner. His major concern now was seeing that Chino calmed down. He could believe it, but didn't understand why he wiled out like that. In the middle of the parking lot, just hitting up everybody's shit. His aim was fucked up. They were running late for their meeting with Paul. The only reason they had stopped by the bar was because Chino spotted the van in the parking lot and noticed the NY plates. Chino expected, but hoped not to see Erik up in the place. Impatience got the best of him, and he couldn't wait for them to come outside, as he should have. Yellow was convinced that his partner had lost his mind. "Fuck dat, I am sick of them New York niggas, and they gon' get handled." Yellow remembered this as the last thing Chino said before entering the lounge.

After passing through the light on Main Street and wheeling by the back entrance to Scooter Park, the Explorer pulled alongside Paul's Land Cruiser. "Julio, do that nigga," Chino demanded. "Something tells me he'll be meeting Erik, or Erik will be trying to meet him later."

"Hold up, Chino. You said before that you wanted me to handle him, right? I got this," Yellow said.

Agitated and frustrated, Chino barked his orders. "Look, I don't give a fuck if Daffy Duck handles him. You met who you needed to meet, right? You know his peeps, so handle him and let's get paid." Yellow was always cool with whatever Chino wanted; he was about his friend. But he wasn't into gorilla tactics, and Chino's outburst certainly made Julio a little concerned. He had been in Columbus one hour before shit jumped off. But like the trouper he was, he rolled with the flow. Yellow stepped out of the SUV and entered Paul's truck from the passenger side.

"What's up, B? You ready to do dis?" Yellow reached into his pants and removed the stuffed nine-millimeter from in front of his nuts. "What do you need that for?" Paul said. He never got an answer. *Tatt!*

The splattered blood went in Yellow's eyes, and he immediately wiped his face with his shirt. After uttering his last words, Paul fell forward, his head hitting the steering wheel and causing the horn to go off. Yellow pushed him to the side, silencing the horn and hopped out of the SUV. He rejoined his posse. "Chino, you really know how to cut out the middleman, don't you?" said Julio.

Chino, Julio and Yellow sat at the table covered with carry-out containers of fish and salad from the local C&S eatery.

"Julio, my plan is to go to New York and scout a connect. You speak the language and we need to get in where we fit in," Chino said as he spiced his whiting with hot sauce.

"I agree with the plan, only I think we should go out of the country," said Julio. Yellow and Chino looked at Julio with confusion.

"I'm on a federal bond; I can't travel out of the country," said Chino.

"Nigga, you ain't supposed to leave the state, but you do," Yellow said, grabbing a french fry from Chino's plate. Yellow sensed the ever present fear in his partner and wanted to be careful not to call it out in front of Julio.

"Man, it's cool. We fly into the city, spend a day, maybe two, talk to my friend over there, and then we back. I assure you, he has a name for us. This will cut down the hunt. We can then hook up with his referral and be working in a matter of days. He's my girlfriend's uncle, and all he'll want is a percentage of what we make," said Julio.

"Well, let's just do the damn thing!" Yellow said as he gave his partner some dap.

"Julio, when can we leave?" Chino spoke up, feeling a little more at ease now.

"In the morning, my friend. We fly in the morning."

PUERTO PLATA

Chino, Yellow and Julio were amazed by all of the military personnel at the airport in the Dominican Republic. Dominicans weren't allowed in the airport unless they were actually traveling. If they were meeting passengers, they had to wait behind tall gates. This was one of the precautionary measures taken to prevent their people from illegally relocating to the U. S.

Chino wondered if he could live in this country—forever. But fleeing from federal prosecution was his major concern.

Chino's conversations with his wife about the possibility of a fugitive lifestyle were not well received. She said, "They won't give you all that time. It's impossible to get that amount of time. Throw yourself on the mercy of the courts. Just believe in the Lord, and He will work this out. Go get a job and stop doing what you're doing."

The thought of living on the run, alone, was not appealing to him.

All everyone kept saying was that it would all work out. Chino didn't believe this, and he knew that deep down no one cared; it wasn't their lives in the balance. Besides, what else could they say? Condolences were polite and proper etiquette in times of despair. They never really mattered.

The three men checked into a resort and settled into

their suites. They then awaited Julio's girlfriend's uncle, Roberto, to arrive at a restaurant on the resort grounds.

"So what's he like?" asked Chino.

"He's cool, Chino—really a lot like you." Julio smiled and looked at Chino.

Yellow almost thought Roberto was a genie that had popped out of a lamp to grant them their lifelong wishes, as he appeared out of nowhere. Julio quickly introduced the men, and Roberto took a seat and got right down to business.

"Chino, I don't want to be a supplier to every corner punk in the city. I have two other clients beside you, and they're out West and down South. You can reign supreme throughout the Midwest. I'm talking giving you a supplier that will put you over the top," Roberto said. Chino rubbed his hands together with anticipation. The look on his face revealed his eagerness for Roberto to continue. "Yeah, with this deal, you'll no longer be small-time, Chino. You'll be the guy to see." No one at the table said a word; they all knew that that was what every real nigga on the streets prayed for—to reach the heights and the pinnacle of the dope game—to be top dog, shot caller, boss playa, don.

"Do we have a deal, Chino? Can you be the person to see in the Midwest?"

Chino scanned the table and said, "Yeah, I can be that nigga, fo sho!"

Yes, the art of the deal was sweet. Chino felt like a kid in a candy store. His ticket was a fronted twelve thousand. His shipment would arrive the last day of every month, of course, for first-of-the-month business. By ground freight, the coca would come packaged in Dole pineapple cans and delivered to a storage facility.

The fifteen percent was due the middle of every month, payable to Julio, who handled the payoff. Chino suspected that Julio kept five percent, but then again, he didn't give a fuck; he had earned that and a finder's fee.

Chino put the wheels in motion and had three vehicles customized per the instructions of Roberto. He really didn't care that his connect was out of New York, and he was given the name of Dragos for emergency use only.

Chino knew the exact person to call for a reference—a top playa from Detroit, Michigan, who ran a crew of money-gettin' niggas—a hookup from dear old dad. This top dog was thorough at putting down his murder game. Chino made the call and scheduled a time to meet them in Columbus to work it out.

Chino thought of how just three years earlier, he was living in the YMCA with his clothes in trash bags after being released from doing his state bid. Now he was a come-up, ghetto-fabulously hood rich. Not bad at all.

YBI

Top boss players from Detroit, Michigan, Young Boys Incorporated, or YBI, arrived behind the main airport in a private chartered jet. They stepped off the luxury plane in dramatic style wearing all black, ready to meet Chino and his posse.

Among them was Dre, better known as Fat Cat. He was from New York, but his family moved to Detroit when he was thirteen years old when his father took a job working for General Motors. He'd been in the Motor City so long that all of his New York traits had been replaced by Detroit ones. He had totally assimilated into the culture of Detroit, which was very obvious by the process in his hair and colorful clothes. He wore suits that had wide lapels, and his glasses had baguette stones on the center of their Cartier frames. Fat Cat was flash without a camera. He specialized in recruitment and public relations in the organization. Recruitment came easy, as shorties followed success.

Dahkil had just done twelve years straight in federal penitentiary and was introduced to Chino by his father. With two months and a wake-up to go in order to leave USP Atlanta, a plan was set in motion. Keyes had given Dahkil all of his son's contact information. As the evening sun set on the compound, Keyes had his last conversation with Dahkil.

"All you have to do is call my son and he'll hook you up. Then pay me monthly, through my woman, ten percent of everything that you make." Keyes reinforced his plan, patting the youngster's leg firmly and looking him in the eye.

"Not a problem, old head. You was like a father to me up in here, and I will do all you ask and look out for you and your son." Even behind the wall, Keyes was still getting money.

Chino, Yellow and two new recruits, Peanut and Bones, the GI Boys, from Gary, Indiana, waited on the runway inside a stretch limo. They would soon meet with YBI.

Peanut and Bones specialized in slangin' crack cocaine. They hustled with the strong arm of the law, and they infiltrated city blocks slangin' rocks. Peanut was not a stranger to the murder game, either, and beating cases against him. Shit, as quiet as it was being kept, he wasn't a stranger to any of the games in the street, including rumors of arson. To make a long story short, he was the wrong nigga to fuck with, and no one—from the biggest man down to the smallest child, and everything in between—was exempt from his wrath.

Bones was known as Chef Boy R Dee in the streets. He cooked up kilos of cocaine like your grandmother would bake cakes on a Saturday night for Sunday morning church. And talk about comeback, snapback; you name it he did it. He brought back shit that others fucked up, for a small fee, of course. While others were flippin' them birds, he was bakin' them birds.

The GI Boys would take an entire kilo and grind that bitch out, raking in about a hundred grand a month, off a seventeen-thousand-dollar investment. Although they had a chance to move weight, it was something about that kibble-and-bit shit that they just loved; something about driving by blocks and blocks of shorties on post, knowing that dollar by dollar it all came back to them, all came home to them in the end.

The history books never recorded it, but you could bet that it was Peanut who started the trend of beating down crackheads and kicking them up the ass. Chino loved him some Peanut, but he found it comical, the lengths that he went through to get his point across. "Man, it's the principle 'bout my shit!" Peanut would argue.

"But it's a nickel rock he short, dog. Let me give you five dollars," Chino would joke with him.

"Give it to me. I don't turn down no money and no pussy. I don't turn down shit but my collar, and again, it is the *P-R-I-N-P-P*—"

"Man, you can't even fuckin' *spell* the shit," Chino would say. Without fail, Peanut always held out his hand and replied, "I'll take my five dollars and anything else you got."

Chino was proud of the meeting that he had put together. He was beginning to feel like a real don. He began to fall in love with himself all over again. With the posse now loaded in the limo, Chino had one stop to make before the meeting could begin. He needed to go see the one woman who could help him tighten his game: Raquel Robinson, also known as *Queen*.

MONTH ELEVEN

By the time the Feds came and picked me up for court, which was actually my first proffering session, I had a plan in place. A proffering session is when they sit and record you as you tell them all your business, or they ask questions related to your case.

I was escorted upstairs on an elevator. I was asked to face the rear so that I couldn't see the buttons on the panel as my escorts stood facing forward. The feds had me shackled and riding backwards out of fear that I would study the elevator panel with hopes of escaping.

I arrived at an office that had four small rooms, and I was asked to sit in one of them. I noticed another inmate leaving the area that I was about to enter. They told him they would do all they could to make this confidential. But how, when, whoever this kid was, he was obviously up here tellin' his business, too.

I was seated at a conference table. My handcuffs were removed and reattached to the chair. My attorney, Myer looked at the officer and said, "Please unleash her. We've agreed to be here."

Myer, was seated to my right and a marshal to my left. One of the escorts from the elevator sat behind me and the prosecutor was at the head of the table. Two more men— the arresting officer and a man I didn't recognize—sat to the right of my attorney. Another officer was present whom I did recognize from the Bob Evans restaurant the day before my arrest. I was the only female, and there was a camera pointed toward me. I leaned in close to my attorney and mentioned that the camera was making me uncomfortable. They repositioned it to the back of my head and started a tape recorder. My prosecutor was well into his forties with silver gray hair—wise old fox was my first impression of him. So much wisdom was in the room, and I was the only black spot in the place.

The prosecutor had a notepad in front of him and began to write down notes. My imagination began to run away with me, as I pretended to know what he was writing. *So you need me now, huh, bitch! Ain't no snitchin' here. Dry those fuckin tears. You can't complain, you gotta still campaign, even behind the wall. Now look at you.* I had to think. The deck was stacked against me, and I couldn't see a way out. I had to use my head . . . had to think.

"Pamela, how are you?"

The DA said my name as if we were friends, which pissed me off. But I answered with a confident "Fine."

"Do you know why we're here?" he asked.

"Yes, I think so," I said.

"We're here because you agreed to talk to us, and hopefully if the information is valid and corroborated . . ." I gave him a weird look and he continued. "That means it can be verified." I knew what he meant. Shit, I was concerned with the verification process and wondered how much I should reveal. I wondered if I could scam my way into a deal.

I got offended and yelled, "I know that!" Myer patted my hand and asked me to calm down.

The silver fox proceeded. "So now, let's just relax and start from the beginning. Okay?" I nodded my head and agreed to relax. It would be hard, but I needed to do it.

"Let's start with your son's father. I know him and

remember you from the courtroom on the day he got sentenced in state court. You were the one crying, and he was blowing you kisses through his handcuffs. I was his prosecutor."

"Okay."

"How did this all begin?" Having rehearsed in my mind what I would tell them and what I would not tell them, I wanted to look good and not be the bad guy. I had to think like a snitch, and what did most snitches do? They put the blame on someone else. Or I could have told the truth and got more time.

"I was going through a rough time in my life, having separated from my son's father. In my state of desperation, I sold drugs and then you arrested me. I had only been doing it for two weeks."

Everyone looked at each other and then back at me. My attorney, in a low whisper, said, "Pamela, you need to tell the truth or this will not work."

The prosecutor must have picked up on what he said or read his lips, because he told me the exact same thing. "Pamela, you need to tell the truth or this will not work."

"Okay, I was separated from my son's father, and then this man called the house. He threatened me and said that Chino owed him money and I had to work in order to pay him back, so I began to collect from people who had owed Chino money 'cause Chino had disappeared. Then I just started sellin' drugs."

The DA shook his head in disbelief and sternly said, "For the third time, you need to tell the truth. We have debriefed the informant, and he said that you started with an escort service."

Now they keep talking this informant shit. Well, you need to get rid of G's snitch-ass. And you know his ass ain't nowhere but in hiding on Livingston Avenue or up in some bitch's house . . . motherfucker ain't saved no runaway loot . . . Go into hiding with what? With who? Puh-leeze. My counterintelligence was working. I wanted to know just how much they knew about me. *That bitch-ass G-Money. When he tried to sell you those used tools, you should have faded that nigga. . . . Again, a lesson learned the hard way, yo. Dead men tell no tales. . . . I tried to help that nigga—tried to help him make a come-up, and this is how I'm being repaid.*

"Well, he's lying," I said coldly.

G is waiting on the feds to keep their promise to him. Remember when Rico snitched on the GI Boys? And a week later, the nigga was on the basketball court, thinking just because his partner was in jail that couldn't nobody touch him. Well, he got fucked up right on the court. Rico came down off a lay-up and got stomped. Guts were splattered everywhere for all to see—an example of what happens when you snitch. Girl, stop acting like you ain't got nobody for protection.

"Pamela, or should we call you *Carmen?*" the prosecutor said. I froze. We were definitely playing hardball now.

"Okay, I'll tell you the truth," I said.

"Good, let's start from the beginning. How did you meet Chino?" he asked. That thought put a smile on my face. I took a deep breath and exhaled and began to reminisce from the beginning. Now I was curious and wanted to get to the bottom of this shit myself. I, too, wanted to know how in the hell was I sitting in khaki tans, flip-flops and a disco bracelet on my wrists. I agreed at that moment, if they wanted to listen, then I would talk. I would take them all the way to the beginning, and perhaps I, too, would realize and have the answers to how I got to this point—how in the hell had I fucked up my life. Yeah, going to the beginning was how I would find out—I hoped. With my last bit of pride still intact, I raised my head and reflected.

"I was sixteen and a freshman in college. I had graduated high school early with honors. My mom was a teacher. She always wanted the best for me and would even help me study."

My attorney gave me a look of approval. He said, "Make them know you. Make them understand how you are and that your crime does not define who you are."

"I was invited to a cookout given by the men of Omega Psi Phi fraternity. My college roommate and I went to the party. I was at the party for, say, about ten minutes when all of this commotion was heard from the front of the house. Out of nowhere, this guy pulled up in an IROC-Z convertible, with music blasting. He parked behind me, blocking me in the driveway. It was, for me, love at first sight. He had the most beautiful eyes." They wanted to stop me, as they were not interested in Chino's eyes, but my attorney allowed me to continue. It was my belief that he allowed me to continue because he knew what I had to say, what I needed to say, and I did. My Chino was not a monster. But how could I have been so wrong about him? Chino was an asshole for leaving me for dead and he was a deadbeat, but he was and would always be my love, my baby's daddy.

Playing along and using a game that playas would envy, the prosecutor continued. "Okay, so you fell in love. Then what happened?" He began to rush me to answer his specific questions.

"Well, he was a drug dealer and he taught me his hustle, and we began to hustle together," I replied.

"That was when he caught his first state case. What did he teach you?" said the prosecutor.

"In regard to what?" I played it slow.

"In regard to the life, Ms. Xavier—about hustling, slanging dope. Come on, let's not waste time."

Damn, he's been listening to rap records, I thought. For all I knew, all I had was time. But I answered his questions before he got irritated.

"He taught me how to sell twenty-five-dollar bundles of powder cocaine. I would make runs with him, selling bundles of cocaine to snorting customers. Mostly that's all I saw; he hid everything else from me, but I knew that we . . . I mean . . . he . . . didn't make our . . . I mean . . . his money legally, and that he was doing something that was against the law that kept us from having visitors at the house and we kept secrets."

"What sort of secrets?" the prosecutor asked, tapping his pencil on the desk.

"About how and where we got our money and where we hid the money—where we lived, you know, secrets. It made our life mysterious," I said.

"Okay, fast forward to when you started hustling." Another agent jumped in, trying to speed up the pace.

"I was broke and hungry and knew there was money in selling cocaine. I had some friends that were from New York that hustled or got down, who had access to cocaine."

"Would that be Timothy and Erik?" the prosecutor asked.

"Yes." I was happy to say that shit.

"We figured that much."

"And I got cocaine from them." I couldn't name the supplier and had to use someone, so why not the mofos that left me for dead? Still, it felt wrong to speak against those two. No human belonged behind bars for trying to eat. All the memories of T-Love and Erik weren't bad. I wanted so badly to charge their action—the stick-up move without a pistol—to the game and not their hearts. I continued. "Yeah, I got my dope from Timothy and Jamaican Erik."

"Now, when you say *dope*, are you talking about cocaine or heroine?" the DA asked.

"Both, but mostly cocaine. I would only get an ounce here or there of the heroine," I replied, trying to minimize my responsibility.

"How much were you paying for it?" he probed. I looked at my attorney for assurance. I was aware of how he had cautioned me that they would convert the cash into drugs, and so I didn't want to get jammed. I whispered in my attorney's ear, and he responded back in a whisper, as he patted my hand to assure me of his confidence.

"Pamela, answer all the questions. This information cannot be used against you; you have an agreement. This information is to be used for their investigation, but not against you. Trust the process. I know you're scared and feel like you ain't got shit to lose; that's what the feds and G-Money are counting on. They're banking on you sitting in there, thinkin' about your baby and folding like a card table. This is the beginning of the death of the game. The game is on life support. Check the scheme. The feds told G this same shit, that's why he felt so comfortable flippin' on you, aside from hatin' on you and your slack hustlin' ways."

"I can't really remember how much each of them thangs went for." Everyone looked at me like I had used improper English.

"By that, you mean a kilo, right?" the mysterious agent asked.

Another black federal agent had entered the room. He was young and black. When everyone introduced themselves, he spoke with a New York accent. I guess he was their secret weapon, the one who would be released to the streets to portray a New York bad boy to capture others utilizing the information. He looked like the police, though; his posture was too damn straight from his military background, no doubt. The prosecutor continued.

"So, how much were you paying for it?" He said it like he was looking to do what they do on the news and inflate the amount of money to be earned from drug sales. I thought about deflating the price, but then decided to bump it up higher so that they'd think I didn't get that much money in the streets.

"I paid about thirty thousand for each of them thangs," I said.

The narc looked at me and shook his head. He said,

"There is no way she could buy a kilo for that amount; they cost much less." He busted on me yelling, and the prosecutor's eyes darted back and forth, from one man to the next.

"Again, Pamela, G-Money said that you sold them to him for twenty-five grand, so how could you have paid thirty grand for them?"

That fucking G-Money—snitch-ass buster brown. I hate that muthafucka! You should have been telling Delano to take that murder weapon and put it to the back of G's head or put a hit out on him.

My attorney pinched my leg and asked the officers to leave us alone for a few minutes. It was evident that he, along with everyone else, was tired of my charade. Everyone exited the room, and the two of us sat there. He looked into my eyes. "Pamela, stop all the damn lying. Just tell the truth and let's get this over with. You are blowing your credibility as a witness. You must be credible and trustworthy. I can't tell when you're telling the truth or lying, and you really need to stop that. If you keep it up, they'll lock your ass up and throw away the key, so stop it!"

Myer motioned for them to return to the room and the prosecutor whispered in his ear. Myer then turned and spoke to me. "Look, all these people are here to see you. We have to coordinate our schedules to see you, and you're wasting our time. One more lie, and the deal is off. This session has ended and we'll continue next week. That will be your last time to tell the truth. Don't waste their time again, Xavier. Keep playing and you'll regret it." *Damn, I thought my attorney was on my side.*

A wave of emotion swept my body like bees around a honeycomb and I heard her, crystal clear, creep back into my mind. It was Carmen.

Call them escort bitches and put them whores to work. You had them getting money, taught them how to eat and fend for themselves. Them bitches owe you. Make them do for you now. Call in some favors. Academy time, like Joe Bub Baby use to say: Put the "m" on ackin' and make it mackin'; put your mack hand down. Flip this motherfuckin' script.

Carmen was back. She was mad, and she was holding court in my head, giving me the Street Solution.

With the prosecutor's last words, I was snatched up out of my chair and returned to the county jail. During the ride back, I had only one question on my mind, and that was: *Can I do this? Can I flip and become a snitch or pick twelve and take this shit to the box?*

QUEEN

Queen was what you would call a "vet" in the streets. Now, a vet was quite different from an ol' G, an old head, a ballerette and all the other words commonly used. Very seldom did you hear the term "vet" when a female was being referred to; they were rare and far between. It's been said by old school pimps that a vet comes along like an eclipse—about every ten to twenty years, and one survives and reaches that height even less often.

A vet was a woman who quite often started out in the life by being turned out. She could possibly, but not necessarily, be the survivor of an addiction. She could have raised several children from her womb, or even the offspring of others. She could have turned more tricks by trade or choice and been a wife-n-law to a pimp or the city's most thoroughbred hustler to boot.

Queen earned her title later in life and would qualify in more ways than one. She never worked a job a day in her life, was approaching seventy and lived like royalty. Her battle scars were deep, but they showed up only in her heart. Her face gave them away when she was caught in deep thought. She could use a switchblade and pull it out like a magician pulls a rabbit out of his hat, seemingly from nowhere.

Raquel "Queen" Robinson began to get her own money

when her man did his first bid. A top-shelf booster, using a girdle was her thing. It was Raquel that made the girdle a criminal's tool. After catching several cases and doing short stints, she braved the choice and had acid placed on the tips of her fingers to avoid the identification print process with the police.

The longest bid she ever did, laying her down and changing her claim to fame, was shooting a police officer. Well past fighting age, Raquel was still boosting at age forty and hit a lick in the store. She was pursued by a cop, and too old to run and determined not to go to jail, she pulled her gun, aimed and tried to put him down like a horse. That shot cost her an attempted murder bid.

She did her six-year bid, came home to her five children, and it was business as usual. By this time, her youngest daughter had picked up where she left off—going up in stores with her girdle. Queen had a legion of grandchildren and those of others she helped raise. The children grew up doing well—legally and illegally.

Raquel inherited the family home, given to her by a local drug dealer in appreciation for all of her advice. It was there that she began to nurture her own family. And, it was there that, in spite of her past and the continued tendency to hit a lick every now and then, that she became affectionately known as Queen.

The limo proceeded south on James Road, swinging a wide right onto Broad Street and headed west. Traveling through the suburb of Bexley, Ohio, Chino slid down his window. The March spring air was brisk on his face, but he could take it, and this community was his favorite. The elite of Columbus occupied these posh addresses. Chino's fellow passengers pointed out the plush estates, as the driver cruised ten miles per hour below the speed limit. Bexley just didn't play that speeding shit, and everyone knew it. Jaywalking was absolutely out of the question. It seemed as though the cops sat up in trees, waiting for an outsider of the community to make their day and increase their ticket revenue. Bexley gave out more violation tickets than any other community. It wouldn't be hard to believe if the town supported itself through the infractions of visitors. All of its residents had stickers on the dashboards of their cars, indicating their resident status, and they never got tickets. It was those brave persons who decided to take Broad through the city, as opposed to continuing down James Road and taking Livingston through the hood to get to the downtown area that were always stopped.

Using the blinker to signal his next right turn, the driver cruised up Cleveland Avenue. The line of demarcation between the haves and the have-nots became apparent. Passing tattered buildings and geekers on the stroll, looking for a rock or a date to turn, they knew they had entered the hood of the city.

The driver made a left turn onto Kohr Place, a quaint street nestled in an all-black area called Linden. This block didn't look like it belonged in the area. It had held its own since the white flight. In the sixties, the Irish dominated Linden community. In the seventies the Jews occupied it, and in the eighties, along came the successful blacks. Now, in the nineties, it was a crime-ridden community. The limo stopped in front of a house that represented this fact. However, the architecture and structure of the single family, two-story homes on the block gave hint to a past of affluence—even with the boarded-up doors and windows that were now crack houses. Those that remembered the area back in its heyday still smiled from the memories.

The crew sat patiently in front of an average, in-the-hood-looking house, and the driver awaited the signal to open the doors. Sitting in the car for a moment, Chino placed a call on his cell phone. *Ring, ring, ring, ring* . . . Chino snapped the phone shut. "Damn! She's supposed to be home."

The driver let down the center glass and said, "I see someone peeking out the curtain. There's someone in there. You want me to go knock on the door?"

"Nah, partner. I wouldn't advise knockin' on Queen's door unannounced. Shit, she's old and living in the hood. She'll use that excuse to shoot a nigga." The group broke out in laughter.

"Word, for real?" Peanut thought it comical that an old lady would just shoot someone for knocking on her door.

"For real, Peanut. If I didn't know any better, I would think she was your grandmomma or something," Chino replied.

"Shit, she might be on my daddy's side of the family, for all I know. I want to meet her." Peanut joked back with his friend. No sooner than those words left his mouth, the shadow of a figure was seen approaching the car. The passenger side window rolled down, and there stood Queen.

Queen was 5'7" tall and weighed approximately 160 pounds. She had warm, beautiful honey brown skin, and her shoulder-length hair was pulled back into a ponytail. On top of her head rested a pair of glasses. She had on a pair of black slacks with black leather loafers and a pink summer sweater. Her neck was adorned with diamonds, and her wrist, holding a cane, sported a matching diamond bracelet. A diamond laced each of her fingers. Her face glowed with peace and serenity. She held her left hand behind her back for a moment, but then it appeared—holding a .38 special.

"Queen, it's me, your son!" Chino yelled from the far side of the limo.

Queen placed the gun in her pants pocket and leaned on her cane. "Motherfucker, get that fucking limo from in front of my house. Shit, ain't nobody died or going to the prom. You making my shit hot!" Queen stated. The men were amazed at the brashness that came from such a lovely older woman's mouth.

"Okay, Queen, calm the fuck down, damn!" Chino tapped the limo driver on his shoulder and said, "Drop us off here, and I'll call you for a pick-up, if we need one." He pulled several hundred-dollar bills from his stash and paid the driver. "Okay, fellas, get out!" The men piled out of the car taking what carry-on bags they came with. The driver assisted in unloading them curbside and sped off. They followed a cursing Queen up the walkway towards her home. Dahkil looked at the surrounding area and wondered: *What in the hell am I getting myself into?*

THE GAME IS SOLD, NOT TOLD

Once past the common, screen-enclosed porch and dusty welcome mat, Chino stepped upon plush, off-white carpet through a double, stain-glass door. Only Chino had seen this place before. It was no wonder why she was called Queen—nine-foot ceilings with original woodwork, trimmed pillar and window casing. Oriental decor and antiques adorned the living room. In the center of the living room was an all white, C-shaped sofa. Pictures of everybody and their mommas surrounded the room like wallpaper. Queen walked them toward the rear of the house.

Passing through French doors that opened into a formal dining room set for ten, a huge chandelier hung over a marble table with cloth high-back chairs. Three-tiered candlesticks were on each end of the table. Every piece in the home was an original.

Damn, this old bitch is paid! She old but her body still looks right, thought Peanut.

This has got to be a joke, thought Dakhil.

My baby gon' grow up and be a vet like this one day, thought Yellow.

Look at them niggas foaming at the mouth over Queen.

One day, my Pooh gone be a vet—after the feds spank that ass, thought Chino.

Queen seemed to glide now as she neared the rear of her house, sauntering across hardwood floors to a sunroom off the kitchen. The entire room was glass, decorated in rich burgundy colors with hues of tan and custom floors.

"Gentleman, please make yourselves at home," she advised. They were all seated on a sectional sofa. In front of the sofa was a glass table with beverages, a leather-bound photo album and finger snacks consisting of nuts and pretzels. A yard, surrounded by a six-foot fence, could be seen from where they sat, through a window in the sunroom. Also in the yard, was an in-ground pool, surrounded by a wrap-around deck. In the very rear, were two tents and children's toys.

Chino embraced Queen and kissed her on the cheek. An elderly gentleman appeared, pulling a chair to the center of the room for Queen to be seated.

"Queen, let me introduce you to the fellas," Chino said as he began pointing out his men relaxing on the sofa. "That right there is Yellow, my partner." Yellow stood to shake a seated Queen's hand. Chino continued. "That's Dahkil. He's from Detroit, and his shorties, Dre aka Fat Cat, and Twan."

They replied in unison. "Hi, Queen."

"I love your home in the hood, Queen," Yellow politely said.

"Darling, a home is where you lay your head at. You can live in the suburb and still not have a home. Did you know that?" Queen asked as she began to size up each one of the men.

The gentleman, who was more like Queen's aide, finally spoke. "Anyone hungry or want a drink?"

"Yeah, straight up!" said Peanut.

"Cranberry juice for me," replied Chino. The others

nodded that they were fine. The aroma of something delicious peeked Fat Cat's interest. "I'll take some of whatever is cooking," he announced.

Queen smiled and said, "We'll eat dinner after we talk. I just don't break bread with anybody. I have to know you first." She lit a Virginia Slim and blew the smoke in the air over the heads of her guests. Beside her ashtray was a small, square-shaped porcelain container. She opened it to reveal a chalky white powder. In a side holder was a silver, three-inch tube. Queen lifted the tube and jaws dropped. Everyone was put off guard. "Whew!" Queen blinked the water from her eyes. She tilted her head back and deeply sniffed twice. Her voice was slightly hoarse now. "Now, that is some good shit!" She dipped her pinky finger into the powder and placed it to her lips, sucking the powder from it. "Have some, men?" All but Peanut shook their heads no.

"Shit, hell yeah, I will have some." Peanut opened his lapel pocket and removed his own platinum powder case. Around his neck, he wore a small container of cocaine, resembling an African piece of jewelry. "Queen, try this China white." Peanut handed the vial to Queen, and she dabbed out a portion using the side of her pinky knuckle and snorted it into her nose.

"Daaaamnnn!" She turned to Chino and then to Peanut. "Okay, Peanut, your ass can eat with me, 'cause at least we both know, if you do get high on your own supply, to use the good shit," she said.

Peanut broke out smiling. He knew from the gate that he liked Queen. He cocked his legs wide open, as he was getting comfortable. He rested back and said, "You know that's right. Hey, homeboy, bring me my drink. I gots to chill." The fellas were still staring in disbelief.

"Look men, ain't nothing closet about Queen. One, you in my house; two, I pay the bills up in this place; and three, ain't no shame in nothing I do, so we all good." They nodded again in unison.

Peanut eased back into the seat sipping on his Martel. "It's good," he said, slowly licking his lips to savor the taste of his drink.

Queen lifted the leather-bound photo album from the table and began to leaf through the pages. She stopped about halfway through to rub her hand across a picture. She rocked back and forth slowly in her chair, eyes closed.

"Dahkil, you are my first love reincarnated," she said as she passed the album to him. Dahkil was blown away. In one of the photos was a younger Queen, accompanied by a man in a full-length mink coat and matching hat. Queen wore a short mink, and her hands were gracefully clasped. They were standing beside what looked to be a very expensive car. The man in question *did* remind Dahkil of himself. The expression he held, peering pensively into the camera, gave Dahkil goose bumps. He passed the album around the room and everyone nodded in agreement.

"Your first love, huh? What happened to him? You believe in reincarnation?" Dahkil asked.

"Yes, I do. Before we get started, men, I need a grand on the table." Queen ignored his questions, knowing that one day, sooner or later, she would provide him with the answers.

"What?" asked Dre.

"I didn't stutter! I said I need a thousand dollars each. Put your money on the table, please," Queen demanded.

Chino reached into his pocket and dropped ten one-hundred-dollar bills into her outstretched hand. Queen noticed the hesitation in the men, so she offered an explanation. "Gentlemen, game is sold, not told, and Queen charges for her conversations; my game is not free. It cost me too much to know what I know. It cost me too much pain to go through all that I went through. I am here to help you, and fair exchange ain't robbery."

The men obediently counted out their money, not even sure why, but Queen just had a presence about herself that demanded respect, and now, she demanded their hard-earned cash.

"So, what you like Ms. Cleo or somethin'?" asked Yellow.

"You could say that," replied Queen.

"Why do you say I remind you of your lover?" inquired Dahkil.

"Because energy doesn't change. It's not necessarily reincarnation; it's energy or makeup. Have you ever gone to another city and seen people who you thought you knew, who looked familiar to you?" Everyone nodded in agreement. "Well, from hello, I can tell you about a person. There's nothing new under the sun—same games, different people, same energy transferred. A whore got a certain energy about herself, just like a person who got larceny in their heart. You can see it. You can tell an honest person from a dishonest person, and an ethical person from unethical person. How many times has someone done something to you, done you dirty, and you were not surprised? You knew what was inside them all along. Think of that girl that crept on you. You knew she was a whore when you met her. Why? 'Cause you met her out tricking with someone. When you catch a case, the one that snitches on you or sets you up, they don't surprise you. You knew they had that in them, but you chose to ignore it. It's called instinct or trusting your very first impression. That's what you boys must learn to do. See, old people have gone through too much not to trust their first impression. That's where all that wisdom comes from. When I meet a person, from the gate, I take my initial reaction and impression of that person and I don't give them a chance; fuck giving a person a chance. I don't let them prove themselves. I trust my heart. Your heart never, ever fools you. You all have caught a case before. Do you remember that morning or minutes before your instinct tried to warn you, but you went against yourself? Never go against yourself. To thine own heart be true."

Queen's words had them all thinking of their past. She let her words marinate a bit in their minds before she proceeded. "Men, let me tell you about a woman and the game. If you have a woman, never make her choose between you and the game. You will lose." The men pondered her words momentarily, not adding anything to her comment.

Chino pulled his high-back chair closer to the other men. "Fellas, what we need to do is join forces and move the product. I have five hundred of them thangs coming through every month. The question is, who can take what, and can you handle the responsibility and the consequences?" he said.

"Let's work it out. Me and Bones can't do much 'cause we ain't gon' let go of our kibbles and bits, no matter how much we can get. We're grinders," said Peanut.

"I got you, Chino. I can move two hundred a month through my sources," said Dahkil.

"Chino, I can take the rest. You need to relax and take care of yourself," Yellow said. The rest of the crew remained quiet.

Queen put out her cigarette and stood. "Gentlemen, let's break bread," she said. They walked into the dining room and sat before a lovely, set table. The men dined and thought of what lay before them as they stepped into the next level of the game.

After dinner, everyone departed to go their separate ways via limo, cabs and pick-ups. Chino stayed behind with Queen to have a final talk. "So, what do you think of the men I've selected?"

"Good job, they all have good energy about themselves. None have outright larceny in their hearts. You genuinely like each other, and they want to get money. They just don't make hustlers like they used to. Back in my day . . ." *Here she go with another shoulda, woulda, coulda story*, Chino thought. "Dahkil will be your best soldier. He has the energy of good peeps all around him. Peanut I like a lot. If he had been born another time, he would have been a pimp, numbers runner or murderer for hire. He has the beast of the hustle in him. It's never about the money; it's about the hustle."

"Queen, how can you tell? That's Peanut for real," Chino replied, amazed at her assessment.

"Peanut is a good-time dude. He loves life and is driven by the passion of excitement. What goes around comes around for him, and the penitentiary won't take him out; his crimes are too petty. He's afraid of doing big time, that's why he chooses slow-roll hustles; he's avoiding biting off more than he can chew—wise on his part 'cause somewhere along the line, he knows what he's got in him, and it ain't doing time. The most he could ever do is five years without folding."

"But Queen, Peanut will put that murder game down in a minute," Chino said.

"Shit, black-on-black murder still only carries five years; Peanut knows that. I like him."

"What about Dahkil? You seemed to really like him."

"I loved a Dahkil once. He'll climb higher than you. He's hungry and don't care about prison, so when he say he'll move the two hundred a month, he'll do that and eventually more. He's not afraid. He knows what he's up for. How much time did he do?"

"Twelve years."

"Yeah, Chino, he's going for broke; so he's going to ball for paper, prison or death. That's your trouper right there. But you're so much alike that you'll clash. It's only a matter of time before he loses respect for you. You met him through your dad, right?"

"Yeah."

"Well, he respects your dad, and on the strength of that, he'll never do you dirty. But when you show him weakness, he'll lose respect and get his money another way.

He lives by the creed and he expects you to be just like your father. You're cut from the same cloth as your father, but you're different."

"What do you mean? I *am* like my dad," an irritated Chino replied.

"Yeah, you're like him, but you are so full of pride. Your dad doesn't have the pride that you have, and that's what makes you different."

"My dad is a proud man," Chino stated.

"Man, pride is nothing good. That's why the Bible says, 'Pride cometh before a fall.' Dignity and integrity are not the same as pride. Pride keeps you from doing right when you know you're wrong—simple as that, so where will you go from here, my wonderful Chino? Can you humble yourself and let someone else get the money and you go do that time that's waiting on you?" Queen schooled.

Chino hated her openness and her riddles. But he knew they were only for his own good. "I *want* that money and I *am* humble," Chino said.

"If you were humble, you'd let someone else get that money instead of you always trying to run things. If you were humble, you would seek another way of life. And, if you were not so full of pride, the police would have never gotten Pamela."

"What?" Chino asked, even more irritated now.

"Have you ever asked yourself what would have happened, or would you have a pending case if you would have just supported your son?"

"I've asked myself that many times."

"And what is the answer?" There was silence.

"I don't know," Chino replied.

"Liar, you *do* know, that's what I mean by pride. If you were humble, you'd tell me the truth. The police would have never got her . . . should have never got her. She wasn't a material girl. All she needed was help, and what you need to see is that she *sold her ass* to support her child;

she sold her *body*. Why do you doubt her telling to be with her child? I hope you've learned enough to know that she has no pride when it comes to her son, and she can and will tell on you to be with him. Chino, you left her for dead. She owes you nothing. She doesn't have to be true to the game; the game hasn't been true to her. Why I gotta keep droppin' jewels on you?" Queen smiled at her young protégé and continued.

"Get out of the streets and give up the connect to Dahkil and collect money. Do your time and go see Pamela and tell her you're sorry and make it right. Otherwise, the cards will fall where they lay. And believe me, she won't do all that time. What dirt does she have on her hands? The blood from drug money . . . she *will* do some time for that. But God is gon' bring that girl home to her son. Go get that baby. I know you can't take the child home to your wife, but Queen will help you raise him while you're still a free man and when you're both doing time."

"Queen, I can't do that. I told everyone the child ain't mine," Chino said.

"Pride, son, pride. You would rather care what someone thinks than do the right thing by your own seed. Again, pride is when you won't do the right thing when you know you're wrong. Courage is doing the right thing even when people think it's wrong. It's caring about the truth of the heart and not the minds of men. You're asking me to size up these men. They're not who you need to be worrying about. Your demise will come by way of a woman. The woman may be Pamela, but I doubt it, Chino. Be careful of the women around you—even the girlfriends of your crew. And keep in mind that you are your own worst enemy. Those niggas gon' get money, kill, rob, do what niggas in the street do. But if you are the head, how can you lead with pride? Now, that is all Queen gon' say, and I will end with what I tell hardheaded niggas in the streets—you will see."

Chino stepped closer to embrace her. He knew that she loved him and that she was right. How many times did he want to make right what he had done wrong, but his pride kept him from doing it? He was stuck on the notion that he was right and Pammy was wrong. That's what it came down to—his struggle against being wrong.

"I love you, baby. Queen don't tell no lies. She knows what God loves, and that is the truth," she said as she turned to walk up the staircase, leaving Chino to let himself out.

"Queen, I'll think about it. In the meantime, I got moves to make, money to count and people to see."

"Goodnight, Chino."

MONTH TWELVE

I stood by and watched Mychala play a few hands. I admired the way she finessed the other players into thinking that she didn't have the trump card when she did, or vice versa. She created an uncertainty in them that she used to her advantage with a vengeance.

I wanted to talk to her, but I didn't want to pull her away from her game, so I lay down and started thinking about what the feds had said about Chino. How could he continue to be involved in the dope game? Didn't he know that the feds would be watching him? I turned my face into my pillow and went to sleep.

The next day, at breakfast, Mychala and I talked about what the feds wanted me to do. She listened like a good friend does. She did not make any comments for or against what I told her, for she knew that whatever decisions I made, I would have to ultimately live with it.

Mychala had begun showing me how to make soap powder out of shaved pieces of soap. She would rub the bar of soap against the metal bed frame until little slivers of soap came off. Then she instructed me to include it inside my laundry bag for pick-up by one of the inmate trustees.

Mychala was always making up some sort of concoction or another. She would crush up small pieces of candy sticks, mix them with Kool-Aid and make sugar candy. She would take a maxi pad and roll it into a tampon or take leftover food, mix it up with a bag of chips and make a treat that was not easy to look at but delicious to taste.

"Trays up!" I heard the deputy yell. The menu indicated we would be having Johnny Marzetti, black folk's spaghetti. However, on our trays was a huge pork chop—not the processed kind that they usually serve, but a real stinkin' pork chop. I had always hated pork, but everyone else in the room was jumping around like they'd been given filet mignon. I gave mine to Mychala and settled for a bag of chips and a Nutty Bar.

Another visit with my mom helped me finalize my decision. It was the most practical thing to do. It was the only way that I would be able to move forward. By owning up to my responsibility, I could then change. Despite that, I didn't feel good about it in any way. Frankly, I was sick to my stomach, as there were three questions in my mind that continued to haunt me: *Is honesty truly the best policy? Is truth too much of a burden to bear? In times of trials and despair, do we really want to know the truth?*

I returned to my dorm after my visit. The place looked like the Tazmanian Devil had whipped through it; all of the mattresses had been stripped of their sheets, which were scattered all over the floor. The mattresses, still barely on their steel bunks, were tossed about with such force that the corners were ripped open. Women's personal belongings had been dumped out of their paper-bag storage compartments, leaving them complaining about things missing or taken from them.

"What happened in here?" I asked Mychala.

"Shakedown," she said.

"What were they looking for?"

"They said that all the pork chop bones weren't turned

in, so they came in here and tore the place up. Look what they did to my T-shirts; they're all dirty now. These people get on my nerves with this shit. Excuse me, Lord, but they do. They even lined us up and made us get naked. . . . For a bone! I am sick of it, Pam, and guess what? They didn't even find the stupid thing, so now we're on TV and rec restriction for three days . . . or until it turns up."

Mychala then spoke as if she was addressing the entire dorm. "Somebody better stop fuckin' playing and cough the muthafucka up. I'm not trying to go without TV for three days." Other girls grumbled in agreement, but no one said anything that would release the sanctions.

Later that evening, Mychala and I got a chance to talk about my visit with my moms and what I was planning to do—not because I trusted her, but because I just needed to hear myself say it, because I still couldn't believe it, and she became my sounding board over time.

When I told her about the fears that my testimony might bring, her mouth twisted ever so slightly. There was a look of contempt and dismay in her eyes, but the next thing she said to me was spoken from the depths of her heart.

"Xavier, when you first asked me about my husband, I didn't say anything because everybody's experiences are different. I hear all these stories about wanna-be gangsters who do cowardly acts on innocent people—like shooting up someone's house or their car to send a stern message while the stray bullets kill the little girl down the street. But some of these men in the game are ruthless; their acts of terror are calculated and executed with precision and malice.

"When Emanuel got knocked, I stayed with his brother because of all the death threats that he had received. One day, Emanuel went on a visit and someone from the organization he worked for was out there. He didn't say a word to Emanuel. He just held up a picture of me coming out of my house. Then he lit a cigarette and put the match to my picture. As the picture burned, he stared at my husband to make sure they understood each other.

"Emanuel was so shaken up about the whole incident that he called me and told me to pack up and move in with his brother until things cooled off. But Pam, there was nowhere to run, no place to hide. They knew everything. Two weeks later, right before Emanuel's trial, I came home to find my brother-in-law hanging, his hands tied behind him, from the railing of the staircase by a rope. He was cut from ear to ear and his tongue was pulled through his throat. They even plucked his eyes out, Pam."

"Unun . . . uhh . . . what did Emanuel do?" I asked.

"Humph. He did what they told him to do. He kept his mouth shut for my sake and he was found guilty of conspiracy for his involvement in an international drug trade. The lesser of two evils was life without the possibility of parole.

"The same people that did this to Emanuel are the same people you've been doin' business wit'. I can assure you that your supplier will stop at nothing to get his way."

Mychala's story crushed and enraged me . . . the thought of them fuckin' with my baby, my brother, me. I felt like Tony Montana in *Scarface:* Fuck these cockroaches. *You wanna fuck with me? Okay. Say hello to my little friend. . . . Carmen!* I was tired of crying. I was going to continue to fight for mine, no matter how big my adversary was.

Mychala inviting me to be her spade partner interrupted the uncomfortable silence between us. We both needed to get our mind off things. I definitely didn't want to have to play against her; there was no telling how many tricks she had up her sleeve.

Mychala was already curled up under the covers by the time I got off the phone with my attorney. I was drained myself, so I opted to take a shower and lie down as well.

I dreamed about my first trip to New York to meet Dragos. I stayed at the Waldorf Astoria Hotel honeymoon suite. That place had it goin' on! And I was plugged. There was a black baby-grand piano and a huge bouquet of yellow roses in the room. Left on the bed were two fluffy white embroidered bathrobes and a beautiful view of New York's skyline through the floor-to-ceiling window. On the right side of the room in a cozy, dimly lit section was a marble floor leading to plush, thick wine-colored carpet and a huge, garden-style bathtub. I soaked in the whirlpool Jacuzzi tub, sipping on Dom Perignon, toasting myself to success, my smooth, shaved legs raised and French-manicured toes showing through the lather of bubbles. Room service delivered lobster tails and steak. Life was so good. . . .

I was awakened by the presence of someone near me. My eyes flung open to see Mychala kneeling beside me on one knee. For a moment, I thought that my dreams had once again turned into a nightmare without warning, but this was real. My eyes met hers. I needed some explanation. I knew that something was wrong. She would have never invaded my space otherwise. What could it possibly be?

I was about to ask her, but she put a finger to her lips. That's when I saw it.

A feeling of horror swept through my body. I wanted to scream, but I didn't—not at first, anyway. It seemed as though we were frozen in the moment, like sculptures on display at Arlington National Cemetery.

I shook my head in refusal of the truth about the woman I had befriended. I would have never imagined this, but it was happening. There was no doubt about it, though, as I looked at the pork chop bone that she held tightly in her grip. It was attached to an empty toilet paper roll that had been tightly folded and wrapped with a strip from her T-shirt to make a smooth handle. The bone was sharpened to a point. I had seen people using cement bricks to sharpen their pencils in the middle of a spade game (the deputies only made their rounds once every hour), and had heard stories of the men grinding their toothbrush into deadly ice pick-like weapons. But Mychala's bone knife, as she held it high above her head, looked more menacing than anything that I could have ever imagined. What she manifested was the vilest thing on the face of the earth—an abomination— and she wanted to stick me with it.

I wanted to scoot from under her, run to the door and beat on it with all my might until the officers came busting in with their riot gear of shields, billy clubs and pepper spray. They would back her down into a corner and beat the living dog shit out of her ass. But I knew better; such an attempt on my part would bring sure death, for every scream for help would be matched with a stab in my back.

She brought the shank down hard, but I managed to catch her wrist, holding the knife just a few inches away from my eye. Her determination was equally matched with my will to survive as she threw her weight onto her hand. I could feel the bone scraping my eyelid, and I knew that if I didn't do something quick, at best, I was going to come out of here looking like Slick Rick.

I don't know what made me try this maneuver. Perhaps my subconscious stored it from all the episodes of WWF that I teased my brother about watching every Saturday. Instead of trying to resist her attack, I raised my head, placed my foot on her stomach and pulled her forward, flipping her into the wall.

I jumped up to take my boxing stance, but my sheets were tangled around my feet and I fell in the middle of the dayroom. By the time I had a chance to recover, Mychala plunged into me, knocking me into the TV. Excruciating pain ripped through my back. Instinctively, I knew that the edge of the steel platform that the TV was bolted to had cut me. I didn't have time to worry about that, though, because Mychala was already bringing the knife down into the muscle of my shoulder. The knife ripped into my skin like a switch on a wet ass. I recovered and instinctively hit her with an open palm to the nose. She stumbled back, blinking the moisture from her eyes, while I gulped for air like a near drowning victim pulled from the water one second from death.

"I tried to warn you, Xavier, but you wouldn't listen. I didn't want to do this, but you left me no choice. I got to kill you now," Mychala screamed.

The other girls in the room had gathered around to form a circle. The dayroom had become the Thunder Dome: *"Two men enter, one man leaves."* I didn't know what to do next, as Mychala adjusted the shank in her hand. All I knew was that I wasn't going out like that. I was reminded of back in the day when kids were told by their parents not to come home with their ass whipped, or they'd get whipped. I had to go for mine.

From what seemed like miles away, I heard the faint cry of the white girl, calling for help.

"I left out one part of the story about my brother-in-law. When they found him, they also found me. This was *my* alternative. Snitches get stitches, bitch!" Mychala screamed as spit flew out of her mouth.

Mychala lunged at me, but I dodged her advance. She lost her balance and I was able to push her against the glass window. I grabbed her hand that held the weapon and twisted her arm around her back. I pushed it so far up, that I could've broken it. I pushed harder as my assailant screamed, but she didn't let go of the shank. I pushed more until I heard her elbow crack. Mychala's screams elevated into a shriek. The pork chop bone bounced on the floor. I tried to follow where it went, but one of the inmates kicked it out of my reach. I must have let up on her arm because Mychala spun and backhanded me with her left fist. I fell, pulling her down with me as we crashed into the picnic table.

I landed on top of her and put both of my hands around her throat; my thumbs pressed against her windpipe. I continued to choke her as she clawed my face.

Mychala opened her mouth as if it could no longer hold her tongue, and the color of her face turned a bluish purple.

"Step aside! Move! Xavier, get off of her!" I heard one of the officers shout. Then I heard a thud. It was a billy club smashing against the back of my head. I was knocked out cold. In the meantime, the feds were watching. . . .

FOR EVERYTHING THERE IS A TIME AND A SEASON

The Mazda van pulled in front of LaShone's loft and parked. "Okay, I'll go upstairs and get her keys. Pull around the back, and we can switch the dope and make our drops," T-Love said hopping out of the van.

"Infa, hit P up on his cell and let him know we're here," Erik ordered.

T-Love rode the elevator upstairs to LaShone's floor. Stepping off the elevator, he walked into LaShone's loft. She was in the kitchen, wearing a baby doll nightgown and looking fine as hell. LaShone ran over to greet T-Love, kissing him on his lips. "What's up, baby? Long time no see."

Chino pulled his SUV into the rear of LaShone's building, having arrived to her place by taking all back streets. Sitting in the alley checking the messages on his cell, he saw a Mazda van drive past, or so he thought. He was listening to messages from his wife. It was her seventeenth phone call saying the same damn thing. "This is your wife, please come home."

A black man around the age of thirty-five stepped out of the emergency exit door of the building. He looked around suspiciously, and Chino began to wonder whether or not he knew this nigga and if he was coming from

LaShone's place. Chino had used that same exit door to creep out of LaShone's as it was just off her kitchen fire escape. Suddenly, he began to feel tingly all over, and an eerie feeling struck him in the pit of his stomach. He watched as the figure stood curbside and a car pulled up to get him. In the front seat of the four-door sedan were two white men, and the black man entered the rear of the car. It was obvious that this scene was out of order. *Follow your heart, your first instinct. Don't second-guess yourself.* Queen's words rang true in his head. He had the urge to call LaShone to see if she was okay or confront her about the guy to make sense out of the scene. But knowing what he knew, he didn't ignore his jitters. Instead of calling or going upstairs, he placed the car in drive and pulled off. "Fuck LaShone, I'm going home," he thought to himself.

Chino hit 315 North and headed home to Delaware, Ohio, to his lovely wife and two children. It had been two weeks since he was there, and he decided to go to the place where he found rest. As he hit the highway, the jitters left his stomach. He understood what Queen was trying to teach him: Follow your first instinct.

The Mazda, having circled the block twice, was now positioned in the same spot where Chino had just been parked. T-Love came down the fire escape with LaShone's car keys in hand. "Go handle the business. I'll be talking something over with LaShone." T-Love turned to leave with a devilish grin on his face.

"That nigga up there gettin' some ass," said Infa.

"Fuck him, let's get this money and get the fuck out of Columbus," said Erik.

They turned up into the parking garage, transferred the dope into LaShone's Mustang trunk, leaving all but two weapons, and headed out of the garage to make the drops.

"P's phone just kept ringing," Infa said handing the phone to Erik.

"Don't worry. I think I know how to find him; if not, we can leave the dope with his cousin," Erik replied.

A roadblock of cars suddenly appeared at the bottom of the entrance to the garage. Before Erik could get "What the fuck is going on?" out of his mouth, it was apparent that they had been followed or set up somehow.

"Get the fuck outta the vehicle!" yelled a federal agent. Infa tried to bust out of the van, but the escape route was too narrow, blocking him. Guns were in the air. The shit was over.

Weapons drawn and doors opened, the police ordered the men out of the Mazda, handcuffed and placed them in the other unmarked vehicles that accompanied them.

Special Agent Newsome pulled the kilos of cocaine from out of the trunk of LaShone's Mustang. Now captured, each of the men began to think how they could explain fifteen kilos of cocaine.

"We need some identification, fellas," Newsome calmly asked.

"I want my lawyer," yelled Infa.

"Didn't I tell you this shit was hot," Abdullah said to his brother Erik.

"Shut the fuck up and don't say shit," advised Erik.

An officer found the Mazda keys in Erik's front pocket and walked over to the Mazda van. They all headed to the federal building on Marconi Boulevard.

LaShone and T-Love were upstairs in the loft getting it on. R. Kelly's music was playing in the background, and LaShone had T-Love on her bed, laying that deep throat on him.

"Mmmm, I missed you," LaShone whispered. She got up from her knees as T rested on the bed butt booty naked, thinking he had died and gone to heaven. LaShone pulled some K-Y jelly from her nightstand and climbed up on the bed with him. "Daddy, I have a surprise for you. I want to get freaked." LaShone began rubbing the lubricant all over her asshole, and then stuck one finger, followed by two more, up her rectum. T-Love got so excited that he was about to nut. Although he had fucked her several times, he never noticed that her rectum was wider than normal, revealing that she was into backdoor action, which turned him on so much.

"You gon' let me hit that from the rear?" T-Love asked.

"Yes, T, fuck me in my ass, baby," LaShone purred. T-Love couldn't contain his excitement. He flipped her over, rubbed his dick with more lubricant and began to stroke the head of his penis. LaShone lay on her stomach, snuggling a pillow underneath her chin. T-Love got so excited that he didn't care about pain; he just had to get his, and up LaShone's ass, oh yeah. She was his bitch. "Come on baby, fuck me," LaShone instructed.

T-Love placed the head of his large penis into her asshole, opening it slightly. He continued to push his hardness into her. Her walls felt really tight at first, and even though he had originally planned to go for his, he thought of stopping. But it felt so damn good he couldn't. He always wanted to fuck a girl in the ass, but they all pretended that his dick was too big or they weren't down with it. Now he was finally having his turn.

T-Love pushed harder as LaShone coached him. "That's it, baby, deeper, deeper, it feels sooooo good." T-Love slowly got the head in, and the rest of his dick seemed to slide in without effort. LaShone's shit was so tight and warm that he just had to rest in it for a minute. Lying on top of her back, his hands grabbed her titties as he whispered into her ear.

"Who's ass is this?"

"Yours, baby, fuck me, fuck me hard. Tear that ass up, baby." Her instructions only fueled him on, as he began to pump in and out of that tight juicy ass. It began to feel so good to him, and the more she screamed, the harder it made his dick. She got up on all fours, allowing him to see his dick going in and out of her asshole. He began to pound that shit over and over, moving in deeper and deeper, until his entire rod was high up in her rectum.

"You nasty bitch, this ass feels so good," T-Love panted.

"Fuck me, fuck me, fuck me, fuck me, harder, harder," she yelled through clenched teeth. T-Love came harder than physics, collapsing on top of LaShone's small frame. She motioned for T-Love, now exhausted, to roll over, and then she climbed on top of his face. He began to hungrily eat out her pussy. "Suck my clit," she demanded, assuming the position, placing her hands on her headboard and fucking his face with her pussy. T began to stick his fingers up her ass as he, for the first time, ate her pussy, not caring about whom she had been with. All he knew was that she had freaked the shit out of him, and it was erotic as hell. He continued to lick and suck her clit as she spread her pussy open, letting her juices flow down the sides of his face and chin.

They lay in each other's arms, exhausted, before bringing up the subject of taking a shower.

"Let me go first, and then you next. I'll change the sheets while you're in the shower," LaShone said.

"Okay, baby," T-Love said, before turning on his side and drifting off to sleep.

LaShone headed for the shower and took her cell phone with her. She played her voice mail as the water ran. She placed a phone call to Chino and left a page for him to call her. She was in and out of the shower in no time. T-Love was half asleep, but she pushed him out of the bed into the shower.

"Come on, baby, you smell like sex," LaShone said as she handed him a towel, coaxing him to end his slumber. During his shower, she changed the sheets on the bed and popped a new tape into her recorder. She placed the tape recorder in the side railing of the bed, concealing the device, and lay in her birthday suit awaiting T-Love's return. "Come on, baby, let me massage you with oil." T-Love obediently lay on his stomach, and then the pillow talk began.

"So, what brings you back to Columbus from New York?" LaShone quizzed.

"We out here gettin' that money. That's why I needed your car," T-Love said, relaxing as she rubbed his shoulders, hitting the tight spots.

"What ya'll been up to?"

"Well, we had a shootout at the Bottoms Up lounge. We even went to go see Carmen and dropped her off some money. Erik and Infa needed to get rid of about twenty kilos of cocaine this weekend."

"Are you still selling drugs, Timothy?" LaShone asked.

"You know I got to get that money, baby," T-Love replied.

"So, who all came with you?" LaShone continued. The typical nigga in the street would have deaded all those damn questions, but shit, she had his nose wide open.

LaShone had been undercover for three years. She was tired and ready to end the Triple Crown Posse case, so she was breaking some rules, fucking T-Love like this. It was becoming increasingly more difficult to crack these cases, and although a federal undercover agent, having violated several regulations, she knew she wasn't going to get anywhere going by the book. She had to roll with the way of the streets and really become a sack chaser, but in court she would deny sleeping with anyone. That would be considered entrapment, so it would just have to be her word against theirs. After the tape was done, she would have T-Love arrested and no one would be the wiser. *They all think Carmen is telling, anyway, so why not blame her?* They'll all eventually blame each other and no one will know what is what, that is, until they're all in federal prison.

The government's war on drugs not only consisted of mandatory minimum sentencing and conspiracy laws, but

it included stings with undercover officers working the
streets. The last player on LaShone's list was Chino. Trying
to get him to incriminate himself was tough. No matter
how much cum she swallowed, he would never, ever talk
about his case, his money or what he did, and every time
she questioned him he pulled away.

If she could just get him to her place, he could at least
be arrested at the same location as the others and the government could create a tie, making them codefendants.
The feds could use this arrest for leverage on deals. They
wanted this group and they wanted it bad. The net was getting bigger, and the bigger the net, the bigger the fish.

Chino noticed the cell phone page from LaShone as he
pulled into his four-car garage resting on a cul-de-sac of a
tree-lined street. Looking at her number made the butter-
flies come back. *Something ain't right about that bitch.
She's cancelled. "Pussy's good, but can't fuck with her, yo,"*
Chino thought as he got out of his SUV and tossed his
phone in the garbage so she could never call him again. He
would get a new phone and start all over.

Chino's wife was in the large den with the children
when he walked into his home. She smiled and he smiled
back at her. He was blessed in so many regards, so why
couldn't he be happy and leave the streets alone?

"Hey, family, Daddy's home."

Peanut and Bones nabbed their target coming out of the
Bolivar Arms Projects on East Fifth Avenue. "Put your motherfuckin' hands up!" Peanut screamed into the man's ear.

"Search him, B!" Peanut ordered. Bones searched the
man and found a nine-millimeter in his rear waistband
and a wad of cash in the side pocket of his jeans.

"Bingo! Got it, let's bounce," Bones said.

"Nah, let me check his wallet, too," Peanut advised. He

ruffled through some papers inside the wallet and found nothing. The man's body twitched slightly to the left, and Peanut, on reflex, blasted him once in the face.

"Damn, what happened?" asked Bones.

"Shit, the nigga moved. Don't be moving while you gettin' robbed." The two scurried off on foot.

Yellow and Chino were at the moving and storage space, stuffing kilos of cocaine and heroine into the Toyota Previa's hidden compartments. Their second monthly shipment had arrived, and Chino was going to make some drops. "Man, I keep getting these jitters," Chino said.

"It's just your case. When do you go back to court?" asked Yellow.

"I go back in two weeks. My attorney said it'll be postponed again, though."

"I want to go with you. Just think, you been out on bond for a year and a half now. You could have done that time. Do you need anything? I can run this shit for you and have it together when you come home."

"No, man, I'm just trying to stack dollars and stay free," Chino said.

"Yeah, but that time is gon' be there and you could be done. I'll let you work your own program, or do you think the case is going to go away?"

Chino laid the last kilo flatly into the van's compartments. "I don't know if I want to plead or take it to trial, or what. I try not to think about it."

The two men hopped into the Toyota, placed the lock on the storage room and headed toward Toledo, Ohio, to meet Dahkil at Bowling Green University, the midway point between Columbus and Detroit. "Yellow, something ain't right. I think you should stay here, and if I don't come back, you know who I went to meet," said Chino to his long-time partner as they approached the highway.

"No, fuck dat. I go with you or we don't go at all," Yellow insisted.

"Man, I ain't got shit to lose these days. Just stay here, and I'll go meet Dahkil and them myself. I'll hit you up after the drop. Call me on my wife's cell phone; I lost mine."

"Are you sure?" Yellow asked with concern.

"Do you remember what Queen said about them jitters? Well, I'm feeling them and they ain't about you. It's about me. If I don't go, I won't be able to stop 'em. Something's in the air . . . Lay low, partner." He gave his friend some dap, and Yellow exited the Toyota.

Chino hit Interstate 71 going north and all seemed well. He proceeded onto Interstate 270 toward Interstate 23 and headed for Detroit, Michigan. While being careful not to go over the speed limit, Chino thought about his choices before suddenly noticing a highway patrol car in the rearview mirror. His forehead broke into a sweat. Chino swerved from nervousness, and that swerve cost him dearly. The disco lights on the patrol car went on, and Chino was faced with two choices: either stop and take the risk, or flee to remain free. He gunned the large, heavy van, doing a slow, ninety miles per hour, keeping in mind that his first instinct would never steer him wrong. The patrol officer hit his radio. "This is Officer James and I am in pursuit of a red Toyota Previa van on Interstate 23 heading north. Officer requesting backup."

Chino hit the switches on the van and began to dump the cocaine within his reach out of the windows. He grabbed a bag of money on the floor and began to toss the loot out of the windows as well. The flying money and cocaine caused cars to come to a sudden halt, crash and made drivers wonder what in the hell was going on. Chino took the first exit off the highway toward a residential area and planned to jump out the first chance he got, as he tossed weapons and paraphernalia out of his vehicle.

"Gotta get rid of this shit!" he yelled as he jammed the pedal to the metal.

Skidding to an abrupt stop, he jumped from out of the van and hauled ass, going in zigzagging directions. Chino was running as best as he could, but with sagging jeans, he wasn't moving as quickly as he needed to.

Chino saw a mall in the distance and sprinted toward it. When he reached the mall, he ran into a store and purchased a change of clothes. He went into the closest restroom and changed his clothing, tossing what he had previously worn into the trash. He searched for his phone and realized that he had left it in the van. Peeking out into the corridor, he walked swiftly to the other end of the mall and spotted an exit. There were two ladies with a child in a stroller leaving the mall. Chino decided to give them a hand and act as if he was with them.

The ladies welcomed the help from the handsome man. As one of them folded the stroller in half, Chino swept the little girl up in his arms and motioned to the mother that he would carry her if she held the bags, or vice versa. The child was having so much fun that the mother obliged. As they entered the parking lot, they could hear sirens nearby and saw a helicopter flying overhead. The police chopper noticed people in the parking lots, but none fit the profile of a suspect in blue and tan denim gear running for cover. Chino politely asked the ladies for a ride to the bus stop, and they were more than happy to be of service. He was free.

Chino couldn't believe how he had escaped like a runaway slave. He headed home to gather his thoughts and make a phone call to the waiting party in Toledo.

Dahkil and his partner sat on candy-painted Ninja ZX11's and drank bottled water as they wondered what in the fuck was taking Chino so long; he was over an hour late. *Ring, ring* . . . "Yeah?" Dahkil spoke into his cell phone.

"Man, shit is fucked up. I need to chill," Chino said.

"Cool. Get with me when you can," Dahkil said. He secured the backpack, full of money, to his back, reached for the switch and popped the clutch on his bike. "Let's roll. The shit is fucked up in Columbus." Dahkil and his partner began to move out, heading back to Detroit. Dahkil rolled his bike over to his girl, who was waiting in a nearby van for the shipment. "Baby girl, we have to get back. Something went wrong," he said.

"Okay, Dah, I'll meet you at home. You want me to carry the money?"

"No. When I do dirt, I like to keep it on bikes, 'cause we can outrun police on them; you know that." Dahkil winked at her, and she pulled off. Dahkil and his partner burned rubber in the parking lot of BGU and headed toward 75 North to Detroit, thinking of their next move.

Watching the six o'clock news, snug as a bug in a rug inside his home, Chino listened as the reporter told of a shooting of an ATF agent in the Bolivar Arms Projects. *Fuck 'em!* The phone rang, taking him from his thoughts, and he picked up the receiver. He wondered who was calling his home. "Hello?"

"You have a collect call from Angela," the operator said.

"Yes!" screamed a nervous Chino into the phone. He heard sobs as the phone connected.

"They came on my job and arrested me. I'm in jail, Chino," his wife informed him.

"For what?" Chino asked.

"They said they found my cell phone in an abandoned van full of cocaine and money. The authorities traced it back to me. I haven't been charged, just arrested for questions. Come get me!" Angela demanded. Chino's heart sank. For the first time he felt like shit, having his wife arrested on a humble for some shit he did. He had left her cell phone in the car—the phone her state job had given her. She was a daycare inspector and did field work. Chino didn't think it would matter that he used her phone to conduct illegal business. It was just a couple of phone calls—detrimental ones. *Damn!*

"Chino, are you there?" Angela asked.

"I'll get a lawyer and come get you," Chino promised.

"Okay. I'm scared. I cannot do this," Angela explained.

"Do not say anything!" The instruction came a little too late. Chino had never coached his wife on how to be silent upon arrest. After all, she would never get arrested; he never involved her in anything and kept her safe from harm. Well, she spilled her guts to the police, and they were overjoyed to find out that the only person that would have had her phone would be her husband, whose name was Christonos, and they needed to let her go. Of course she was innocent and had never been in trouble or did anything a day in her life. Her background check substantiated that. However, the feds did a vehicle registration search and found three other expensive vehicles in wifey boo's name. Further research revealed that they were leases all from the same car dealer, all fully paid up front in cash.

After receiving a Delaware address, a property search revealed Mrs. Christonos Franco lived in a seven-hundred-and-fifty-thousand dollar home. This amazed the officials, as income verification revealed that Angela only made twenty-eight thousand bucks a year. Something was definitely amiss.

The feds put together an indictment for wifey boo, and they called it "aiding and abetting" for the authorization of the cell phone use. They also labeled her little phone a "criminal tool." Then money laundering was added to the paperwork for the concealed source of revenue used to maintain her lifestyle, which was suspected of being acquired illegally. Additionally, all of the expensive vehicles were impounded, and the noticeable, six-carat wedding ring on Angela's finger was confiscated. Indeed, she was married, and because of the law, she became her husband's codefendant.

MONTH TWENTY

SEGREGATION

Twenty months on lockdown, and my case had gone to trial seven times. I wanted to go home.

I awoke in the infirmary with a painful knot on the back of my head the size of an orange. I wasn't allowed to return to general population due to death threats and the attempt on my life by Mychala and her pork chop shank. I was in "seg" because someone had tried to kill *me*, and I had to give up my privileges as if *I* was on disciplinary. Fortunately, there was a lot to read in there, and by that time I had already read over a thousand books.

I couldn't believe that someone had tried to kill me over this case. They tried to have me killed with a pork chop knife. My attorney was scheduled for a visit with me to clarify what was really going on. There was a knot in my stomach in addition to the knot on my head as I waited. It had been almost two years, and I still hadn't seen my son. He was almost four now. My mother told me that he was potty trained and learning to ride his bike. As I reflected on his photos, I thought about how much he had grown. I spent my days missing him, and I spent my nights crying and wanting to the leave the county jail. When I had spoken to him, it caused me to break down; he wasn't even talking when I left, and now he was speaking in full sentences.

Hi, Antonio, It's Mom.

C-come get me. The tears fell down my face as my son said those words to me. I missed him. I wanted to go home. I needed nobody less than God to help me.

"Xavier, pro visit!" The words snapped me out of my reminiscing. The door to my one-man cell slid open, and I walked to the front of the segregation door.

"Xavier ready for visit," I yelled into the speaker that was on the side of the wall. The door opened and I walked through it. A guard who I was unfamiliar with was on duty, and this was rare. After being housed in this facility for almost two years, I was practically on a first-name basis with all the guards. Since being in this fuckin' detention center, I had missed two Christmases, two Thanksgivings and two of my son's birthdays.

I walked into the professional visit booth and sat across from a man who I was definitely tired of seeing—my attorney.

"Pamela, how are you?" Myer asked.

"Fine, now what? Another continuance, or, let me guess, we've had our three limit, the prosecutor has had his three extensions and my codefendants have had theirs; so who does that leave to request a continuance—the fucking deputy or the K-9 police dogs?" I said sarcastically.

"I know that doing all this time has been rough on you, but we're almost there. I've requested a separate trial for you, and we'll take a plea from the government."

"Whatever. I just want out of here so I can hold my son."

"Pamela, do you know these people?" Myer said, laying a stack of papers before me along with some photos.

"What is this, more proffering? I thought they didn't want to talk to me anymore since I was lying and uncooperative."

"They didn't and they didn't have to. Apparently there was an undercover on your case," Myer said.

"Who, that motherfucker in the proffering session? That guy from NewYork?" I asked.

"I can't tell you, but it wasn't him. He was her contact," Myer said.

"*Her?* Myer, who is it? I live in solitary confinement, and I get two phone calls a week. Who am I going to tell?" I blurted.

"Well, you will soon find out. I would rather that you not know anything. That's in your best interest." As I shuffled through the papers, I noticed names on the new indictment paper: Erik Williams, aka English, or E; Timothy Hutchins, aka T or T-Love; Abdullah Williams, aka A; Scott Hardaway, aka Infa; Christonos Franco, aka Chino; Angela Franco . . . *Chino's trick-ass wife.*

"What's going on? Are these my new codefendants? Is this another superceding indictment?"

"No, Pamela. These are people that have caught other related cases while you were already doing your time. They've taken all of the spotlight off of you and opened up an entire new can of worms."

"So, what does that mean for me?" I asked.

"Well, that just corroborates one thing."

"So that's still like snitchin'," I said.

"Call it what you want. Do you want to go home?" Myer said.

"Okay, what do they want to know?" I asked. I had decided that missing two of my son's birthdays was enough.

"I have someone I want you to meet." Myer stepped outside the visiting booth, and I sat looking through the papers and couldn't believe all the shit we had gotten ourselves into. About fifteen minutes passed, but it seemed like an eternity. I wondered why no one was guarding my booth. I stood to peek out the door window into the hallway and it was empty. I thought of running, but shit, where could I go? I sat back down and laid my head on the table and began to pray. *God, please help me. I'm sorry and I want to go home. Please, just give me another chance.* Moments later, the door opened and I heard a familiar voice.

"Carmen?" I looked up and saw the face of LaShone. Only she didn't look like LaShone anymore. She had on a navy two-piece suit with a starched white shirt underneath. The hair weave extensions were gone and she sported a short Anita Baker haircut.

"LaShone?" I said in disbelief, eyeing her more closely. She sat down and extended her hand.

"Please, call me Tasha. My name is Agent Tasha Coleman." I left her hand suspended in midair.

"What the fuck is going on?" I looked around the room in a panic and began scratching my arm, trying to awaken myself from this dream.

"Carmen, or should I call you, Pamela?" she asked. I remained silent, and she continued to speak in a professional manner as she placed her badge on the table. "I've been working undercover on drug cases for three years, and I know how you got involved; T-Love mentioned that much. But I'm here because we can help each other, and this is off the record," she stated.

"No. I want my attorney," I said.

"There can be no witness to this conversation, although your attorney has a statement from me. I want to read you my report that I'm going to turn in regarding your involvement with my investigation." I sat back as she removed the statement from the manila folder in her hands. "I, Tasha Coleman, special agent 3214 became aware of Pamela Xavier, aka *Carmen*, during the summer of 1995. From investigation and further research, it has been discovered that Carmen was a former girlfriend of Christonos Franco, aka *Chino*, and a college associate of Erik Williams and Timothy Hutchins. By admission and further investigation, it was determined that Pamela was threatened and coerced into making drug transactions for this group. She suffered from extremely low self-esteem and was repeatedly asked to do favors in exchange for money to care for her son. A visit to her home revealed modest living and it was substantiated by her immediate associates that she was clearly a contracted employee of Chino and T-Love's. It is this agent's observation that Ms. Xavier suffers from duress and should be tried for aiding and abetting and money laundering. These are my findings from my surveillance and investigation; so swear I, Agent Coleman. Do you know what this means?" Agent Coleman aka LaShone asked.

"No," I answered stupefied.

"This means that you will be charged with the sale of two kilos of cocaine to an undercover agent—that you will be charged with aiding and abetting and money laundering. There will be no enhancements, and this will support your attorney's motions for separate counsel tables."

"Why, what does this mean?" My ass was still dumfounded.

"It means that your guidelines will be lower, and you could be going home to be with your son," she said smiling.

"Okay, like I'm supposed to believe this."

"Well, you can. Can you believe I am a federal agent—the same person you talked shit about?" This whore actually smiled in my face. She did actually have a point. She continued. "But I need something from you. I need you to forget about me ever sleeping with anyone, or even knowing anything about me. So far you haven't mentioned me, and if you forget me, I'll forget you."

"Oh, so now I gotta make a deal with you?" I asked.

"Pamela, one hand washes the other, and both wash the face." We sat in complete silence, reflecting, as she continued to talk. "I could lose my job and blow this case. You can lose your freedom, and I will make certain of that." Her demeanor was now demanding. I was in a position that I had to trust the trick of the week's word. "I have enough money saved that all I could lose is my job. I saved enough off those men, you know," she said smiling. "They treated me like shit, and none of them cared about you. Care about yourself. Take this out."

With every temptation, there will be an opportunity for relief.

I studied LaShone's face to see if she was sincere. I felt in my heart that she was, and I had no choice but to believe it. I had prayed so hard for someone to come help me—for me not to have to be a rat and to be able to honor the code. I raised my hand toward LaShone and she shook it. "Why do you want to help me?" I asked.

"Pamela, you don't deserve to be left for dead. This much, I know is true." LaShone winked her eye at me. "Sometimes we girls have got to stick together." She turned to exit the room, and I looked at the statement envelope that she had left.

My attorney entered the room smiling. "Pamela, you'll be fine. I need one more thing from you. You must take a psychiatric evaluation to be labeled competent. A presentence investigator will come visit you to prepare you for PSI paperwork for sentencing."

"Really, is this going to be over soon?" I asked.

"Yes, Pamela, it is. I expect to have your sentence date within sixty days. You could be out of here within four months."

Tears began to stream down my face at the thought of going home, or at least to a prison where I could touch my son and feel fresh air on my face. "Myer, how much time will I get?" I queried.

"Let's look at the PSI report and I'll get back to you." For the first time in twenty months, Myer put his arms around me. I sobbed into his lapel, and he whispered in my ear as he wiped my tears. "You are special. It has all worked out in your favor." *Says who?*

MONTH TWENTY-ONE

I sat in my cell thinking of how things were turning out. My mother was overjoyed that the Lord had heard our prayers. My mom swore up an down that my grandmother had implored the angels and that they bombarded heaven. It was unbelievable that there was even an out. That LaShone, trick bitch, was an undercover. I wondered if sucking dick was a legal way to arrest people. But, hey, the government was desperate. If you really think about it, how else, other than entrapment or a set up, could someone be captured? The government needed help doing its job.

I decided to keep my mouth shut and go with the flow. The hand I had been dealt didn't look as bad as it did twenty-one months earlier. My attorney felt confident that LaShone, aka Agent Coleman, would keep her word. After all, we had a notarized statement, and only she and I knew the additional terms. She was very confident that I would keep my end of the deal.

My presentencing report was done by a fresh-out-of-college, racist asshole. She had no understanding of why a person would break the law. I was advised to be nice to her, as she wrote my version of the incidents. My prosecutor agreed to the separate counsel tables and the charges as discussed. The PSI report was used to inform the court of a clear picture of the accused. It covered background information as well as the facts of the case reported in the indictment. It also included any statements regarding the case. It began with a point system that was then used to place the offense on a level with a punishment comparable with the mandatory guidelines. I received a three-point reduction for acceptance of responsibility—simply meaning that I had pleaded guilty. Without all the shit in the game, my score was 29. I was in a criminal history category of 1, chapter 5, part A sentencing table.

The probation officer recommended that I be sentenced at the lower end of the guidelines, pursuant to U.S.S.G.5C1.2, which meant that the court should impose a sentence in accordance with the applicable guideline without regard to any statutory minimum sentence. This left me facing 87 to 108 months in federal prison, and escaping the mandatory minimum appliance of 10 years or 121 months.

My attorney argued and my prosecutor agreed that some leniency be shown for my lack of criminal history, my initial willingness to cooperate and my time spent detained in the county jail facilities. Things were looking better by the day. I just wanted everyone to stay on point and for me to get the fuck out of here. With the feds the rules changed daily, and it was impossible to ever know what to expect.

"Xavier, visit!" the guard announced.

"Pro or personal?" I asked as I was slipping my tan shirt over my long johns for my visit.

"Personal."

"Who the visitor?" I asked Deputy Allison.

"Let me see." She lifted her walkie-talkie and called into the visiting area. The officer there uttered the name *Sheila White* into the receiver. "Sheila White," Deputy Allison repeated.

Sheila, Sheila White . . . I didn't know who in the hell *she* was. I began to twitch with nervousness, as I needed no more surprises. I approached the visiting booth with dread. I stood back, against the wall, as the seated visitors waited for other inmates to arrive. A woman, who was vaguely familiar, smiled at me. She motioned for me to come over to her. I lifted the receiver and she did the same. Upon closer inspection, I recognized her. Next to her was a young boy about ten years old. He looked just like Delano. It was Delano's baby's momma and their son, Little D.

"Sheila," I said into the receiver.

"Carmen." For a moment we both stared at each other. When I looked at Little D, I began to cry. Looking at him was, for me, like looking at Delano for the last time. Noticing the tears in my eyes Sheila said, "Carmen, please don't cry. I'm here to talk to you about something. It took me a long time to come and visit you. I was so angry at you after Delano's death."

"Why were you angry at me? I loved him," I said defensively.

"I know, but I thought somehow, someway, you were involved with his murder and I held you responsible . . . but not anymore."

"I wished I could have been there for his funeral. How are the kids?" I asked, glancing at Little D.

"Little D took it extremely hard, but we're all making it and hanging in there. I recently got married, and that allowed me to bring closure to that part of my life," Sheila explained.

"Delano always said you were wonderful," I admitted.

"I'll mail you an obituary; they wouldn't let me leave it at the visit window," Sheila stated.

"Thank you. Where is Delano buried? I want to visit his grave when I get home."

"His body was flown back to New York and buried at Cypress Hills, a cemetery on the borderline of Brooklyn and Queens."

"Will you please send me that information in a letter so I can go see him?"

"I can do that."

Silence fell between us, and I wondered why she came to see me. I soon stopped caring why she was there; I was just glad that she was.

"Carmen, I'm here because I found something going through Delano's things. It was in a box with your photos and mementos. There were some letters from you to him, and underneath it all was this item. Because you were already in trouble I didn't want to turn it in; I didn't want to get involved. At first I was going to throw it out. Dee said that it was yours and you needed him to keep this box. He left it with me before he got killed. What do you want me to do with it?"

I couldn't believe my ears. Sheila had the gun—the gun Chino used in the murders. I could go home free with that. I could go home and use it to put Chino's black ass in the clinker for life. Somehow I knew he was responsible for Delano's death, too. I just knew it. *Vengenence is mine saith the Lord,* said a voice inside my head.

"Sheila, you've had that box all this time?"

"Yes, and I just went through his things and got rid of everything. We're building a new home and getting ready to move into it. I decided to give my marriage a chance and get rid of Delano's things." Part of me wondered why in the fuck his things were at her place. Were they still messing around? Then I realized how unimportant that was, and how typical it was for a female to think this way—even at a time like this.

"Sheila, I need a favor," I said.

"What?" she said with a slight attitude. I knew that this was hard for her. I mean, we loved the same man and here I was asking her for a favor.

"Sheila, please take those items and just dump them into a garbage yard or drop them off the Broad Street Bridge for me."

"Really? Everything?" she asked.

"Yes, everything. I don't want to hurt anymore. I want to be rid of the past. I need to let go and move on with my life," I said.

"Broad Street Bridge it is! I'll do it on my way home. The box is in the car. Consider it handled."

"Thank you. May I please speak with Little D?"

"Sure. Little D?" She tugged on the back of Little D's shirt and handed him the phone.

She stood so he could take her seat.

"Hey, put your hand up to the glass; let me see how big you are." As he put his smaller palm to the glass, I lifted up my larger one, placing it against my side of the glass to match his. He smiled, revealing the same grin that his father had. Looking into the innocent face of D's son made me feel loved again.

"How are you, Ms. Carmen?" Little D said.

"I'm fine. How is school?" I asked.

"School is fine; I get good grades." Looking at him made me imagine what my son would possibly look like when I came home. Seeing Little D made me feel as though I *did* get a chance to say good-bye to Delano. Delano choosing such a wonderful baby's mother, whose heart was good, allowed me to have closure. The deputy signaled that the end of the visit was near.

"Little D, it's almost time to go." I put up two fingers, making the peace sign. This was something that Delano did all the time. Little D's eyes sparkled at the gesture.

"Let me talk to your mom," I said.

"Carmen, I am praying for you. Do you need anything before I leave?" Sheila said, now sitting back across from me.

"No, you have already given me so much," I replied.

"He loved you," Sheila said.

"I know. I loved him too. Thank you!"

Click. The phone line went dead and little Delano waved and smiled at me. I waved back at them both and stood against the wall, waiting to go back to my cell. I knew Sheila would dump the contents. I knew I could have made a different choice, but I didn't want to bring harm to others.

Although I could now go home with the information about the murders, I didn't want to be responsible for sending my baby's daddy to prison for life. I just didn't want that.

MONTH TWENTY-TWO

Chino pulled up in front of the Bolivar Arms Projects and waited for Peanut to show up. He was there trying to collect money that was owed to him. The clock on the dash of his suburban read 1:30 P.M. Peanut was running unusually late. Chino sat and could not believe that his nigga, his homie, was playing him. Peanut knew that he needed the money to bond out his wife and get his shit in order. But as the dash light on the digital flipped to 1:45 P.M., Chino knew that his friend would not be showing up. He thought of calling Peanut or stopping by his baby's momma's house to search for him, but he knew it would be useless; never in their dealings had he ever had to search for him. Chino was that nigga, and when he called, everyone came running . . . or so he previously thought. Chino put the car in drive and drove off, passing the staring shorties on the corners slangin' them rocks. Peanut had played him and wasn't paying him his money.

Peanut and Bones sat in Legends Barbershop talking shit about Chino. "Yeah, that nigga is hotta than a VCR in a crack house," Peanut said, as Sean cut his hair.

"Word?" Sean asked not really giving an opinion either way.

"Haven't you been watching the news?" asked Peanut as other patrons nodded. The case was plastered all over the TV news—including the highly publicized chase of the van dropping money and dope out the windows.

"When I saw that money coming out of that van, I *thought* it was that crazy nigga," the barber at the next station added.

"But, hey, he won't tell, will he?" Sean asked.

"I ain't gon' find out," Peanut said as he stepped from the chair and Bones took his place. They smiled at one another, knowing that they had just jacked five kilos from Chino, and, after they grinded those bitches out, they would be heading back to Gary, Indiana.

Peanut left the barber shop, and Bones got in the chair for a cut and shave. Peanut made a U-turn in the middle of the street and headed out West to collect. At the second intersection, he was road blocked and arrested, as cops swooped down on his shit in broad daylight. *It's cool, 'cause a nigga ain't dirty, yo,* Peanut thought.

Peanut sat stupefied in the rear of the car, as he heard that he had a federal indictment for the distribution of crack cocaine. Still, he managed to feel somewhat confident, because he remembered that crack didn't carry much time. That was true for the state courts, but the feds put the jumper cables to their shit and made crack a 10 to 1 ratio to powder cocaine. One of the runners got caught with an eight ball of crack; he had set up his supplier with three sales, bringing the crack purchase up to a big eight. At the very least, homeboy was looking at twenty years. This was his third case, and it didn't look good.

Bones lay back in the chair, oblivious to the events going down just two miles away from the barbershop. Sean placed a hot towel on his face to soften up the pores for his straight razor shave. Bones relaxed as he thought of how he was going to spend all that money.

Suddenly, three figures appeared at the door. "I'll be open after this shave," Sean said.

"I'm open," said the barber at the next station, raising his index finger.

"Nah, we straight." The trio walked over to the chair where Bones was getting his shave and the younger gentleman with dreads snatched the towel off his face. Bones squirmed a little in his seat.

"Stop playing Sean, that was feeling good—" A pound to his midsection cut off his words, and he bellowed in pain. Patrons scattered out of the way as the three men dragged him to the rear of the shop. Bones's arms were flailing and swinging about; he was desperately trying to grab a hold of anything in sight.

"Nigga, you think you gon' just up and rob my peeps?" dreadlocks said.

"What, what the fuck! Who are you?" Bones asked nervously. *Pop!* Bones was hit on the side of his dome and knocked dizzy. Sean couldn't believe that they were fucking up his business, but being more concerned about his safety, he ran down the street for cover. In the distance, what sounded like four shots was heard. Bones was placed face down in the rear of the barbershop and shot in the back of the head. The trio ran out on foot. No one dared to identify them, and they were never seen or heard from again.

Chino pulled up in front of Queen's home and sat for a while, listening to Jay-Z, his favorite rapper. Queen saw him from her window, came outside and sat in the passenger seat of his truck.

"Hey, baby," she whispered.

"Hey, Queen." Queen could see the tears welling up in his eyes.

"Now you got to pay the piper, baby," Queen said, as she turned to him. "You got that money for me to hold?" she asked.

"Queen, I can't collect; everyone thinks I'm hot."

"Shit, nigga, you *are* hot. Your wife done called everybody in her phone book collect; so people think you gon' try to spring her any way you can. They don't know what you know or told her, 'cause it's apparent you ain't told her to keep her fuckin' mouth shut!" Queen scolded. "See, Pammy got pinched and we didn't hear a peep. If it wasn't for the news, we would've never known she got knocked. But, hey, what do I know? You chose Angela to be your wife."

Chino sat silently, not knowing what to say. His pants leg vibrated, signaling an incoming phone call. He looked at the caller ID on the small compact phone and noticed that it was a call from out of state. "Yeah."

"Hey, you gotta do something. Your wife is blowin' up the spot. Peeps is lookin' for you, dog," Yellow warned his friend.

"Yeah, I figured that much. I can go out like Young Mike, end up stankin' or rot, right?" Chino confirmed what he knew to be his three choices: Commit suicide; get got, 'cause dead men tell no tales, or fight the case, facing rot and ruin in jail numbers.

"You know the drill. Handle your business. Me and Jewel will hold you down," Yellow said. Chino believed his friend, but with the time he was facing it didn't even matter anymore.

"Yeah, I want my family all right," Chino said, making certain his wishes were communicated to his comrade.

"And they will be. One, baby!" Yellow said with remorse in his voice.

"One!" Chino said snapping his phone shut. He turned to Queen. "Well, fuck it. Let's do this." He put the car in drive and drove slowly down Cleveland Avenue toward downtown. "Queen, can I depend on you?" he added.

"No, you can only depend on God. Shit, don't put that pressure on me and try to lock me down like I'm some sixteen-year-old tramp 'cause you headed to the joint. I will do what I can for you, but don't call my house until you get where you're going; don't make me hot, too," Queen warned.

They finally reached the federal courthouse. "Do you think I'm doin' da right thing?" Chino asked.

"This is what you should have done before, but if you want to turn yourself in now to save your wife, go right ahead. My ass would be in Mexico somewhere," Queen said, lighting her cigarette.

"I have my kids out here," Chino said.

"You didn't seem to mind when you left that other one out here. . . . But hey, Queen is not mad at you. I don't want this for you, and you turnin' yourself in won't help your wife."

"I gotta do it, Queen. You know I can't talk about it," Chino explained.

"So you gon' cut your wife loose and take her time, huh?" Queen pressed.

"I told my attorney I would, even if they had to give her a plea or whatever. I want my wife home," Chino said.

"Handle your business, then," Queen said, blowing smoke out of her nose like a dragon. Chino leaned over, kissed her on the face and turned off the car.

"I guess the legend is true: Niggas do give you they shit," said Chino as he got out of the SUV. Queen positioned herself behind the wheel of the suburban truck. "Didn't you know? I'm Queen," she said with a toss of her head.

Queen drove off slowly and watched Chino from the rearview mirror, standing in front of the courthouse building. A tear slid down her face. Again, another vehicle would temporarily be in her possession while someone went to prison. Queen figured that the bag of money in the back seat would be used for Chino's commissary and other things he would need while away. *I hope I live long enough to see him come home. . . . Damn fool.*

The Suburban looked strange, being driven by a sixty-something woman, but Queen gunned that big truck, and it floated on the highway back to her home.

Chino glanced at the United States flag as it flew in the wind, and then he turned to walk into the federal building. He knew the rule all too well: *The catchin' comes before the hangin'.* But with his wife in custody, the rule had changed. Chino began to rethink his choices: *Suicide—no way! Get got? Hell no! Fight the case???*

MONTH TWENTY-THREE

I lay back on my bunk and thought of my life again. Another indictment was passed down and it looked like war. Everyone was flipping on everyone. Diaz was telling on Dragos, Paul's crew was telling on him and his body wasn't even cold yet. Car dealers were coming out the blue to avoid tax evasion and abetting charges and explaining car purchases. Western Union clerks were taking polygraph tests. All I could do was thank God that I was no longer their codefendant, but merely just tied to a related case. That made a big difference. A hearing was slated for all to answer the indictments.

I was placed in a holding cell. As I waited for court to begin, in walked Angela Franco, the beloved wife of Chino, and I spazzed the fuck out. Carmen appeared and beat the cow-walkin' shit out of her before she could even yell for help. That little episode got me an assault charge, but it ran concurrently with my other charges.

During the preliminaries of the court sessions, I was transported to the court building in a federal van, stopping to pick up others for court. It was like a family reunion in July. I saw all the old faces from the streets. I was gawked at as though I had become a totally different person. I had my cornrows pulled back into a ponytail. My hair had grown out of the relaxer and into an all natural state. The marshal tried to keep order. The sight of me had niggas heated, and they began to yell out shit. "Snitch!" Erik had the nerve to be the first one to open his mouth. T-Love just sat silently.

We were lined up to go into the federal building like ducks in a row and were instructed to walk through the underground garage. Climbing up a set of stairs, we passed the back seat of the Mazda van that had been taken apart. It made me snicker a bit. When we entered the building, I saw my brother for the first time in over a year. I leaned toward him, and he kissed me on my forehead.

Ramon was also there. *"Hola,"* I said to him.

"¿Cómo está?"

"Bien," I answered back as we walked slowly to the holding area behind the courtrooms. The marshals, with sawed-off shotguns strapped to their sides, watched us as we moved along the corridors. Entering the rear of the courtroom, we were placed in separate holding cells. There were six holding tanks that lined the wall. Chino's wife was placed, all alone, in a cell. I had a cell to myself as well, in case I got the urge to slap the shit out of her again. Chino, Young Ty and Ramon were put in a cell together. Erik, T-Love, Infa and Abdullah were placed in another holding area. About four cells down from me was Joseph Jamison, the detainee from a related case. He was on a federal writ to testify against our case in order to satisfy his agreement.

We waited. My attorney, Myer, finally came to talk with me, and soon after several of the other attorneys appeared to speak with their clients. This was a pretrial hearing, and I didn't understand why I was here if my case wasn't related to theirs. My attorney explained. "Pamela, this hearing is to request separate counsel tables, or separate you from their trial. It's also an opportunity for them to enter their initial pleas. Don't worry about them. Just let me do my job," he coached. I just looked at him, not wanting to say another word, as our conversation was being overheard and echoed throughout the hallway. All ears were on me. Once the attorneys left and announced that court would begin in twenty minutes, the drama began.

"You snitch bitch!" someone yelled. It sounded like Infa. I ignored the shouting, assuming that LaShone might appear or something.

"Chino, she hit me," yelled wifey boo from her haven.

"Pammy, you hit my wife, huh?" Chino said.

"Fuck you, Chino!" I yelled at the top of my lungs.

"Fuck you!" Chino replied.

"Chino, hold that shit down!" Young Ty said.

"*¡No problemas!*" Ramon said, afraid of any possible violence.

"Fuck you, Pooh," Chino said again.

"No, fuck *you*!" I screamed.

"As much as *you* tellin' you need to be free, star!" Erik cracked.

"Motherfucker, I ain't tellin', and you left me for dead. Where that money you owe me at?" I screamed. Everyone just started wilin' out, yelling back and forth and arguing with each other about who said what and who's fault it was that we were in there. If they had installed a recorder, they would have ended their case, that very day.

Chino and Young Ty were now beginning to go at it. "You sorry-ass motherfucka, tryin' to make a come-up off my sistah!" Ty said.

"Shit, I taught her what she know," Chino replied

"Please, why won't you take care of your baby? That's what a real man would do—got my sister up in all dis bullshit 'cause you wouldn't be a man," Ty retorted.

"Fuck you, what you wanna do?" said Chino, obviously posing a threat. I was waiting to hear the sounds of Young Ty beatin' that ass, but instead I heard something I didn't expect to hear.

"Chino, I don't want to fight you. You were like my dad." My heart began to sink as the reality of his words rang true in my head. Ty continued. "I believed in you and wanted to be you. This is how you did us—just turned your back and said fuck us? Fuck you! Chino, you ain't shit!" The marshal entered the room and yelled for us to be quiet. Satisfied that he had everything under control, he turned and went back to his post.

Chino smirked at Ty and gave him a menacing look. As he was about to sit down on the floor, Ty, out of nowhere, swiftly retrieved a sharp-edged razor that he had secured underneath his tongue. He grabbed Chino from behind, deeply sliced him in the jugular and released him before Chino got the chance to defend himself. Chino, who usually had an answer for everything, could only gurgle and choke on his blood. He lay dying, with no assistance from a soul. There was an eerie silence. The only sound that could be heard now was Ty whistling a slow, gloomy tune.

"Hey, what's goin' on? Baby, you okay?" yelled Angela nervously from her cell. "Baby, are you all right? Chino? Chinoooooooo!" The marshal raced over to Angela's cell. She was doubled over with agony, and there was a sick look in her eyes. "Please, go see about my husband! Something is wrong! Oh my god!" The marshal inspected each holding area until he came upon the cell where Chino lay dead in a pool of thick blood. It was evident that Ty was the main suspect because of the bloody razor that he still held in his right hand. He wore a look of total serenity.

Each of us was led out of the courtroom, and the motions were tried in the courts. The prosecution made the arguing points, and the defense counsels agreed. Motions for separate counsels were approved. Suddenly, the prosecutors called for the undercover agent to make a statement, and LaShone appeared.

Everyone in the room almost fell out with shock. T-Love turned to look at me and then back at LaShone. Everybody began whispering into the ears of their attorneys. T-Love stood up, and kicking and spitting on the tables, started calling LaShone foul names. The media reporters, loving the circus before their eyes, were busy scribbling on their notepads.

It was a long and silent ride back to the detention center. Nobody had shit to say. Chino was dead, and Ty, my beloved brother, would be on lockdown for life.

The following morning, my attorney came for a pro visit and told me that everyone on the case was taking a deal. Then he mentioned something that startled me. "Pamela, I received a phone call from the attorney that was working with Chino. Chino had mentioned your involvement in an unsolved murder case from about four yeas ago. Do you know anything about a murder?" *Chino was trying to get me for those murders. He told, thinking I would tell. . . . Or he was trying to get me more time.*

"No. I don't know anything about that."

"He also had said that you shot him. Is this true?" Myer sternly asked.

"No. I don't know anything about that," I repeated.

"Pamela, he also said that you were his supplier."

"No. I don't know anything about that," I said for the third time

"Well, as you can see, it was extremely easy for you to be separated from codefendants, and Chino was digging a hole for himself. Excuse the pun, but I hope, for your sake, that he was the lying wonder you described him to be." He began to stuff his papers into his briefcase "You get sentenced next month."

"Really, Myer? I get to leave here?" I happily asked.

"Well, you should be out of here in about three months. I'm recommending Bryan, Texas. They have a camp and an RDAP program there."

"What is that?"

"It's a residential drug program that will reduce your time by one year," he explained.

"You have got to be kidding," I said.

"Or, you can do the boot camp and go home eighteen months earlier. Pammy, you really could be home in three years if it goes the way I think it will," said Myer calmly as he removed his thin frames.

"And my brother? Ramon? What about them?" Knowing that my brother would be doing life, I asked about him anyway, not yet fully accepting what had just recently happened.

"Ramon got mule status, and that's three years and deportation, so he's almost out the door with good time. And your brother, uh, well, you know . . . he's going to be away for a long time," said Myer, not being able to look at me.

I sat there, upset about my brother, confused about Chino and relieved that this shit was almost over. I wanted to know about the others, but I said fuck them like they said fuck me.

"I'll see you at your sentencing date. You've got the most lenient judge, and I also think you've got someone up above watching out for you," Myer said smiling as he stuck his pen in his lapel.

"Myer, thank you!" I said.

"Pamela, your life deserves a sentence reflective of a second chance. I hope to help you get that. I'll see you one week from today."

THE CHOICE

It was a dream, but it seemed so real to me. . . .

I had fought sleep and finally dozed off. "Xavier, visit!" the correctional officer yelled through the segregation intercom. As I walked toward the visiting booth, I noticed that the officer was someone I had never seen before. She didn't speak any words, and I just followed her.

There appeared to be a ray of light cast from the far right corner of the visiting area. I eased into the room and saw the back of a person resting in an armchair. The door closed behind me and I stepped farther into the room, cautiously and slowly. The fragrance of Cartier filled my nostrils and the faint scent of honeysuckle and citrus lingered in the air. The scent was clean and fresh as if I had just stepped out of the shower. I saw the top of what looked like a woman's head and a well-manicured hand rested alongside the chair. I called into the tiny room.

"Hello?" Suddenly the chair swiveled slowly in my direction. That was when I saw her. She was wearing a salmon-colored, single-breasted silk Chanel pantsuit. Of the four C-embossed buttons, only the first two were buttoned, revealing a Chanel belt that graced the loops of wide-legged slacks with two-inch-thick cuffs at the bottom. I noticed her French-pedicured toes resting in Gucci, stiletto-heeled, strappy sandals with one strap encircling the big toe. They were pearly white in color, with silver heels to match the silver buttons on the jacket of the suit. Her lips were lined with the recognizable cinnamon hue by Mac and covered with lip gloss, adding a shine and a simmer to her pouty mouth. On the right side of her face was a penciled-in beauty mole just above her lips. Her skin was a bronzy, brushed brown, upon which her makeup was flawlessly placed. Her hair was cut shoulder length into a layered bob that had much body and screamed come touch me. The soft layers framed her face and hung over one eye more so than the other.

The figure stood before me, matching my 5'7" frame. We stood eye to eye. It was like looking in a mirror. Her doelike eyes were mine and perfectly lined in dark brown liner. Her top lids revealed a pale pink eye shadow that matched her suit. This woman was clean as a whistle—polished like platinum shining in the night. There was nothing out of place on her. Her neck was adorned with a diamond-studded choker. Its clasp was the figure of a leopard, encrusted with diamonds. The leopard's eyes were garnet, her birthstone and favorite color. Her wrist sported ice and her finger nested rocks with flawless stones. Studying her ever so closely, I saw she was all I had been and strived to be. A ballerette in the game, polished like a jewel, looking like a hundred grand.

Carmen had come to visit me, and she was as alive to me as I was to her. We stood face-to-face, eyeing and then comforting one another without words. I . . . she . . . Carmen . . . I was so pretty. Not one stress line was on her face, and not one ounce of fat was on her waistline. She began to give me that pearly white smile that she cherished so much.

I smiled back at her knowing that she was me back in the day. She was me on my absolutely best days. She was me when I was at my weakest point. She was me when I couldn't see.

Carmen cleared her throat and asked, "So what is this I hear about you thinkin' about snitchin'?"

"Look, I ain't even trying to go there with you. I am sick—"

"Oh, we gon' go there? Good, 'cause I want to know. I deserve to know."

"I don't owe you. . . ."

"Look, bitch. You definitely owe me."

"What?"

"How many people did you leave for dead, Pammy? Niggas and shorties got picked up who put in work for you and didn't say shit. They didn't say a word. As long as motherfuckas ain't droppin' dime on you, the law of the streets is righteous. Now that you got pinched, you on some fuck-the-streets-type shit."

I backed away from Carmen, crossing over to the other side of the tiny room. There was nothing dividing us but a small table. I checked her. "Let me tell you somethin'. You ain't runnin' nothin' 'round here. I'll take yo' ass out and put it back in when I get good and ready. I don't need your funky ass right now, Carmen. Get back in the box, bitch. When I need to be gangstress, I'll call on you. But I don't need that shit right now, so like I said, bitch, get back in the box."

"Listen to me. That baby daddy we had is stankin', and you don't owe your momma or your sister. And you sho don't owe the feds a helpin' hand to do their job." I began to shake my head in disbelief. I couldn't believe what was going down. Carmen continued. "Like I said, you owe me. You owe the streets. The streets showed you love. The streets held you down. Now you gon' turn on the streets like you don't owe nobody nothin'. Oh, you owe. You owe big time."

"I don't owe anyone anything. I'm a mother now, ya hear? I have a son. That's my loyalty. Fuck dem streets. I'll flip just like dem street niggas. It suits me to be a mommy, and right about now, I'm facing football numbers and—"

"I don't give a fuck if you facin' basketball numbers. This ain't no game, baby. We ain't on the playground, and this here," she said, and began pointing to the surroundings "ain't no motherfuckin' sandbox. Do the godamn time! Period."

"I miss my son. I am his mother," I replied.

"Ain't got no time for no Mother Goose fairy tale shit. Fa real!" Carmen screamed.

"That street code, death before dishonor, is dead. The streets weren't true to me—"

"You chose the streets, the streets didn't choose you!" Carmen said, cutting off my words. She swept her hair back away from her face. "All choices have consequences and repercussions, ma."

I pointed my finger directly in Carmen's face, only inches away from her nose. I reminded Carmen of her words. "You said be true to the streets and they'll be true to you. Well, they wasn't. The streets snitched on me," I reminded her.

"No you fucked with a snitch. And injury is par for the course. You take a foul, you gon' get injured." Carmen began to walk around the table coming close to me—so close that I could feel her breath on my nose. I stepped back from her as she shot me a piercing look. "That's right, take a good long look at me. Do you see me? A bad-ass bitch. I had to be twice as good as any man—the only female on a case with eighteen men. I served them motherfuckas. I fed them. I made them and I made you, too. Shit, you owe *me*—nobody but me. And I don't want to go down like no snitch. You owe me the honor of going down like the hood legend I am. I want legend status and you fuckin' it up by trying to snitch. I can't let you do it. I worked hard for my rep. Don't you know, all the shorties know the name Carmen—that bitch that got down for her crown. Do you know not one of them niggas can say I ever sucked they dick, ever lied to them, ever borrowed money, ever begged to get put on. Money never came up short. I was that bitch. And here you go trying to make all I worked for go down the drain. I cannot let you do this to me."

"Well, what about my son and me?" I asked.

"What *about* you? There would be no you if it weren't for me. Don't get it wrong, negress. You owe me. I clothed you. I fed you when you couldn't feed yourself. I saved you and your baby from skid row. You definitely owe the streets and me. We loved you. I turned them escort dates for you. Where was your momma, your sister, Chino, when your ass was spending WIC coupons?" Carmen began pacing back and forth and then stopped in front of me. "I want to be a legend. I want to go down in history that I was that girl and I held my own. I want to walk that yard with my head held high, knowing all I went through was worth it, and I carried it like the vet that I am."

"I don't care about legend status."

"Darling, that much is painfully obvious."

"I am a mom and I was given this life to care for my son."

"Fuck your son," Carmen replied.

"No, fuck you, Carmen."

"Look darling, mommy dearest. You were a horrible mother. That's right. You were horrible, throwing bricks at the penitentiary as a mother. Your son played second fiddle then, so why not now?" I got up and walked slowly toward her, and she met me halfway. I looked at her shoes and guessed that they were about $375. "You see these shoes?" Carmen asked after catching me staring at her toes.

"What about 'em?" I asked.

"They're the shoes that are on the feet that stood up on corners waiting for niggas in the cold so I could collect. You see this Chanel belt, Pammy? Remember when I had to shake my ass to get dollars put in my G-string belt—dollars that kept the lights on?" She inched closer to me, held up her nails and wiggled her fingers. "These fingers that cut and bagged coke now have rings on them. They went through countless stacks of dollar bills, which ain't fun. This high-maintenance look didn't come cheap." Carmen was outraged and continued to defend her position. She pointed at her neck. "Look closely at this diamond-studded choker. When motherfuckas left me for dead, they tried to choke the life out of me. There were times when I literally couldn't breathe and fought for life. This choker symbolizes courage and the will to survive."

I had had it with Carmen's self-righteous tirade. She wasn't the only one who had made sacrifices. I turned to face her again, and this time I wasn't going to back down.

"You see, I'm a female first, no, a woman, which means I bring forth life, and I have a higher calling, because it is I, meaning woman, who perpetuates the species. Ain't no fuckin' man havin' no babies. He ain't carryin' shit, so excuse me for my attachment being stronger, 'cause my biology is a lil' different from his. And as long as I have this mandate from God—to be a passageway for our species, fuck you, fuck your streets, fuck your weak-ass, whack-ass gangsta code, the horse you rode in on, your spurs, and your muthafuckin' cowboy hat. I got pussy between my legs, not dick. Dick may go in but baby comes out. My son came out. You know what? I'll do the time. I'll do it and hold to the street code. I'll do it as soon as one of them street mufuckas is on his back with his legs open and the nurse and doctor is tellin' him to push. Until then, kiss my left tit, rub my right elbow, suck my clit, and then, bitch, get back in the box!"

I wasn't trying to hear what Carmen was saying. I knew I was wrong, a horrible mother, even. I had done what I thought was right. The quick money came so fast that I thought it was okay and then greed kicked in. I continued to plead my case. "I felt there was no other way," I said.

"Of course there was: welfare," Carmen said with a smirk. Then she sucked her teeth and rolled her eyes at me.

"You was playing ass-out chick. Your son was a pawn, so why not now?"

"I have a chance to make things right—to do something different. I love my son," I said.

"Love is what love does. Save that drama for your momma." I turned my back to Carmen and she reached for my arms, turning me to face her. I could feel that same positive energy that was between us earlier. I began to cry, and she wiped a tear that was cascading from my left eye.

"Don't you want to be able to look in the mirror? I need you to be there for me for once, Pammy. Don't let me down. You owe me. You owe me to represent. Don't make me into no motherfuckin' snitch-bitch. We just can't go out like this. I am here for you. You still got me. You will always have me. I will never ever leave. I will never turn my back on you." I broke away from her embrace trying to make her understand what I was feeling—what my heart-strings were telling me to do—what was needed of me. I walked over to the chair and sat down for a moment. Carmen came and sat across from me and held my hand. Looking at the diamonds on her hands. I wanted to be her again for just one moment—to feel that confidence and be free, if just for a second, to be fearless again.

I snapped out of the trance and was determined to make Carmen understand. "Listen, Carmen. Let me just talk to you for a moment. Just like that dope called them addicts to me back in the day, what do you think calls me now? The voice of my son is calling me. He is calling into my spirit. He needs me. I owe him." Carmen began to breathe hard, and I could see sweat beading on her upper lip. She was furious, and I understood why. I owed her; she had saved my life on numerous occasions and I loved her, but I just couldn't let her control me anymore. I needed to love me. I needed to love myself. I, Pammy, needed to be there for Pammy.

"You owe me. If we must go down let's do it royally.

Don't make me crash and burn 'cause you scared. Let's do the time. I am with you. You still got me. Together, we can do this." I sat there staring blankly into her eyes, and for once, I saw something that I had never seen in Carmen—desperation. I, Pammy, had the power. I had the ability to choose consequences for my own life.

Carmen stood and began to get angry again. What she wasn't realizing was with all that she taught me, I could now see—without her. I could see that fair exchange wasn't robbery.

"Is being a hood legend a fair exchange for not being with my son?" Carmen looked at me, no crack in her armor.

"Wrong question. Is being a snitch fair exchange for being with your son? Is lack of loyalty to those who made you, rode with you, backed you, got down for your mother-fuckin' crown fair exchange for being with your son?"

"You know who gave me a second chance, Carmen? It wasn't the streets, it wasn't the feds and it damn sure wasn't you!"

"Oh, really?"

"Yes, really!"

"Then who?"

"God!"

"Don't go there. I ain't tryin' to hear no Holy Roller shit!"

"I listened to your loyalty-to-the-hood shit, and now it's my turn." I pulled a chair out for her. "Have a seat, Carmen," I said, still standing.

"I'll stand."

"Suit yourself. When I was left for dead in the streets, do you know who I called on? I needed a way. I asked for a way. I got on my knees and pleaded for a way. I didn't specify. I just wanted, no, *needed* a way." Carmen rolled her eyes and shifted her weight back and forth from one impatient foot to the other. "I asked God for the way. Carmen, you became that way—through God. God didn't let me down.

God didn't abandon me. God didn't judge me. God just showed me that way."

"Bitch, please!" Carmen said, and took the seat before her, not trying to hear what I was saying.

"This time I've asked God to save my son—make him safe—make him whole. I do love you, Carmen, but I can't serve two masters or a master and a mistress. If I have to choose between you and God, Carmen, well then . . ."

"So, I'm ass out?" said Carmen jumping back to her feet. She continued. "Look, I'm not playing with you any-more—turn on me and you can fuckin' forget me. You'll be on your own, and don't think you won't need me when you come home, either; you'll still have to survive. You're no better than Chino. . . . No good, dead muthafucka. He fuckin' used you, and now you're using me. Are you finally telling me that after all this time, I, Carmen, got what my hand called for? Are you a leave-for-dead person? I helped you, and now you just say fuck me, right?"

What was I thinking? Carmen was right. I knew I needed her. She had saved my life. I was now convinced that every woman needed a Carmen in her life. Carmen was the only one who ever cared about my well-being. Car-men cared if I ate. She cared if I looked badly and she gave me the secrets to success. I could have another child. My son was in safe hands with my mother. I had already done two years. Every day got easier, not harder.

Carmen began to rapidly tap her nails on the table, glancing back and forth at her diamond-studded watch as the time for our visit dwindled. She rested back in the seat and looked me dead in the eye. She said, "This is my last time asking you the same motherfuckin' question: **Bitch, what you gon' do?**"

AFTERWORD

I received thousands of letters in response to *Let That Be the Reason*, the novel that introduced the story of Pammy and Chino, or should I say Carmen and Chino? I am so grateful for the love and support this story has received. You, my readers, have made it yours and came inside the plot with me. Thank you. I wrote *this* story giving you the choice. *Imagine This* was about you imagining yourself in this situation and then having to make a decision. Everyone wants to know what Carmen did. Well, you will have to keep reading—just kidding. I know you guys don't like cliffhangers, but I served a mandatory sentence under the federal guidelines, and my choice was my choice. I would never want to influence anyone to lead a life of crime with serious consequences like the characters in this story. That's why it's told in a manner for you to make your own decision—use your own judgment. There are no rules, no absolutes.

By God's grace, I walk the same streets I did dirt on with pride. I continue to reside in the same city that I lived in before I did time. I'm with my son, and I live legally as a writer and a publisher, thanks totally to you. I've been home for four years now. On my first outing, I went to Cypress Hills Cemetery in New York to visit Delano's grave. I tell him how much everyone loves his character and our story. I miss him a great deal and often wonder what kind of life we would have had together. Delano was my knight in shining armor, and I was his Princess, trapped in a fortress that he could not rescue me from. Rest in peace, my Prince . . .

It gets greater later,
Vickie M. Stringer